The Two Feelings

To Una

Jacqueline Smith

all best
Jacqueline Smith

Independent Publishing Network

Copyright © Jacqueline Smith 2018.

The right of Jacqueline Smith to be identified as the author of this
work has been asserted by her in accordance with the Copyright,
Designs and Patents Act, 1988.
All rights reserved. No part of this publication may be reproduced,
stored, or transmitted in any form, or by any means electronic,
mechanical or photocopying, recording or otherwise, without the
express written permission of the author or publisher.
British Library Cataloguing-in-Publication Data
A catalogue record for this book is available on request from the
British Library

Print ISBN: 978-1-78926-230-8
Ebook ISBN: 978-1-78926-723-5

Published in the UK

REVIEWS

"I enjoyed the beautiful descriptions of places and of the people's experiences...really uplifting and mesmerising. The characters and settings are very convincing and believable, and the descriptive language is memorable...lovely." Carol McKay, author of *Ordinary Domestic*

"Fabulous...and really well written. I enjoyed it...It really is brilliant."
Ruby McCann, author of *Duke Street Rhapsody and other poems.*

"What I loved most about the book were the descriptions. The author described details stylistically and vividly. It was almost as if I was standing in the past and observing everything that was going on... The book was very thrilling and I enjoyed every...aspect. The characters were well-developed. The storyline was compelling and enlightening. The book also had action and the elements of surprise and suspense... I'm therefore rating this book 4 out of 4 stars." OnlineBookClub.org

DEDICATION

For **Ben Okri**

Who told me to dream the book,
trust the dream; then write.

CONTENTS

Prologue

*"We consider bibles and religions divine - I do not say they are
not divine,
I say they have all grown out of all of you, and may grow out of
you still.
It is not they who give the life; it is you who give the life.
Leaves are no more shed from the trees, or trees from the earth
than they are shed (from) you."*
Walt Whitman

Speaking Woman Whispers

I am Speaking Woman and I am with you always.

This account chronicles the effects of a task of helping to awareness; giving an individual consciousness encouragement to continue evolving, and who was ready to be reminded that there was important work for them to undertake for the benefit of humanity. For such a one, like each of us, has gathered both negativity and positivity in the evolution of our consciousness; but in order to advance further spiritually we must, in full awareness, remember what has come before to move forward in the present.

Look well to your dreams, your visions and those Chronicles passed on to you from others, for it is the nature of Divinity to speak through those who have ears to listen, eyes to see and the courage to speak.

Morag MacAulay was such a Volunteer. She has returned willingly many times in an attempt to enhance both her own and others redemption and evolution. Come with me now. Learn how each life seemed a consequence of others where she sleepwalked through time, unaware of how her actions could affect the lives of many innocent people.

DÉJÀ VU-- France-1981

Morag could feel her feet throbbing as she dragged one in front of the other. Her shoulders felt raw from the chafing as the rucksack's weight bounced at every step.

"Can we stop soon?" she asked, hearing the whining tone in her own voice. Gareth beside her, his face pale and drawn and in no great humour responded with a contemptuous look before replying with exasperated weariness,

"Where are we going to stop, there's nothing here?"

She couldn't argue with this. Looking down the quiet country road ahead there was nothing but fields on either side, empty of any visible signs of habitation or people.

It was a warm dry afternoon, the hot sun making them sweat in the jackets and jumpers they'd yet to remove. The hoped for happiness of a trip together without their usual family entourage of respective brothers and sisters had been fast evaporating over the last few days on the train journey through north and central France. The final destination on their tickets was Chateauroux, but having impulsively jumped off the train at an in-between stop with no obvious town or village, they hadn't much of a clue where they were.

They trudged miserably on for another few hundred yards before coming round a bend in the dust-laden road, sighting a building coming up on the right hand side.

"Look!" Morag exclaimed, pointing out the obvious. Gareth ignored her enthusiasm but both were walking faster with anticipation in their steps. Morag felt a welcome relief at the prospect of somewhere to sit down and rest for a while.

Reaching the building Morag began to feel breathless from a sudden tightness in her chest, then dizziness overcame her. She stumbled under the force of her sense of déjà vu. Time seemed to slow down. It was as if the moment was expanding. Underneath a strange fear and excitement was taking hold of her.

"I need to go in there!" she cried. Gareth looked back at Morag sharply on hearing the urgency in her voice.

"Hold on a minute, what for? It doesn't look like there's anyone home. You can't just barge in to someone's garden. What if they've got a guard dog?"

"Yes, but I have to see. Let's knock the door. The gate's open and if there was a guard dog it'd be after us by now." Striding up to the front door, not waiting for Gareth's approval for a change, her determined knock was greeted with silence. No dog; no people. Morag stood for a few moments waiting in expectation, unsure why her breathing was still feeling inexplicably erratic, before shaking her head to clear her confusion. Then she felt small, a way she often felt in Gareth's company, as he did his 'I told you so' voice,

"There's no-one here. Let's look around the back."

The grey brick cottage looming over her looked inhabited. There were lace curtains hanging at the windows with no sign of peeling paint on their frames. The thick wooden door overshadowed a garden in full bloom. There was yellow jasmine and red flowering geraniums with bees buzzing happily amongst their petals. It all seemed well looked after but Morag sensed an ominous stillness in the shade below the cottage eaves that bordered on creepy.

"Don't you think this place feels a bit strange?"

"Naw, maybe they've just gone shopping or are out in the fields somewhere." Gareth abruptly dismissed her doubt, continuing around the side of the house leaving Morag standing there unsure whether to follow or not.

She reluctantly trudged after him round the back hoping for nothing more now than a place to rest. On coming round the corner of the cottage, the feeling of excitement jumping in her belly coupled with a ripple of fear returned as she saw an orchard a few yards away. Morag could smell fruity sweetness and decay, an alcoholic odour of overripe fruit drifting from the direction of the fence separating the orchard from the back yard. Some trees were laden with pink apples or still-green pears, while those already fallen were surrounded by insects enjoying the feast. The scene felt so familiar that she almost remembered the last time she was here. She shook her head again realising that that wasn't possible. This was her first trip to France ever, though it was a place she'd wanted to visit as long as she could remember.

Morag thought she must just be tired and hungry and her aching muscles weren't helping much either. She didn't dare mention anymore of her weird thoughts or feelings to Gareth. He'd been so snappy the last few days. As if he regretted coming at all. She'd had enough dismissal for one day. Morag continued gazing at the neatly lined trees lost in a frightening sense of familiarity until she heard Gareth's tone of irritation behind her,

"It'll just have to be a seat on the grass, there isn't anywhere else." He watched her quizzically then as she wandered past him, her eyes no longer registering his presence.

Morag struggled out of her rucksack hearing the dry grass crackling when the heavy bag hit the ground. She wandered over to find a tree to rest against, glad to be free of the weight on her back. Rotating her shoulders a few times to ease out some of the tension, she settled under the shading branches, her water bottle in hand.

"Hey, look at this. It looks so old. Isn't it wonderful?" She felt her eyes water and a quiver close her throat as she put out her hand, stroking the ancient trunk, looking up through its thick branches laden with apples. Her brow crumpled in confusion as she let out an exhausted breath. Rather than trying to figure it out Morag lay down to enjoy the rest. That was when Gareth shouted her over.

"Yeah, but this is much better. Come and see this!" He motioned to her with a wave before disappearing from sight.

She harrumphed, pulling herself back up and followed his voice. He'd found a Nissan hut sitting close to the side of the house about seven feet high and eight wide of corrugated metal sheets with large doors that he'd discovered were unlocked. On opening the metal doors all they could see were mounds of loose, but not old, clothing and electrical items like lamps and toasters. There were also two bicycles in great condition. Gareth wondered aloud if they should take the bikes,

"What do you think? Should we, could we? It'd save walking and humphing the gear?"

"We might not be able to take them on the bus or the train though. Then what would we do with them?" Morag wasn't much of a cyclist at any time never mind in a new place, so was relieved when Gareth shrugged.

"Okay, just a thought."

The clothing wasn't packed in bags but piled into the hut in no order. And there were boxes of books, photographs and sketches.

Do you remember?

"What was that? Did you hear that voice Gareth?" Morag swung round to see where the voice had come from but there was no-one there.

"What voice? You're imagining things." He snapped, but nevertheless, looked over his shoulder towards the house just in case someone had returned or been there all the time and he somehow hadn't noticed. Gareth felt a sense of menace in the atmosphere now.

13

"Really? You think so?" Morag reluctantly agreed that it must have been her imagination but was sure she'd heard an old women's voice whispering urgently. Her heart lurched then at the sound of shifting movement from the hut. She stepped back, landing on Gareth's foot.

"Ouch! Watch what you're doing."

"Sorry, but something moved in there. Didn't you hear it? Did you see anything?"

Morag was slowly craning her neck to look back into the darker reaches of the hut for the cause of the noise while Gareth hopped around behind her. The sliding sound came again but this time she saw that it was boxes nearer the back moving forward and emptying onto the piles of clothes. Black and white photos tumbled from a box.

There were images of several men lined up against a wall, others fallen at their feet. Morag gasped on noticing the fear on the faces of the standing men and the bullet wounds of the prone bodies. The boxes moved again and the images disappeared as heaps of papers and more photos of burned out cars and blackened ruined buildings cascaded down to bury the startling view she'd glimpsed. She turned abruptly and went to quickly shoulder her rucksack. Feeling a cold sweat erupt and a tremble shudder through her body, Morag became anxious to leave the place.

"Let's go Gareth. I think we've seen enough. We need to find a campsite or hostel where we can stay for the night."

Gareth had been rummaging at the other side of the hut and looked up, surprised at the fear in Morag's voice. He did feel nervous now too, the feeling of being watched without knowing who by or how it was happening made him uncomfortable and he unusually acquiesced. After picking some fruit, they moved on.

The day didn't get much better. As it turned out, they weren't close to any camping sites. The rain began before they got much farther down the road, making them hurry to find somewhere to pitch the tent before dark but the night seemed to race ahead of them. After some cursing, with jackets and sleeping bags piled over them to keep in small warmth and the relentless rain out, they huddled under a tree with the densest branches they could find. They spent the night shivering, getting little sleep and were still more irritable by daylight.

They wandered back along the long empty road in the direction they came, heading for the train station. They needed to get back to Paris that afternoon for the connecting bus to Calais later in the evening. Coming upon the house again Morag felt the tremors of fear strengthen, this time locking the image and sensations inside, which as she came to realise, would haunt her long after returning home.

Glasgow- 1991-The Medium

In the study I sat reflecting on my life to date while looking at a wood-framed leaf skeleton depicting an Asian woman carrying baskets. It was propped up between Chinese hand-carved candles at each side; both of which were cracked long ago by the careless throwing of a ball in a child's game. The weight the young woman bore seemed somehow symbolic of the drudgery I felt as if I carried now. The image had drawn me from across the street the day I discovered it several weeks ago, sitting lopsidedly in a junk shop window.

The leaf had seemed to jump out at me and I'd managed to haggle with the shopkeeper and buy it for less than he was asking. I could ill afford any money, but felt the leaf held some deeper significance for me and decided whatever sacrifices were needed would be worth it.

Life went on as usual as I tried with difficulty to stay positive for the kids.

"Drink, Mummy, drink?" whined my twenty-month old daughter, Paula. A blonde blue-eyed, cute and curly-haired child with the face of an angel.

"No. Leave me alone!" I barked, not wanting to wake up to yet another day of fetching and carrying, cleaning and cooking. Pulling the covers back over my head, I forced myself back into sleep again, feeling petulant and put-upon; hating my lot. The accompanying guilt was made worse by the knowledge of conscious decisions to bring my children into the world.

After continued cajoling and whining from my daughter, I finally give in to her demand. Resentfully, I dragged myself out of bed. Taking the bottle from her hand I made for the kitchen and half filled it with milk and boiled water. I needed to keep enough milk for tea and cornflakes, among other things. A reality I also resented. Hoarding not wasting; always worrying if there would be enough. The list went on every day.

The baby was smiling now as I brought her back the bottle. I warmed to her cuteness,

"Here you are darling," I murmured, snuggling close under the warm covers with her, feeling guilty for my bad temper. "I'm sorry, baby. Mummy's very grumpy this morning, isn't she?" Paula nodded, her curls bouncing and her lip petted. "I'm a mummy Bear; grrr…who's been eating my porridge?" I growled softly in her ear and tickled her till the petted lip spread into a smile and she chuckled.

These days I often felt like this. Most mornings I woke with a heavy head from too much sleep, troublesome dreams and discontent. Every morning analysing and pinpointing how I felt. I'm very good at that: analysing, working things out, making plans.

I loved my children dearly but they're only a part of my life. I've always recognised this. Not a 'live for my children' mother. But the children were often able to bring me back to the present, helping by reflecting back to me both my best and worst self.

With my first child I was content. There was little else I wanted to do that having only one child could prevent. Besides Jane had been at day nursery, which provided the space I felt we both needed. At that time some of my plans were dreamt up. Hatched with great optimism but since then torn down with even greater disappointment.

For a few years, life had been philosophical, full of friends and fun though not without some measure of heartache too. But now, there seemed to be only isolation; much of it self-imposed. That and my two children. My faith and positivity in life was gradually becoming chipped and tarnished. I was almost getting lost in the daily grind of the children's emotional needs, physical dependency and the slip into poverty. Now, on the inside I often felt empty and indifferent. And on the outside I had an edge; a cynicism and defensiveness with both strangers and people who were once friends. I had developed an air of aloofness that was born not of superiority but insecurity.

We had lived in our four-apartment ground floor flat for five and a half years now, a place I felt at least a little secure. It was ideal for the girls in many ways with front and back gardens to choose from, but being overgrown were of limited use.

Inside the house there were six rooms, three to either side of the long narrow hall. A small rather cramped bathroom to the right at the front door, a newly painted ample kitchen; the concrete floor still bare and carpet-less. Further up the hall at the top, the largest room in the house was given over to the two children.

There was a heap of toys in one corner: bike, scooter, doll's pram in another, with storybooks piled high on a shelf above. Against one wall were two single beds, given to the family by friends when the baby no longer slept in a cot. On the walls around the room were paintings done by my eldest daughter Jane, now a bright six-year-old with penetrating blue-eyes. These pictures were favoured more for the memories they held for me rather than the children. At the bottom of the hallway, on the other side, was my bedroom. The most interesting item there was the white metal, three shelved bookcase containing books that I considered precious.

I was presently engrossed in some research for a renewed interest in one of the oldest world philosophies, Buddhism and its origins. My interest had begun in my late teens and flowered at the same time as my first pregnancy with Jane, when I'd learned to meditate. The Buddhist culture and its system had once again begun to fascinate me amid the occasionally unbearable gloom of the days. A need to change something in my life had provided the impetus to go deeper. I felt the truth of the Buddhist assertion that everything is impermanent and holding on to the wish for it not to be so causes that dissatisfaction; that discontent I felt now and somehow always had.

At the other side of the room in a small recess stood an antique pine chest: brass-handled and grand, with deep old-fashioned drawers. The bed was set against the opposite wall and flanked by a small dark square table to the right. These days, broken objects waiting to be mended were piled in my room. Then there was a small sitting room. Its royal blue carpet gave a cool hue to the pale green walls, on one of which hung a painting in acrylics, a good attempt of a woman on the telephone, done by my youngest sister. Better than I could achieve. A thought I held somewhat enviously; nurturing aspirations to an ability to paint and draw myself.

This last room is where I tried to improve and enjoy my own attempts at putting colour and shape into form with whatever medium moved me at the moment. These days it was pastels I used in the study room. One attempt was of a 'could-be' lover, Enrique, from another country (in whom some of my dreams still lingered) and a new one, just begun, of my dead father. A powerful and imposing figure in life, his true likeness eluded me when I tried to immortalise him by design. He resembled an ageing man, nothing more familiar as yet.

Each drawing seemed to show less improvement, less confidence than the last. The character, the essence of the person would not shine through despite repeated attempts. Never knowing when to stop, I seemed to be guilty of making the same mistakes time and again. The pictures left unfinished yet overdone disappointed me, for I gained a much treasured release from bringing the bright and soft pastel shades to life; when successful.

As well as the easel on which I occasionally worked, the room, my favourite, housed a dark brown varnished desk. It looked fine and its deep drawers held many notes and books relating to past events and ongoing interests. Atop were books on alternative medicine, my chosen yet unrealised vocation. Unrealised because just at the time almost three years ago after applying and being accepted on to a four year course to study Aromatherapy, I had found out I was pregnant with Paula. Rather than try to juggle both: the course, a pregnancy and eventually a new baby, I opted to let the course go. Books on the Spanish language lay there too, for a class recently started at the local college to explore that 'could-be' lover's culture, which held inexplicable fascination for me.

Against the opposite wall was placed a two-seater club sofa in dark blue velour, an antique club chair and a fire to take the chill off the room. There was a modern but moving lamp of a naked women holding a globe as if carrying the world on her shoulders, surrounded by a crescent moon, a last reminder from the short but tumultuous relationship with the father of my youngest daughter Paula; she of the angel face.

Looking at the framed leaf again I realised that the illustration on the leaf skeleton struck me as appearing perhaps Indian. I decided to take it to the meditation class and ask if anyone could give me a clue about its origins. When I arrived Subhrata was at the reception.

"Hi Subhrata, could you have a look at this for me? I picked it up in a shop the other week and wondered if you could tell me anything about it. It looks Indian to me but what do I know?" I unwrapped the framed leaf carefully and showed it to the friendly-faced middle-aged man in front of me.

"That's a *Bodhi* Leaf!" he immediately exclaimed.

"Is it?"

"Yes Morag, you know, from the *Peepal* tree that the historical Buddha Shakyamuni sat under until he became enlightened?"

"Really!? I didn't realise that, a *Bodhi* Leaf, wow, I'm stunned. I felt really drawn to it when I saw it, no wonder!"

"Yes and it looks very old. I don't think I've seen one like that before, not in Scotland anyway." Subhrata looked impressed and mumbled something about Karma working in mysterious ways.

The meditation class was good but the leaf turning up now gave me an excuse to become distracted from the focus of the practice. As he led the practice Subhrata's voice helped bring me back.

"If you find yourself becoming distracted by sounds, sensations or thoughts just gently but firmly bring your attention back to rest on the breath. Just resting the mind..." Yes, I was supposed to be being mindful of the breath, but my mind wasn't interested in resting and it continued to wonder at this synchronistic event with excitement, further distracting me, but I managed to settle for the last few minutes before the session ended.

Subhrata later told me that events correlating and falling into place, was known in Buddhism as 'Auspicious Signs', to be appreciated as indications of inner and outer development moving towards integration and was often accompanied by the ripening of Karmic seeds. I was glad I'd trusted my intuition and bought the leaf but naïvely didn't realise that this could also mean seeds of *negative* Karma.

On returning home with the picture I discovered the frame was in a worse state than I'd realised. The wood was splintering and the frame would need replaced if I wanted to hang it. I began to take the picture apart and once I'd removed the frame was left with a fragile and transparent leaf mounted on stained and discoloured card covered at the back by rotting paper. I slowly and carefully peeled away the paper to reveal below it some writing in fading blue ink, scrawled in a spidery hand. There was what seemed to be a verse or poem, but I was going to need a magnifying glass to read it.

The rest of the study where I worked with the leaf was tastefully decorated, aping affluence the budgeting-by-poverty way. It still smelled faintly of burning from the fire of twelve months ago. We had been lucky that night no-one having been injured in any way. This room though, had been reduced to a burnt-out shell. I hoped hanging the picture in here would bring some 'good karma' and laughter to our lives again now that the room had been redecorated.

This room was my sanctuary, my sanity: my soul in material form. 'Burned-out' was a feeling that'd been hovering around me for the last eighteen months. At twenty-eight, five feet four inches tall with black hair, that frustratingly tended to become frizzy, and blue eyes. I'm sometimes described as 'cute' though I'm never sure that's quite what I want to hear. My only feature worth talking about is a birthmark in the shape of a diamond on my neck, not big but striking, even under the gaze of others. I'm beginning to feel the despair of never-realised dreams, yet I know patience is the only answer. I can do as I wish; but only if I wait. A book I once read, a philosophical science fiction novel suggested, "Waiting is…."

How much longer would I have to try to survive alone with my wings clipped in this Scottish inner city? Until my children flee the nest in fifteen or twenty years' time? It seems too long. Like the clanging as the jail door slams, the thought resounds to wrest away my freedom. But as I think this I can hear Avhiragoma's voice from a previous discussion at the centre about dealing with children and family in the spiritual life; pointing out a great teacher's view of children,

"Remember, *Padmasambhava* talked about the importance of children in our lives. He described children as our 'Karmic Creditors'. Basically, we owe them big time for bringing them into the world. They are here to teach us about ourselves."

So, despite my bouts of self-pity I knew I was lucky. There were lessons I could learn from my situation. I'm the girls' mother because I chose to be. Besides, there were many more like me, finding themselves by choice or circumstances, alone in the city with young children. Many were in a more desperate state of poverty with more children and smaller houses. Some living in vertical concrete towers like cell-blocks with minimum-sized windows that let in only a token of the sun's light.

I felt more fortunate, for around my house were parks, trees, a river. Greenery on each side, giving a freshness that at times could uplift my weighted spirit. Especially in the coming season of autumn when the colours began to change to those that were my favourites, with golden, orange and deep red flashes of leaves fluttering down to the earth. This was the season I felt most affinity with. It was time to take stock and renew my sagging spirit. And go on waiting?

Not likely, I wanted to live now. I wanted to create some quality of life for myself and the children. My love of reading and writing had always been able to transport me to other worlds; helped me walk in other people's shoes even if only for a short time. And my recent foray in the local charity shop had bagged me some very old and interesting books (not to mention another strangely-shaped skirt to add to my modest collection) which, like the discovery of the *Bodhi* leaf, added to my burgeoning sense that for the first time in a while I felt enlivened and purposeful.

I wakened the next morning feeling excited and eager to get back to my research. I got the children ready and walked Jane round to school with Paula in the pram under leaden grey skies amidst a deluge of freezing rain that, unusually, didn't dim my enthusiasm. The towering concrete blocks on each side of the street had glistening tidemarks sliding down the walls. They constantly overshadowed the daily goings-on of us locals but gave no cover from the rain. I greeted other parents dropping their children at school and for the first time in a while managed a smile that didn't go unremarked upon by my friend Maggie, who shouted over from the other side of the street,

"Mornin Morag, whit you smilin about? Have you met anither man or somethin?"

"No, Maggie, don't even mention men in my company!" I shot back, thinking that another man was the last thing I either wanted or needed right now. "I'm just heading round to the library. I'll catch up with ye later, ok?" Maggie was fast becoming my main relief from self-imposed exile. Her situation was akin to mine but this red-headed, green-eyed hellion took no nonsense and didn't suffer fools gladly. She and I were total opposites. She was outgoing and devoid of self-pity and dealt with life by managing to always crack a joke even at her own expense, while I was well...

I waved goodbye to Jane and then Maggie and strolled happily with the pram, glad that Paula was asleep and I could have a good look in the library for what I needed without too much interruption. I arrived back home two hours later laden with books just as Paula wakened looking for elevenses. I changed, fed and read her a story from one of the books and then gave her some toys to play with while I glanced over some interesting leaflets I'd picked up when checking out the books.

The one that had particularly caught my eye gave details of a Women's Day on alternative health organised at the local borough hall for the next day. There were workshops on the likes of massage and aromatherapy. This is what I'd been waiting for and just round the corner too! Luckily they were offering a crèche; so no need for a babysitter. The day was getting better and better.

I was up and out early next morning getting Jane to school, waving to her as she ran to huddle with her friends before the bell rang. Then I slowly walked to the borough hall for the event starting at ten o'clock. As we entered the creche Paula began screaming her objections,

"It's okay love, I'll just be a wee while. Look at all those nice toys." I tried to prise her arms from round my neck where she clung, pulling at my sweater.

"Hello Paula, is your name Paula? We've lots of friends for you to play with," the helper crooned, holding out a brightly coloured toy and when Paula reached out for it, encircled my daughter in her arms, gently lifting her from me, settling her so that I could slip away. I sighed with relief as I closed the crèche door behind me and felt a welcome, if small, sense of freedom. I was temporarily childless and intended to make the most of it. I headed straight for the massage stall and put my name down for the first available session and then went from stall to stall, slowly savouring all that was laid out before me.

The day passed quickly, during which I felt totally indulged, especially when being kneaded and gently pummelled with knowing hands that found every knot of tension in my back and shoulders. This of course resulted in bringing me close to weeping as the knots unravelled, bringing long-held emotions to the surface. Before and after the massage I visited several stalls at which I delighted in being able to follow up some of my lingering interests. I left the stall giving information on aromatherapy courses till last.

Checking the time to make sure I could chat without rushing, I made my way across the hall. I spotted Maggie sporting her usual multi-coloured scarf, while smiling and acknowledging some of the other women I knew from the area.

"Hi Maggs, enjoying yourself? Did ye no get a massage? I did and it was amazing! I'm just waiting to talk to the Aromatherapy School. What about you?"

"Naw, none o that for me, Mo. I'll jist wait till you've done yir trainin and get ma massages frae you, eh?" Maggie clasped my arm affectionately as she spoke.

"What? Your messages!? You can get them yourself, can't you?" I teased her with a gentle push, which had no effect on her generously rounded frame.

"Ha ha! Very funny, jist remember me when ye need a guinea pig tae practice on!"

"Guinea pigs are a bit hairy Maggs. You'll just have to be a baldy Glesga pig." I was pushing my luck but Maggie could take it. "I'm just winding you up, but listen: did you want to come over tomorrow night with Claire? After the kids are in bed I'll make us something to eat. "

"I can see ye're on form the day, hen. No worries, that'd be great. About seven? See ye then." Maggie walked off to talk to another acquaintance from the school and I checked the stall, noticing that the person I wanted to talk to wasn't free. Just as I was picking up some leaflets about courses to study Aromatherapy someone touched my arm. I thought it was Maggie again but on turning saw a woman in her early sixties, smaller than me with shoulder length, silver-streaked dark hair. She wore glasses, a grey skirt and blouse with a cream overcoat. Without any pre-amble or small talk, the woman drew me closer and in a quiet, husky voice said,

"I've been trying to catch your attention for a while today. I have message for you. I'm not sure who from or why but the sense of having to pass this on to you is very strong." I was surprised and apprehensive at the woman's words for I had no recollection of seeing her that day or at any other time before.

"I see, what's the message?" I replied cautiously, suppressing a smile, thinking she must have heard the banter between me and Maggie.

"If I said, '*The leopard never changes its spots*'. I know it's a common enough adage but would that mean anything to you?" I felt the hairs on the back of my neck stand up and my feet were rooted to the spot. I immediately recollected one of the last conversations with my father before his death some years before. Dad had been giving me yet more unwanted advice about my life and latest boyfriend at the time, with whom I'd had my first child.

There had been some violent episodes during my pregnancy and I had returned to my parents' house for a few days to decide what to do: end the relationship or forgive him once again. I had tried to hide the bruises on my arms while there and even if my mother had noticed she would never have told my father. Somehow he had intuitively guessed and had spoken the very same clichéd words that I now heard from this stranger, both of them without knowing my situation.

"I'm sorry I didn't mean to frighten you." I heard the woman say as I snapped back to the present, seeing the concerned face gazing at me with a direct look.

"It's something my Dad would say," I replied with false lightness, trying to steady my voice.

"Yes, that explains it. He passed over some years ago, didn't he?" I struggled not to show my continued surprise, coughing to cover the intake of breath.

"I'm a clairsentient dear. There's more to tell you but it would be better if we spoke somewhere else. Can we arrange for you to come to see me very soon? This feels quite urgent." The woman hastily scribbled her phone number on the leaflet that I was holding. "My name is Mhairi. I live just at the roundhouse further up the road. Call me," she said as she handed back the leaflet and turning, disappeared through the groups of people milling about. I stood unable to move for a few moments till Maggie jolted me out of my reverie.

"A thought I'd find you here. I'm just goin roun tae the school, are ye coming? Hey, are you OK? Ye look a bit pale."

"Aye, aye, I'm alright. Did…did you see that woman there?" I stuttered.

"Whit wummin?" Maggie looked about her as she said this. I quickly dismissed her question and hopefully the woman,

"Och, it's OK, she's away now. I'll just go for Paula and get you round to the school." The important chat about aromatherapy I'd meant to have was forgotten in my confusion and then the rush to make it to the school before the bell rang and Jane spilled out of class, expecting me to be standing there waiting to collect her. My future plans were submerged below the oddness of the encounter and once more to the children's needs.

For the rest of the day I was caught up in cooking, washing, then homework and bath-time with the girls who were lively past bedtime. All the while during these activities I was quietly thoughtful and a little distracted with my mind being pulled back to other times.

I had remembered that soon after my father died I could feel his presence around so strongly that I would hold doors open behind me to let him through. Then, not long before I found out that my request for a house swap had been successful, I'd gone to a clairvoyant to have my tarot cards read for the first time. On turning over the card known as the King of Swords, the woman immediately exclaimed, "Oh, there's an Aries man here! He's all around you." This was something of a relief to hear, as I'd sometimes felt I was going a bit mad and imagining the sensations I felt regularly. "It's someone very close to you. Do you know who it is?" she asked. I'd known who it was immediately,

"Yes, it's my father." I watched her turn over the next card, the High Priestess.

"Ah, and there is another spirit with you. A very ancient soul. I have the words 'speaking...woman'. Does that mean anything to you? It's Speaking Woman - like it's a name?"

"No, I've never heard that before. It sounds a bit native American."

"No, this is an advanced spirit of all cultures and none. She also watches over you and keeps counsel of your soul. She has been with you always." The psychic looked in her late forties with a kindly face surrounded by a mane of unruly blond hair running to grey, which she kept having to push back as she continued to turn over the cards. "On a more mundane level, I see a move in these cards too, a new home in the next six

28

months". Eva Moon went on to tell me many things that the near future promised.

When I did move to this house four months later, strange occurrences took place in the house from then on. Like inexplicably plummeting temperatures in the corners of rooms and occasional sensations and whispering voices of other presences besides my father's. What did he want now? Was he seeking me out again and to what purpose? No doubt I'd find out if I called that woman, but did I want to?

The children had sensed the distance in my mumbling responses and seen my faraway look during dinner, making them more demanding than usual. Now they were making sure I made up for it.

"Can we have another story, mum? Pleeeease?" Jane wheedled.

"Okay, one more and that's it! What's it to be then?"

"The rainbow fish, the rainbow fish!" They chorused, bouncing up and down.

"Okay but remember this is the last one, girls. We'll have no stories left for tomorrow night if we read anymore. Are you ready? Lie down now. You can see the pictures tomorrow and maybe we'll draw our own rainbow fish? Would you like that?"

"Yeah!!" they shouted.

"Sh...sh...sh. Okay, Once upon a time..."

After the children were asleep I tried to get back to the needs of here and now by bringing out the *Bodhi* leaf again to attempt deciphering the scribble before replacing the card and reframing the picture. I hunted out my magnifying glass from the bottom of the drawer where I kept my art materials and settled at the desk to have a good look.

I carefully removed the last of the paper stuck to the card on which the leaf was mounted and laid it on the desk. Gazing through the convex glass I began to read what was written on the stained yellowing paper. I tried to copy out the letters and words in the sequence they were written.

Some of the ink seemed to blur making several letters and words run together as I read it out loud. I felt a little dizzy when I tried to focus and as I began the second line, to my astonishment mist appeared blurring the colours. My heart raced and my hand began to tremble but I couldn't tear my gaze from it as I continued to recite the verse. The words were now illuminated from inside, pulsing through the misty colours then spiralling quicker and quicker as I got to the last line. As the mist cleared I could now see a dark-skinned young girl who looked as if she was milking a thin, humped white cow. In the distance I thought I could hear the sound of a flute playing. The images got bigger, came closer or was it me who was moving closer to them? I could see the spiralling again but this time it was me who seemed to be spiralling! I spun faster and faster till the last sound I heard was the thud of something hitting the floor.

FIRST CHRONICLE

*"The vision makes such a lively impression upon the seers
that they neither see nor think of anything else,
except the vision, as long as it continues"*

Martin Martin, *A Description of the Western Isles of Scotland*

The Silver Swan-Indus Valley - 4 BC

Gita was dark in complexion, her face a warm brown with bright mischievous hazel eyes. Her skin became a deep rich umber with the sun's sometimes fierce attention as she went about her day's work. The only part of her skin that was almost as black as her shiny hair was the diamond shaped birth mark on the side of her neck. Her mother had told her that it was a mark of the black obsidian stone that aided spirit contact and enhanced the gift of prophecy. Its diamond shape held a deeper meaning; its significance not yet apparent.

The people of her race, the Sarappos were relatively small and squat, but Gita still had some growing to do for she was just approaching the dawn of womanhood.

"Stand still until I finish this milking, Leah! You can be a real holy fidget. I'll be done a lot quicker if you'd stop pulling away! I don't mean to hurt you; you know?" Gita was just about finished her morning chores and was as impatient as the cow to be done so that she could go off to the river with her friends.

For much of the year the weather was hot and dry until the rains arrived and the countryside around Sarappo and in the city gardens became lush and green, especially by the riverside.

Here and there were expanses of parched, ochre-coloured sandy soil before the monsoon would come and churn them to mud.

Between June and September after the floods had receded, it was warm and sunny and Gita would go for walks in the daytime and watch the farmers planting crops of wheat and barley. Her favourite place to walk beside the River Indus was along its reedy banks, where she could watch the water flow and meander or rush and rage depending on the time of year.

Gita had to work hard doing chores like tending the family cow, a white hump-backed creature like those used for pulling the plough in the fields; but sacred in the Indus Valley as the totem of the Great Goddess. Her people believed that the universe itself was curdled from the primordial Sea of Milk, of the Goddess-as-Cow.

She didn't mind this chore too much, she seemed to have a special affinity with other creatures and it was an honour to serve the Goddess in this way. She also helped to prepare meals for herself and her parents. Gita was an only child with many friends in the city but for the last while she seemed to be spending much time on her own, or so many believed.

When she'd first encountered the Swan, Gita had been startled and more than a little afraid. It was a beautiful evening as she walked by the river. The streaks of golden red and shimmering pink of the long descending sun of afternoon gave the sky a lilac hue that hinted twilight was close. The clouds on the horizon looked heavy and full carrying sunbeams. In the cooling temperature Gita wandered in quiet peace after her day's work and play. She gazed with awe at the majesty of the developing sunset, hearing from somewhere behind her a bird-like noise of some kind that she didn't recognise. The gentle murmuring came from near the river among the reeds.

Gita turned a little frightened, her arms prickling, in the direction of the sounds. It was about the time she would usually begin to make her way home before darkness fell, but her curiosity was roused. She just wanted to see what kind of bird was making those strange but compelling sounds. Gita moved closer to the riverbank amongst the tall reeds and as she came to the edge she gasped. The graceful head of a long slender, white-necked bird she had never seen before stretched up and returned her startled gaze. Gita let out a squeal of surprise at the unusual and elegant bird and was a little wary of its direct stare. She didn't dare go any closer but instinctively bowed her head in respect, sensing an air of knowledge and wisdom emanating from the bird. She withdrew quickly and hurried home before it became dark and her parents began to worry.

For the rest of the evening Gita could not stop thinking about the bird she had happened upon at the riverbank. Both the sounds and its gaze remained to haunt her even into sleep and that night when she dreamed, she saw wispy clouds shimmering lilac while the water was a beautifully vibrant, turquoise-blue with pure white gentle waves frothing momentarily on its surface. A shape was vaguely distinct on the horizon. It slowly moved closer and the outline of a bird began to take form.

A large bird, the colour of which was as yet indistinct, shone in the light of a beautiful full moon hanging in a deep sapphire-coloured sky behind the clouds. The bird glided gracefully towards the shore looking regal in its plumage of metallic silver, the light of the moon illuminating and softening the glint of the glow which surrounded the Swan.

Carried on a warm gentle breeze, the pure notes of a flute, whose source was indefinable, could be heard. The silver swan came to rest at the shore. It opened its jet-black beak and uttered the words: *"I am of Kali, the Great Mother, Treasure-House of Compassion, Giver of Life to the world, the Life of all lives. Come to me Gita, Kauri awaits!"*

Gita awoke the next morning filled with a deep feeling of peace coupled with a sense of urgency to go immediately back to the river and see if the bird was still there. She hurried through helping prepare and eating breakfast and carried the pannier baskets of washing on her shoulders to justify her visit to the river, just in case it hadn't also been just a dream.

As Gita approached the place she was sure she had encountered the bird previously, she slowed her stumbling run to a halting walk and almost crept in trepidation at what she might find. Her worst fear was that there would be nothing there. She was tiptoeing through the reeds and breathed a sigh of relief as she heard the same strange and compelling murmurs that she'd heard the night before.

Gita parted the bulrushes closest to the riverbank and there was the bird, this time its head and neck were bent and huddled into the feathers between its wings. She immediately noticed that unlike her dream the Swan was white, other than a few stray silver feathers towards its tail.

The Swan uncurled its long, graceful neck and inclined its head in her direction, once again its stare was directed towards her and she felt herself being drawn into its gaze. Then, to her astonishment the Swan spoke to her.

"Namaste, Gita, thank-you for returning so quickly. You may call me Kauri for the time that we will be together, which is not long." The bird's voice was deep and resonant but melodious like the lower notes of a flute, almost hypnotic in its effect and Gita felt deeply calmed.

"I understand that this must be frightening for you, but you are just approaching the dawning of womanhood and I need someone of your gender who has the potential for deep compassion. You are needed to bear and transmit wisdom which soon will become forgotten and despised. I have come in the form of this bird, which is called a swan and is in nature coloured white, as I now appear. But my form will not remain white. During the short time that I have with you these feathers will gradually be transformed into silver, as you saw in your dream. This has already begun for there is conflict growing that

drains my life force. I will die when my plumage turns completely silver, so understand that I only have a little time to impart to you what you must know before great changes take place."

Gita had been listening to the words of the Swan as if she was hearing a beautiful melody that was barely discernible and so subtle that it was as if she more heard it in her own mind, than on the air. When the bird finished speaking Gita didn't know how to reply. She felt many emotions as Kauri spoke of the offered learning, feeling honoured yet wary and sad at the news of the its imminent death.

So Gita said, "I will do what I can to help you in the time that you have here. I don't know why you have chosen me for this learning but I will try to dignify the great honour that you have bestowed upon me."

"Thank-you for listening so patiently to my strange request, Gita. Please don't be afraid. Your compassion is already evident. I know I have made the correct choice. I will rest for now and hope you can return again this evening before sunset so that we can begin The Teachings."

And with this gentle dismissal the Swan, as Gita now knew it to be, curled its head back down in between its wings and remained this way. Gita got up, remembering that she still had to wash the clothes in the baskets she had needlessly brought and went off to join the other young people at the washing stones farther up the river. She took her time getting there, wanting to let the strange experience settle before meeting her friends.

The day could not pass quickly enough for Gita and she had the words of the Swan swirling round in her mind the whole time that she beat and washed the clothes at the stones, tended the cow and helped her mother, Mudita, prepare the evening meal over the cooking blocks. She felt more than a little confused and wished that there was someone with whom she could talk to about her dream or her meeting with the Swan who called itself Kauri. She intuitively felt that this happening was of profound significance and recognised that somehow she had been waiting for this all her short life. Both her friends and her mother had noticed her being unusually quiet. Gita was a happy, bright young woman who loved to share a song or a story, whether she was the teller, singer or listener.

Her mother tried to talk with her about the coming ceremony, which would take place at the next full moon in six days time by asking,

"Are you becoming nervous about the moon change ritual, little one?"

Suddenly it struck Gita in part, as to why she had made contact with the Swan at this time in her life. She had a show of blood three weeks ago heralding the onset of her own moon change. She was fourteen and about to celebrate the arising of her womanhood, a time of great celebration in her Clan. Gita decided to confide her dream of the night before to her mother, if not her rendezvous with the Swan itself. After relating what she remembered of the vivid reverie, her mother sat back and looked at her with a mystifying expression, which had in it traces of fear, admiration and concern.

"My dear, you have been greatly honoured by the Great Mother. This vision of Kali signifies that you are a chosen Apsara or Swan Maiden. Your life will now be in the service of the One as a Shakti, but not until after your initiation by the 'Bearing of the Flower' or first full bleeding at the next full moon. Don't be afraid. I will convey your dream to the women Elders and you must tell me if you have more dreams before your ceremony." After saying this, her mother held her close and let flow gentle tears of joy at her daughter's great honour. Mudita could feel a slightly bitter-sweet tinge of sorrow aching in her heart as she realised that Gita would no longer be just the accepted earth daughter that she was now, but in six days would be more fully priestess to Kali and serve the Spirit of Creation.

Gita was happily disconcerted by her mother's interpretation of the dream and felt closer to her than ever before. It also helped her to understand a little more of the Swan's utterances. She resolved to ask the Swan that evening if she could share the knowledge of their meeting with her mother. Gita remained to eat with her parents before going off on her walk by the river and her first teaching from Kauri, the Swan.

The sky was aglow with the golden rays of evening sunlight as Gita made her way to the riverbank beside the *Peepal* tree she remembered was there. She cautiously approached the area of bulrushes behind where she expected to find the Swan. Pushing the reeds aside with anticipation and excitement, Gita saw the Swan as she had left it, with its head tucked between its wings. It seemed to sense her approach and began to slowly lift its head gracefully to see her.

"Namaste Gita, how are you this evening? Please sit and we will begin the Teaching."

Gita bowed and while making herself comfortable at the river's edge, noticed that more of the Swan's feathers were now silver than earlier in the morning.

"Namaste Kauri." she replied in a quietly respectful voice.

"I understand that you have confided the dream that I sent you to your mother. Don't look so surprised," the Swan countered as she noticed the expression on Gita's face. *"Close your mouth and let me explain to you."* Gita gulped and too late, tried to appear unperturbed by the Swan's foreknowledge of her conversation with her mother.

"Your mother has, since her own 'Bearing of the Flower' or moon change, been a Priestess to the Divine Mother, but was chosen as a Matri, a mother. I have a three-fold nature. Though known as "The One", I am always recognised in trinity;

40

Creatrix-Protectress-Destructress. In the three mortal forms I am seen as Virgin-Mother-Crone.

"As your mother correctly told you, you are to be initiated as a Swan Maiden. This means that you will remain as a Virgin for the next seven years and be announced as High Priestess so that you may contain the teachings in a purified vessel. Your initiation will begin from the Flower Bearing Ceremony and will continue until the age of twenty-one.

"You have much spiritual practice and teaching to undertake during this time, at the end of which you will be given a choice as to how you wish to continue to serve the Mahadevi. The nature of that choice will not be revealed to you until that time."

Gita tried to take everything in that the Swan said. This was made easier by the deep sonorous tones in which she heard the words Kauri spoke. Gita breathed deeply and slowly, her every breath becoming more regular and subtle as she relaxed into the fathomless regard of the Swan's eyes.

"Continue to accept the breath; be the breath that you are. Kali represents Existence, which means Becoming. The world is an eternal living flux from which all things rise and disappear again." As Gita remained focussed on her breath, the words of the Swan resounded in the space between the breaths and she begun to hear a rising chorus of subtle sounds that formed themselves into words she did not yet understand.

"You are both Subtle and Gross, Manifested and Veiled, Formless, yet with form.

You alone remain as One, ineffable and inconceivable…

You are the Beginning of all; Creatrix, Protectress, and Destructress."

When Gita next blinked consciously the Swan was not at the riverside. The twilight had fallen and she felt surrounded by an aura of the most gentle but impenetrable protection. Gita got up, stretched and begun her walk back to her parents house in the near darkness. The whole time, thinking of nothing at all.

On arriving at the house she greeted her parents, noticing that her mother was looking keenly at her. She smiled calmly, sat with them for a glass of sweet Chai and went to bed, falling immediately into a deep dreamless sleep.

In the morning, Gita awoke feeling refreshed and ready for the day. She was up and about as the sun rose, and went with her mother to the forest to gather a supply of herbs, which were used to help heal illness and added to their food to give a richness of flavour no less than for their health-enhancing benefits. She knew intuitively that she would now visit the Swan each evening to absorb more of the Mahadevi's Teaching. Although she had not asked, she knew she should not discuss these meetings with anyone, including her mother. Despite this, Gita was curious about her mother's own initiation as a Matri. She knew that the precise details were sacred and therefore unspeakable, but Gita tentatively asked Mudita if she would tell her something of her own 'Flower Bearing' ceremony.

Mudita talked as they gathered the herbs,

"I was given a beautiful dress of fine red cotton made for me by the Elder women of the Clan. I still have it but I don't think I'd fit into it now. I'm a bit rounder than I was then."

"Did you have a dream like mine matri?" Gita asked.

"No, I didn't receive a dream directly from the Divine Mother, but one of the Elder Women, the eldest who was called Sila, received a dream which indicated that I was to take the red robe of a Matri. Everything felt full of mystery, it was so exciting. I completed the first ceremony with the Elder Women and then went into retreat for seven days until my first moon change was complete.

"During the retreat, I had been granted a vision from the Divine Mother, showing me that when her seven years of intensive training were at a close, I would join with a chosen consort and bear a daughter who would be special to the

Mahadevi. This daughter was expected to become High Priestess of our Clan, the Mesnui, and would be respected by many in the land as the holder of the core teachings of Kali Ma, known as the Primal Deep.

"You are that daughter who is for the moment known as Gita, but the Mahadevi will give you a new name when you are reborn as her Vessel of Knowledge after your ceremony and retreat." She then went on to describe the great celebration, which followed her return from seclusion.

"Was there much dancing and singing?" Gita asked excitedly.

"Yes, and we ate the finest foods available. Okra and curried chicken, many herbs and spices like coriander, turmeric and cloves were used to cook what must have been at least a dozen different dishes. My mouth is watering now when I think of that feast. I ate so much!" Mudita laughed as she remembered.

"Who did all the cooking Matri?"

"Oh, that was done by Elder Women not directly involved with the ceremonies and retreat. They had been preparing and cooking all the days whilst we young ones were gone."

"I know you can't talk much about the retreat itself but did you enjoy it? Were you scared?"

"No, not once it began but I was before it. I imagined all sorts of things that never happened. Gita, it was one of the most momentous times in my life and those treasured memories remain vivid still." Mother and daughter walked together in companionable silence through the trees and reached home in time for a midday snack that Gita's father, Viriya, had prepared for them. They were surprised at their hunger but knew they had worked hard, judging by the full baskets of herbs they returned with despite their long conversation.

Gita's father was a metalworker or smith. As well as producing the functional, practical utensils and tools made of copper and bronze for those in the city, he also had the gift of working beautiful jewellery with detailed patterns such as spirals and symbols of animals like the unicorn; those traditional to their people. Even his utensils and tools were never merely functional but were often inspired in their craftsmanship.

His daughter was a joy to him and he was in the process of creating a gift for her made of the still scarce metal known as *luna* that he had traded gold for, on his last trip to the coastal settlement at Lothal. He planned to engrave it with an image of the crescent moon and set into it smooth blue stones of lapis lazuli. She did not know of this and would not, until she was presented with it at her ceremony in five days' time.

After their midday meal, the family had a short rest before continuing the day's work. Mudita would continue her teaching of other young women who had been signified at their own moon change initiation as those of the red robe, in the skills and knowledge of the Matris. These were skills and knowledge, which would enable them when the time came to become compassionate and caring parents. They would also learn the craft of midwifery and be able to aid and attend the birthing of other Matris. Through this spiritual practice of earthly motherhood they would best be able to honour their positions as Priestesses to the Divine Mother Kali Ma, who was considered the fount of every kind of love, said to flow best into the world through her surrogates on earth: women.

Viriya had some metalwork to complete and later he would go to the Temple. An integral part of his spiritual practice, which included fatherhood, was to attend rites of celebration for the Goddess. He went daily to the communal bathhouse for ritual cleansing, and then gave thanks with prostrations and offerings of poems in her honour. The essential prayer of paradox and rapture was contained in his favourite verse:

By feeling is She known. All is the Mother and She is reality herself.

Sa'ham – She I Am, and all that is sensed is She in the form, which is perceived by me.

Deathless are those who have fed at the breast of the Mother of the Universe.

Viriya had gone through his own initiation at the age of fourteen. At this time he had been given direction by the Mahadevi in the form of a vision that he should be the consort of the newly renamed young woman called Mudita in seven years time to join with her in the Yab -Yum sacrament. He was to take the yellow robe of the Patris and make fatherhood his spiritual practice. Like Mudita he would teach other young men in the ways of the Patris and take on an apprentice in future years when he had perfected his art of metalworking. Of course as a Master Smith, he was given the gift of being able to channel the beauty of the Ineffable One into the metal forms, which he forged and engraved. These metalworking skills when learnt with humility, commitment and devotion often bestowed other powers of a spiritual nature channelled from the Mahadevi. But only wise use, focused towards inner forging of the Sword of Discrimination, resulted both in their appearance and continuance.

When both Gita's parents had both left to carry out their respective activities, she made herself ready to go to the other side of the city to meet her friend before seeing the Swan. She walked quickly through the centre of the city around the main temple, at the heart of their community, beyond the granary where wheat and grain were stored after harvest and on under the fig trees and called on her friend.

Magadhi was Gita's closest friend. They had been friends all their short lives and shared everything from clothes to confidences. Magadhi was only a month older than Gita and

45

was of similar build, but thinner and fairer. She was of a quieter disposition and more introverted than Gita, sometimes bordering on the side of melancholia.

Today Magadhi seemed distracted but was also looked as if she was trying to suppress a small smile as she greeted Gita at the entrance of her parents' home, ushering her in with a warm hug.

"*Namaste* Gita, come in, come in. I have some news to tell you!"

Gita followed her into the room to the front of the living space, which was used for the company of friends. The area was warm and bright from the afternoon sun, which was blazing through a light space in the front wall. There were colourful wall hangings and rugs on the floor depicting spirals and patterns derived from the flora and fauna of the surrounding countryside including birds like the shikra and the kingfisher. The main wall-hanging depicted a beautiful male peacock with its plumage displayed proudly. There were lots of richly coloured, large cushions of woven cotton scattered around this *Mitra* space, predominantly in many shades of green and blue.

"What is it, Magadhi ? What has happened, you look different. What have you heard?" Gita felt very curious about what could have made her friend so anxious despite the excitement around the town among the young people. Being normally one who kept much expression to herself, it was unusual to see her so eager to share her feelings.

"Let's sit before I tell you." Magadhi replied, which they did, sinking into the cushions on the floor. Magadhi spoke quickly and anxiously,

"I have been told by the Elder women that I have been chosen to train as a Matri to the Goddess. I didn't tell you before because I wasn't sure you would understand and I didn't know what to do! I was supposed to have 'Borne the Flower' at my moon change ceremony in fourteen days time, but I already started bleeding several moons past! I would have been made a priestess for the next seven years or longer, if I passed my initiation but now I won't be allowed to take part in the ceremony!" Magadhi seemed unusually calm considering she was telling her friend that she could not undertake an age old ceremony and that by missing it, this would leave her adrift from her peers.

"Magadhi, what do you mean? What will you do? Have you told your parents?" Gita asked in a shocked voice.

"No, and you can't say anything Gita. That's not my only news. I'm pregnant." She announced with a strange sense of finality. "What do you think, isn't it wonderful? It's scary but it feels so right, as if I've been waiting for this to happen." There was an air of defiant triumph in Magadhi's words and Gita struggled to find something positive to say. She was perplexed by her friend's news and immediately wondered who could be the father.

"Who is the child's father?" she asked hesitantly, realising just how little she really knew about her friend.

"I can't tell you that yet, Gita. I'm sorry but all hell will break loose as soon as I do, so everyone will hear at the same time. But enough about me, what's been happening to you, any news?"

Gita proceeded to tell Magadhi haltingly of her own news about being chosen as an *Aspara* but did not reveal her meetings with the Swan. Even with the girl she had thought was her best friend, this was not something that could be shared. In a way, both events marked the beginnings of distance in their friendship that already began to feel like a yawning gap. Although, they would have both been serving the Mahadevi at the temple along with another forty-eight women of all ages, Gita knew that she was to be chosen as the next High Priestess and Magadhi would no longer be part of that unless she went to speak the Clan Elders soon.

"Magadhi, you must speak to the Elders soon! At least let them know what is happening so that they can help you! You

47

know they will try to do what's right for you." Gita spoke earnestly to her friend hoping she would listen and act on her words.

"No, Gita. It's not time for that yet. The baby's father and I are making our own plans. When we have decided what is best for us, we'll let the Elders know." Gita was finding it difficult to take in what Magadhi was saying. Pregnant? Not tell the Elders? Decide with the father? Gita was stunned by the words of a very different Magadhi that she did not recognise. Gita wanted neither to take anything away from her friend's defiant joy, nor to reveal that the learning she had undertaken with the Swan was sacred to those given such a position of responsibility. She had already begun to keep her own counsel as would be appropriate more and more, if she were to pass her initiation in a few days time. Magadhi interrupted her thoughts to wish her well,

"I'm happy for you Gita. It sounds like the right choice for you. I would have been surprised if the choice had been anything other than that. I'm sure you will flourish at the Temple."

She stood to leave, thanking and hugging Magadhi. Her friend was seemingly as happy and excited as much about Gita's news as her own. She then made her way down to the river, her mind reeling as she wound her way round the circular streets in the northern area of the city heading towards the pottery and bead-making factory, where many were hard at work.

The city of Sarappo was built in a spiral formation, which moved from the central temple outwards. The buildings were of burnt red brick, uniform in size and made from the reddish ochre-coloured soil of the land. All the dwellings and places of trade and commerce were also shaped in curves rather than angles, which gave a sense of fluidity as she walked. As Gita passed by the entrance to the bead and trade seal factory, she waved to some of her neighbours who worked there. She saw her friend Khanti's father, overseeing the kiln workers, his head bent showing them how to place the seals just so, to avoid them cracking from the heat. Gita wondered what he would make of Magadhi's news when she got around to informing the Elders, of whom he was one.

The factory was situated where the residential area ended and the commercial began and she knew it housed at least a dozen rooms that included the worker's quarters, warehouses and guard rooms surrounding a courtyard, wherein stood the bead-making machine that consisted of a twisted chambered kiln made from mud and plastered bricks. It was used for firing the soft steatite stone beads and moulded terracotta seals, after inscriptions and patterns had been carved, thus making them extremely hard. Gita left the factory behind, thinking of Khanti as she went towards the river, sighting the *Peepal* tree that marked the place where the Swan was to be found and pushed her way towards the edge of the riverbank.

The Swan was present with its head poised in gracious expectancy of her arrival. Gita bowed her head and sat on the grass in silence to await her next instruction from the Great Mother.

"*Namaste, Gita, Let us begin this evening with the significance of the 'Flower Bearing' ceremony, in which all female earth creatures by nature must live with for at least half of their lives, thirteen times a year with each moon. The Great Mother gives birth to the cosmos by the churning of the Primal Sea, the Ocean of Blood.*" The Swan then intoned,

"I invite all other Divine Ones to bathe in the bloody flow of my womb and to drink of it; the gods in Holy Communion may drink of the fountain, bathe in it and rise blessed to the heavens."

Then she continued, "*So, it is sometimes known as the elixir of immortality or Ambrosia, food of the Gods. Dew and* rain become vegetable sap, sap becomes the milk of the cow, and the milk then becomes converted into blood...The vessel or cup of this immortal fluid is the moon.

"When the time comes, you will officiate and take part in the Left Hand Rite of Tantra. The Priestesses must be in their blood flow at this time, so that their lunar energy will be at its height. It can help the males of your race to live longer if they, as Shivaktas join with the priestesses at the Mysterious Gateway and absorb menstrual blood as life-giving female energy. This experience also occurs during the sacrament of the united 'father-mother' or Yab-Yum practice, and when the energy reaches the throat they can generate a special bliss...This is the bodhicitta or the aspiration to delay full enlightenment until all other beings are free of suffering and the dawning of true compassion. These rites are governed by the Elder Women of the Clan who no longer have their flow with the moon cycle but retain their blood of wisdom and are mortal sages."

Gita was distracted during the Teaching, still feeling disturbed by Magadhi's news, blurting out her doubts as soon as the Swan finished speaking.

"Kauri, my friend Magadhi has already borne her moon flower and has had intercourse with someone. She has told me that she is to have a child. What will happen to her? What will this mean for the Clan? I don't remember this ever being spoken of before."

"I can assure you Gita it is not the first time this has happened. I would hope that the Elders would help and support her. After all, she will be a matri just by bearing the child if all goes well. But the father of her child is not one who has strong faith in the teachings of the Great Mother. I sense he is of the element in your Clan who poses a threat to the way things are."

"A threat..? What kind of a threat? Do you know who the father is?" Gita exclaimed.

"I don't know the name but I sense the energy. The threat is one that has so far been mainly unspoken, but is present among those who seek change in the way of life here. Events are unfolding quicker than I had anticipated but we should have enough time to complete what I came to do."

The Swan became quiet and seemed pensive after this exchange and let the silence become full. The cool evening breeze drifted about them as the sun set with its usual royal red streaks setting the hills in the distance on fire as its rays fell on their summit. The Swan finally opened up the silence into speech again, saying,

"Do not be afraid of the unknown in my words, but let go of the known in your heart- mind and try to prepare yourself for what is ahead by remaining in the moment. Stand under these utterances and let them become you… Till tomorrow." And with this final word, Kauri dipped her head into her wings, which were now almost silver and said no more.

Gita sat for a while longer appreciating the profound presence of the Divine bird before rising. The deep sense of peace that she always felt after being in the presence of the Swan followed her like a scent. Once again, her mind felt empty of thoughts as she walked home in the mauve twilight. Her thoughts were no longer tripping over themselves to be heard. Gita welcomed this, especially now as her life seemed to be changing so quickly. The carefree time of milking the cow and playing with friends seemed to be slipping away from her, as if she were waking from a pleasant, playful dream. On reaching the house, Gita sat for a short time with her parents exchanging news of their day. Feeling a welcome tiredness, she went off to bed, closed her eyes and drifted off, her last thoughts being of concern for Magadhi.

The next morning at the riverside whilst bathing with her friends there was an air of excitement. Shouts and laughter pierced the air as the young people splashed and cavorted in the water. Many of Gita's friends were at the end of their middle child-time. They would all undergo their initiations in the coming months and at times there was much apprehensive discussion about who might be next and what the initiations would have in store for them. They had all heard stories from their parents about the celebrations following completed initiations, but they also felt both dread and enthusiasm about the unknown quality of what was to come. Most though, shared the spirit of adventure this required, knowing that finding courage was part of the process.

Adding to their anticipation was the knowledge that the youth of the Mesnui Clan were to attend a gathering that was to take place in the 'Garden of the Lotus' on this very day after the midday meal. Here they would all hear from an important and experienced Priestess of some authority, who would talk on the first noviciate instruction. The twelve young people made their way to the Garden after their food, talking with somewhat subdued animation to each other. This was their first formal instruction in the Way of Truth and heralded the end of not only Gita's middle child-time, but that of each of the six boys and six girls.

The Garden was lush with flowering plants of many varieties and the foliage was various shades of green. There were thirteen log stumps arranged in a circle beside a pool of rippling, azure blue water adorned with lotus flowers floating atop in different stages of growth. At the far side of the pool there was a small waterfall, originating from a mountain stream, which flowed over some large rocks engraved with the movement of many years of circling water. It lent a light, tinkling gurgle to the gentle stillness of the garden.

The Priestess appeared from behind some trees to their left just as they settled on the logs. She was dressed in a black sari of fine, spun cotton. Her shoulders were draped with a thicker cotton cloak of sapphire-blue, which fell in folds around her feet as she bowed to the young noviciates-to-be, before sitting down on the remaining log. The priestess was of an indeterminate age. Her hair was fine, silvery-white though long and curled up onto her head. Her face glowed with an inner calm, so that although the woman seemed to emanate a sense of the ancient, she retained an air of youthfulness.

"*Namaste,* Children. I call you 'children' for you have not yet left behind your middle child-time, though that will come soon for all of you. My name is Upekka and I was initiated as a Dakini priestess forty-two cycles ago. We are gathered here at the pool in the Lotus Garden, as a way of using this sacred but living flower as a metaphor for your development as human beings.

"It is also a way of helping you to recognise that you have a choice about what you do with this precious human life that you have been given and chosen. In the blackest darkness before life forms and on its death, the whole universe is contained in the womb of nature, of Matripadma, Mother Lotus. Look at the lotus plants in the pool before you. Some are only just visible under the water still encased in mud. Others are trying to stretch towards the light and have their buds breaking the surface of the water, whilst others, still in bud have managed to clear the surface of the pool. Then here are yet more, which are beginning to flower and in various stages of opening their petals. And see there! Only three or four are in full bloom." The Priestess pointed to a pair of pure white lotus flowers and then two deep red ones. They were truly beautiful as the unfolded petals languidly soaked up the sunlight with their abundant blossoms.

"We are all at different stages in our lives and our development within each stage. Once the barriers that limit our experiences as children have passed, we are able to begin to choose our actions according to the ways of our clan or people and the strength of the calling of spirit within. We can choose to listen, to try out what we are taught and experience its 'rightness' or we can choose to ignore both our calling and our heritage and remain in the mud, forever a bud of unrealised potential. This time in your young lives is where you begin to make choices about the way you want to develop as human beings.

Today, I have been asked to explain some of the ways in which your lives may change in the next seven years. There are paths which suit some but not others. It may be that some of you already know which path that the Goddess recognises as being the best place to begin the first stage of physical and spiritual maturity before reaching the twenty first cycle. For those who do not yet know, you will be alerted soon by the Elder women and men of your clan if not by some other means."

As the Priestess Upekka went on to describe to them the names and functions of the different roles within the sacred life of the community, every few minutes she would turn her head and mutter as if speaking to someone beside her, except that there was no-one there that the young people could see. A few of them raised their eyebrows, looking at each other questioningly. Upekka, unperturbed by these invisible interruptions continued explaining that the *Shivaktis* or Yogis, the Patris and the *Digambaras* or Sky-Clad were roles given to or chosen by men, which committed them to the work of the Goddess. The roles given to and chosen by women were those that Gita had been told about by her mother and the Swan: the Maidens who could aspire to become *Shakti* or Yoginis, the Matris and the *Dakinis* or Skywalkers. Of course, these young people had heard of most of these roles because within their land, the daily life was the spiritual life.

These two areas were considered to be deeply intertwined and in particular, the bringing of children into the world was regarded with great importance. Hence the long training given to those men and women who were chosen or themselves chose, to become Matris and Patris. Parenting had the potential to aid realisation of a human's true nature as a spiritual being. Gita looked over to where Magadhi sat as the Priestess explained this to the group. She saw her raise her head to smile at a youth at the other end of the circle. He returned her smile then dipped his head as if to prevent others noticing their gaze. The Priestess continued the discourse outlining the purpose of the training.

"This helps each of you to develop the ability to feel compassion or *Karuna* at the deepest levels as you watch and guide your offspring as they grow into themselves. Parents must learn to detach from any need to hold on to their children. They come through you but are not of you; they are not your possessions. *Karuna* is central to the spiritual life of our culture, as is Truthfulness or *Sacca.*" At this point, Gita felt uncomfortable on Magadhi's behalf.

Upekka continued talking for some time, making sure the young people had an opportunity to ask questions about things they did not understand, but no-one voiced their curiosity about the strange mannerisms of the Priestess. It was late afternoon by the time she ended their first instruction by leading them into a short period of silence with a verse to Kali:

"Material cause of all change, manifestation and destruction…

The whole Universe rests upon Her, rises out of Her and melts away into Her,

She is both mother and grave…The gods themselves are merely constructs out of her maternal substance, which is both consciousness and potential joy."

The twelve youths left the Lotus garden quietly, each cocooned in their own thoughts and feelings about what they had been told about their possible futures. Just as Gita said goodbye to Magadhi, having arranged to see her the next day at the river after the midday meal, someone caught her arm. When she turned to see who had stopped her, the Priestess Upekka smiled.

Her hand was raised urgently beckoning Gita to follow her. She followed the Elder Woman back to the circle of tree stumps where they sat down again.

"Gita, I have a message to give to you. I am close to those who have passed on, because I spend so much time in the charnel grounds and hear their whisperings. An ancient soul known as Speaking Woman, has urged me to tell you that there is an imminent death of an important presence in your life and that you must take care."

"What do you mean? I must take care of what, of whom? Gita's eyes were wide in alarm.

"I mean that Speaking Woman sees all and in that all for you now, she sees a gathering of destructive energies."

"What should I do? Where are they coming from?"

"She urges that you be aware of negative forces and remain alert. Trust your intuition about those around you. They may not be what they seem." The priestess spoke with fervent solicitude in her words. Gita looked doubtful and felt puzzled which prompted her to ask,

"How did you know the message was for me Upekka? Did this soul whisper my name to you?"

"No, Gita. She whispered that the message was for the one with the diamond-shaped birthmark on her neck. That could only be you, little one." She replied gently, taking Gita's hand in hers, stroking it to reassure her. She then told Gita that if she needed her help, to come to the burial ground and find her.

Gita felt both stimulated by the group talk and fearful of the message that she had heard from the Priestess Upekka, but had a strong feeling of admiration for the Elder Woman. She could see the priestess's face when she had been instructing them this afternoon, glowing with the joy of her commitment to the Teachings. Her voice had been filled with a gentle but deep conviction as she related the meaning and purpose of the offices of the Temple and full of concern when conveying the message. And of Speaking Woman: how many more spirits was she to discover were watching her? These recollections helped Gita's sense of gratitude strengthen about her coming entrance into a deeper spiritual life as a noviciate in four days time.

It had been another hot day with a clear blue sky. Those at the instruction had not borne the brunt of the sun's heat for they'd had the welcome shade from palm trees and bamboo grass, leaning over to shelter them from behind where the Priestess had been sitting. The glorious sun shining high above for most of the afternoon had begun to slip slowly across the sky on its descent into early evening. Gita remembered that she was to meet with Kauri the Swan after the meal that she was now heading home to help make.

Mudita arrived shortly after her daughter, just as Gita was setting places at the low table making ready for them to eat. Viriya was at the cooking blocks putting the finishing touches to the food with a stir here and a sprinkle there. He had made them a spicy chick pea stew with vegetables and Mudita smelt the aroma as she came into the eating area.

"That smells wonderful, Viriya! I'm starving. It's been a busy day and I can't wait to sit down to rest my feet and eat. How are you both?"

Mudita gave them both a hug, lingering with her arms circling her consort's waist. Viriya leaned into her hug and then swerved away with a pot in his hand to serve their meal.

"Excellent my lovely, but as tired and hungry as you. Gita has been telling me about her first instruction this afternoon from Upekka. Sounds like that old priestess has been working her magic again with the young ones. Gita hasn't stopped talking about her since she got home half an hour ago. Have you, little one?"

"Patra, you'll have to stop calling me 'Little one' soon! I'm to have my Initiation in a few days. I won't be a child anymore." replied Gita pouting playfully.

"That may be so, but your child-time isn't over yet. Maybe you're right though, I'll call you 'chicken' instead!" Viriya teased Gita with another affectionate name that he had always used throughout her child-time. They all laughed and Mudita said,

"So you were impressed by our revered Dakini. She is a wonderful woman and a good role model of what you can aspire to. I've always been a little in awe of her depth of commitment to her practice. The path of the Dakini is one of the most soul-wrenching aspects of the Way of Truth. But you'll learn more about that in time. So, let's enjoy this delicious meal that your father has cooked for us and we can talk more after we eat."

"Can we talk later matra? I wanted to take a walk by the river before dark. It's such a beautiful evening." Gita asked.

Mudita looked closely at her daughter, curious about these twilight walks, but said nothing about her feeling that there was more to this than her daughter's understandable need to be alone at this time. She simply agreed with Gita's suggestion and glanced at her consort who sensed her concern and raised his eyebrows in reply. As was the practice, they ate in silence, appreciating and savouring the gift of food without the distraction of chatter. But sounds of enjoyment were unavoidable, especially when Viriya cooked for them.

Everyone kept these periods of silence except the smallest of children. Silence was encouraged to help develop the skills of contemplation. If communication was necessary, people used the *Mudra* signs which all learned in their first child-time. These consisted of hand postures signifying various attributes and qualities. They were also used to strengthen the hands physically and energetically, helping to release knots of tension that could hinder the flow of prana used in sensing and healing.

After the evening meal, Gita bade goodbye to her parents and set off along the river-side for her meeting with the silver

Swan. She did not like to keep things from her parents. In fact had never felt any need to before; so she once again resolved to talk to the Swan.

Gita ducked under the branches of the tree moving more confidently through the reeds than she had done on her previous visits to the Swan. This time she had more resolve, more determination to undo the seeming deceit that she had perpetuated with her parents in the last couple of days. She felt that the end did not justify the means. The Way of Truth was about being truthful at all levels not only when it suited. Of course, so-called 'truth' could be used to hurt and manipulate. Gita had only just begun to learn the skill of discernment.

She was surprised at the turn her thoughts had been taking in the last week. They had a deeper quality than before. She was more able to follow a train of thought to its conclusion but not by applying any forced concentration to still random and frantic ideas and images. By allowing her attention to gently focus at the heart of a query or feeling, it seemed to rest in resolution when it was ready or rather when she was ready to hear or accept what the outcome would mean for her own conduct. Before now she had not consciously participated in a spiritual life but had been educated and guided to accept that all we do is sacred. Now she recognised that there was a choice to either, accept and develop this learning or to resist it. She parted the tall reeds, hearing the Swan's sonorous voice welcome her.

"*Namaste, Gita. Are you well?*" asked the Swan in its thick, soft vibrating tones.

"*Namaste,* Kauri." Gita replied, bowing her head without thinking, in a natural movement. "Yes and no to your question. I feel good about all that is occurring in my life and happy that I'm able to share some of it with my friends, for they are also experiencing much change. With my parents I feel uncomfortable with not telling them about my sessions with you. It feels as if I am being dishonest with them. This doesn't feel good or right. I wanted to ask if it is possible for me to let

59

them know where I go each evening." Gita rattled this all out quickly before she lost her nerve, only just realising that she hadn't breathed once till then. She then went on to tell Kauri about the feelings and thoughts concerning truth and untruth that had been circulating in her mind.

"Mmm..." Kauri said after a long silence. *"Well, Gita, you're beginning to be able to discern the subtleties of dealing with the ineffable and paradoxical nature of all things. This is good. I understand your discomfort and would seek to reassure you that it has been necessary. I ask that you continue to keep confidence about our sessions with friends and other adults. I would encourage you to tell your parents this evening on returning home, why your walks have had an added dimension and urgency in the last few days. Please refrain from giving details of the Teachings that I share with you. You will pass on this knowledge when you are ready but it is not yet time. You will have others to discuss this wisdom with after your ceremony and retreat when you enter the Temple. You have much to learn from those who have come before."*

Gita thanked the Swan for listening and for her permission to tell her parents, for she was used to being open with them. The Swan shook its increasingly silver feathers, creating ripples on the reflecting water. It then smoothed them down using its slim head and beak in preparation to channel the wisdom she was imparting to Gita.

"This evening's Teaching, to some extent, follows on from the Lotus story that you received from Dakini Upekka this afternoon, but goes much deeper into the significance of the symbolism of the lotus blossom in the Way of Truth. I will give an introduction tonight but we will talk in more detail tomorrow. This is an important Teaching with which you will work on many levels for the next seven years, concentrating on the practice of development and insight at one level each year. You must have both breadth and depth of knowledge, most of which needs to be learned by experience.

"To begin with, the physical human body is interlaced with a web of energy points, which is its unseen but true nature. This much you know. There are seven main lotus centres that channel and receive energy in the body as well as those in the feet and hands. Look now down to your yoni area."

Gita looked down to her pelvic area and as she did so, a red glow begun to emanate between her legs, which gave her a feeling as if the muscles of her legs were being pulled gently towards the earth she sat on. Her tail-bone felt as if it was being pushed gently forward and downwards. The feeling did not last long but Gita had a sense of somehow being more connected to the earth. Then it diminished as the colour faded.

"Look now to the area below your birth knot."

An orange light shone brightly and she could feel warm tingling and pleasurable melting sensations that she hadn't felt before. Gita gasped with pleasure, smiling as the sensation and colour began to fade as quickly as it had appeared.

"Focus on the space just below your ribcage and watch once more." Kauri nodded her head in the direction of Gita's midriff and the area began to emanate a yellow light, which was associated with sensations of energy being pumped around her body. This lent a strange sense of power within. Once again both the light and the sensations quickly faded leaving Gita feeling somehow slightly deflated.

Kauri continued to direct Gita's attention on and up through the centre of her body. Next the Swan indicated her chest area where a green glow appeared and feelings of deep love and an ache pulsed through Gita's heart bringing tears to her eyes. She was aware these tears were not for herself. She could see images of people she knew and loved, some who were alive and others who had passed on. Like her grandpatri; but within this was acceptance for how things were.

The feelings and colour diminished and she felt a cool tingle in her throat as streaks of turquoise light radiated outwards. Her throat relaxed and Gita felt an opening sensation while also noticing her sense of hearing heighten internally. Notes of that ethereal flute were present again but she could not locate their whereabouts. It moved through rather than around her.

As echoes of the music died away the colour changed to a deep indigo, which she felt on her forehead just above the eyes and everything that she could see in front of her including the Swan, was tinged with this vibrant purple-blue hue. Her clarity of thought increased and she could suddenly see the wheel of life and all the phases of growth, with both linear and encompassing vision. The indigo light shifted to the top of her head, which felt at the crown as if it reached up and up, way beyond and around her whole body.

The colour had become a more vibrant shade of purple resting in a warm violet ambience, which was accompanied by a greater sense of knowingness. Gita recognised this from previous experience glimpsed around the Swan. There was a strange sensation of wholeness with all there is and connection to the Divine. All this faded quickly and Kauri directed Gita to remain quiet and rest within the experience without letting thoughts or feelings of excitement overcome her; to breathe quietly and deeply, letting the breaths ebb and flow without force. The Swan spoke quietly as Gita breathed, saying,

"Picture the chakra circle of worship as if it was a large lotus blossom, on which the priestesses and priests sit enveloped in all colours of the spectrum, chanting with one voice, 'Om Mani Padme Hum, Om Mani Padme Hum...'

After some time, Gita lifted her head to look straight at Kauri but the Swan was gone.

She was startled at the bird's sudden disappearance since she hadn't heard any movement but was unsure how long she had been sitting there. She could now though, hear the sound of voices further along the riverbank, singing and chanting:

'Shiva, Great Lord on high
No-one rises above you.

All bow down at your feet
You who danced this world into creation
Shiva, Shiva, Shiva...'

Gita raised herself from the ground a little confused, still sensing the colours and subtle feelings of the energy centres vibrating within her. She stayed back behind the tree and allowed the small procession of people to pass, peering through the darkness hoping to recognise some of the men, and they had all been men, who were singing their praises to Shiva: praises that she had never heard before. It seemed to conflict with the little that she had learned from the Swan, all be it in wonderfully deep and resonant harmonies. To some extent their presence explained the absence of the Swan, though she still had questions. Gita started home with much experience to digest on many levels. She also wondered who that one figure was that had seemed so familiar, but whose features she couldn't quite make out. This raised a new question, which consistently arose in her mind on the way back. Why were they exalting Shiva above the Mahadevi?

It had become quite dark by the time she had wound her way across the city to her parents' home. The sun had set some time ago while Gita was in meditation with the Swan. Her parents looked agitated and more than a little worried when she entered the mitra space inside the house.

"Gita! Where have you been?! We were becoming concerned. You're never this late back from your walks!" cried her mother.

"I'm sorry matra, I was held up with a procession at the river. I had to let them pass before heading home." Her father, who appeared to have been pacing the floor, enjoined,

"A procession!? At this time of night, it's a quarter before the half night. It couldn't have taken that long?"

"Well, there is something else that I was doing and didn't notice the time pass. Can we get some *chai* and a seat and I'll explain." Gita replied.

She then spent the next half-hour or so relating to her parents the circumstances of her twilight walks in the last few days, without going into too much detail about specific teachings. She apologised to them for keeping her meetings with the swan, Kauri, a secret, explaining how she had felt uncomfortable with this omission. She told them that she loved and respected them deeply and appreciated that they had always been honest with her. She had learned from them above everyone else that truth was central to openness with oneself and others.

Her parents listened in silence as Gita spoke of her rendezvous with the manifestation of the Mahadevi and when she finished her father was first to speak.

"Daughter, thank-you for telling us about your 'walks' because your mother and I sensed that there was more to your wandering than just walking, though that *is* a very beneficial practice in itself. Though, preferably not at night!" His worried tone continued as he went on,

"We also recognised and respected your need for space and solitude at this time but after your lateness this evening, we did need an explanation because the possibility of you being attacked by wild animals in the forest at night was a real worry to us. I'm grateful that the Mahadevi has honoured us by being in your presence this way and we do understand there are elements of your teaching that can't be shared. There is much to learn from the silences of speech. I will say goodnight now and leave you to talk with Matra."

He bowed slightly to them both and left the space to prepare for bed. Mudita and Gita talked late into the evening before retiring. Mudita supported her consort in his feelings and remarks to Gita. She added a positive exclamation regarding the deeper and increased significance of the arrival of the Mahadevi in Swan form, rather than only in the dream Gita had related to her some days ago.

"You have an important and difficult task ahead of you, little one. But your father and I will support you for as long and as much as we can. Soon enough you will need to live at the Temple to continue intensified teachings and practice with the Yoginis and Yogis. We are all intrinsically learning to be alone or All One, but this takes time and nurture. Accept what we have to give through our love for you and the Mahadevi."

Gita's eyes filled with tears as she listened to her matra. Deep love and gratitude radiated in her heart area for her parents' care and concern. She thanked her matra with a fiercely affectionate hug and said goodnight.

Magadhi was waiting for Gita at the round boulders by the river, the next half day when the sun was high and hot in a dazzling azure sky. She too, had had much to ponder over in the last few days since discovering her path was to follow in the footsteps of the Matris, with or without the ceremony and initiation.

Magadhi had been given details of the many meetings and practical workdays, which she was supposed to attend for her initiation before she discovered her pregnancy. Now that she had defied all Clan expectations, she was unsure and scared. What most scared her was the fact that she had already chosen her own consort. Who else might have been chosen for her? What would happen to them now that she couldn't participate?

The stirrings that she had been experiencing lately in her body focused on only one boy in particular. Ravi both unnerved and excited her. He had spoken the last evening, of a new devotion to Shiva as the Lord on High, not the Great Mother as she had been brought up to believe was the omniscient source of life. But he wanted to be with her and teach her the new ways. He said she would be his consort and equal no matter what happened. He said he would stand by her when they decided what to tell the Elders.

"There will be conflict soon, Magadhi. The male priests and consorts want more say in how things are run. They have great plans for the city. I want to be part of that change. I won't resist it because I think they are right. For too long the men have been at the beck and call of the women Elders and Priestesses of the temple. But I want you to benefit from this too. I have been assured of a position in the temple and I want you to remain as my consort." Ravi had then planted a soft kiss on her lips as if to convince her of his sincerity. Magadhi was still savouring the kiss and ruminating on his words as Gita deftly climbed up and quietly sat down beside her on the huge boulder.

"*Namaste* Magadhi. Am I interrupting? You look deep in thought there. I'd recognise that frown anywhere, it's so you Maga," Gita teased her friend with a chuckle.

"*Namaste* Gita," she replied with a smile and a hug through which Gita could sense her friend's tension even as she relaxed into being held.

"There's just so much to consider these last few days Gita, don't you think? And you to be a Swan Maiden! Our paths are taking such different turns. Do you think our friendship will last? It's all such grown up stuff. We don't get much time to talk like we used to. I suppose I'm scared inside. I still feel like the child I was last moon, but now everything is changing. Sometimes it feels like the world is turning upside down." Magadhi finished; her voice thick with unshed tears, her melancholy nature getting the better of her.

"Yes, it is scary Maga. I'm sure everyone our age is feeling this way no matter which path we choose at this crossroads. It must be so much harder for you. You will miss out on much of the seven years training since you will be busy nursing and caring for your child. Try not to get too anxious for there is much support, but you do need to tell the Elders soon so that they can arrange for you to train with the other pregnant and new matris. Let's look on what's coming as exciting. An exciting start to a wonderful adventure! We don't know what's to come but we can know that we love and care for each other no matter what, eh?"

Gita surprised herself with these mature words of emotional understanding as she spoke them to Magadhi and it was apparent that Magadhi was surprised too, judging by the look on her face.

"Of course, you're right Gita. Thank-you for reassuring me," she replied quickly with a smirk, looking away as she slid down the side of the boulder to the ground. Not though, before Gita caught the shadow of something negative that had passed across her friend's face a moment before she replied.

"Come on. Let's hurry to the Lotus Garden before the others get there ahead of us." Magadhi said quickly to conceal the brief discomfort the shadow had created.

Gita said nothing about her sense that something had changed and followed her friend, but now with a slight frown appearing on her own brow.

As they made their way to the Garden they met other friends that they had known all their lives and who would probably be feeling akin to the doubts they had just expressed. Gita sauntered whilst Magadhi hurried ahead and caught up with a tall gangly youth she seemed to know well, pulling him closer and whispering into his ear then glancing back at Gita with an expression that intensified Gita's discomfort. The boy Ravi glanced slyly in her direction too with a mirror image of Magadhi's previous smirk then whispered something back and they both laughed and ran on. Gita puzzled over this and in her distraction walked up the heels of Khanti, a boy slightly younger but a head taller than herself with whom she had been friendly with since their first child-time in the *Karrubim*.

"Oh, *Namaste* Khanti, I'm sorry. I was a bit distracted. How are you? We haven't visited together for at least a moon. Have you been given the phasing for your initiation yet?"

"*Namaste* Gita. I'm well, apart from a sore heel!" he replied with a shy grin, checking if there was any cut to his heel. "Yes, we must have a visit soon because I was given my initiation phase to begin in two days. I don't expect there will be much time for visiting after that," he said with a sigh.

"In two days time! That's when my initiation is also taking place. What have you been given as your path?" Gita exclaimed questioningly.

"I'm not too sure yet but I had the strangest dream a few nights ago, and in it was a beautiful golden bird that I've never seen before." Khanti said this just as they reached the entrance to the Lotus garden, so they had to observe silence as they made their way in. Gita's eyes were wide in astonishment and her mouth half open. She was about to ask Khanti more about his dream but quickly let go of his tunic that she had unknowingly grabbed in some shock on hearing his words. Khanti glanced down at her hand, blushing as he did so, and as she let go, he looked up at her face and almost burst into laughter at the expression he saw there. He made the *mudra* sign for 'Later' and held his hand over his mouth to suppress the chuckle threatening to explode. He made his way to the lotus pond and took a seat on the nearest free tree stump with the others.

Gita watched him move in front and to the right of her and just stood for a moment looking after him. She was deeply puzzled and intrigued by this apparent synchronicity of experience and forthcoming events but had no time to ponder further. The *Digambara* giving them the noviciate instruction today appeared from behind the palm tree and gestured to her to take a seat so that he could begin.

Once all twelve young people were seated beside the pool, the elderly man introduced himself as Nekkhamma, a *Digambara* priest who was the counterpart to Dakini Upekkha. He began to explain that the titles that they both carried shared similar meanings. *'Dakini'*, meaning SkyWalker or Traveller in Space and *'Digambara'* meaning SkyClad or Clothed in Space.

"They are complimentary aspects of the same quality aspired to, through diligent practice, pure commitment and devotion to the Way of Truth. This quality, is such, whereby one transcends all notions of and attachments to life experienced through perception of the senses, including what some of you may have heard about or experienced as the 'higher senses'. The Space in which one is said to 'Travel' or be 'Clothed in', refers to inner space which is like the sky above us now," and as he looked up, all eyes followed his gaze and stared at the infinity of blue over their heads. They felt increasingly drawn upwards and into it, while experiencing a calm spaciousness within.

"To this end..." he continued, bringing their attention back to earth with a bump,

"... adepts like Upekkha and myself concentrate much of our practice in dealing with the death and dying of other human beings. We help others to awareness in dying as the passing through yet another stage of life to the next rebirth. Our most sacred places include burial grounds where we attempt to purify the environment for the passage of spirit and move on those energies that continue to resist purification.

"I realise that it may seem unusual to talk of death when you are all so young and presently thinking much about beginning a new stage in your lives. But understand this, death will not ask for an appointment as and when it suits you. Death most often comes unannounced knocking at your door just when you have made plans to do other things. Look at the pond, even lotus blossoms die!" Nekkhamma gave a fleeting smile and on saying this pointed to the dying and dead blossoms, several of which were in a limp and withered state. Then, holding each of young people briefly in his gaze, he willed them to absorb the reality of his words.

"Some of you will already have experienced the death of loved ones but you must consider your own death even as you reach into the heart of The Great Mother for nurture. At the moment life is given, it can be taken away. In that momentous instant of transition from one to the other is Eternity - Deathless and Lifeless - only Space."

Nekkhamma remained quiet after completing his discourse and the mood of the young people was sombre except for an air of pregnant freedom, which lent an underlying tickle to his words. Slowly, each young person gradually felt lightness disperse the sombre aura and smiles began to appear on some of the faces in front of the priest. He nodded gently to them, smiling in return as if to confirm the sense of space that he could see in their eyes. Nekkhamma continued to remain silent but his eyes seemed to glow with compassion especially for those who had not managed to touch the space within. He ended the silent communication with his soft but crackling laugh and bid them 'Good-day'. He immediately stood and smoothly disappeared at the edge of the palm tree. The young people gasped.

Watching him in those few short moments before invisibility appeared, Gita, Khanti and the others saw a rather bent old man with pure white hair and a thousand wrinkles on his face and hands, who made a mudra sign that only two young people understood. He clasped his hands together with the two middle fingers pointing upward. Gita and Khanti looked at each other in surprise and recognition, the meaning passing between them in an instant.

Afterwards, Khanti and Gita naturally drifted towards each other as they all trickled from the Lotus Garden. They both headed in the direction of the river without speaking and returning only smiles to the 'good-byes' tossed to them from other friends. They chose a spot where the bulrushes gave way to some shorter grass and they could sit down.

"Well...! What did you make of that?" asked Khanti. "I don't know about you but I have a distinct lack of confusion since Nekkhamma made that *mudra*. Somehow it seems connected with my dream and you may be able to shed some light on its purpose. True?" Gita took her time before answering his questions so that she could reply with the clarity he had touched upon and she most definitely felt.

"Yes, I feel much clearer now than I did ten minutes ago, but clearer about what I don't yet know. I still have many questions that I'm not too sure there are answers for, but I will try to shed some light on your dream by telling you why I looked so shocked when you first mentioned it earlier today. I also had a dream a couple of nights ago, in which, a large bird appeared to me that I had never seen before that day. The bird was not gold as you said but silver. It spoke to me quite clearly and I was given instructions as to what I must do. Did the bird in your dream speak to you?" Gita asked quietly. It was Khanti's turn to look shocked on hearing what Gita had to say and he stumbled over his words a little.

"Y-Yes it did. It–it told me I must wait for a sign to know what came next. I thought this might be something to do with my initiation, but where do you come into it?"

"I don't know Khanti. I have since been given further instruction by the bird, which is called a swan. What did your bird look like?"

Khanti described a similar long-necked bird to Kauri and told her that it had called itself *Sthanu*, after gliding towards him from the horizon at the time of the day when the sun was at its zenith, burning fiercely in a beautiful, clear blue sky. He described how royal the swan had seemed to him, commanding immediate and unquestioning respect. Gita did not relate the teachings from the swan, Kauri, to her friend but went on to ask him if he knew which mudra Neckhamma had used.

"I don't think I have ever been taught that particular mudra, yet when I do it now," and he moved his hands, Gita moving hers also, into the shape the priest had made,

"I see a brilliant jewel of clear, penetrating white luminosity…it's a…"

"Diamond!" they both said excitedly at the same moment. At that moment Gita realised too that this must also be the sign for the birthmark on her neck but said nothing to Khanti, not being sure of its significance, even though Upekka and Speaking Woman had used its presence in their recognition of her. They smiled shyly at each other and glanced away, then turned their conversation to deciding to meet early the next morning in order to understand more the purpose of events that were happening at breakneck speed and only two days till their initiation ceremonies!

Gita finished her work for the afternoon and started preparing the evening meal. Her father came home whilst she was still peeling and chopping vegetables.

"*Namaste* daughter, did you have a good lesson this morning with the *Digambarra*?"

"Yes patra. It was very different from that given to us by Uppeka, though the priest talked about aspects of similar duties we would have to undertake. Patra, do you know this mudra?" Gita asked her father, showing him the hand sign that Nekhamma had made to herself and Khanti.

"But that's the sign for the mark you were born with! Did Nekhamma show it to everyone today?" Viriya asked, looking puzzled.

"Well, just as he finished the instruction he made it before he disappeared behind the palm tree. It was a bit strange because it seemed like only Khanti and I actually saw it though all of us were still there."

"Khanti? That very shy, gentle youth?" asked her father.

72

"Yes, his initiation is in two days time and he had a dream like mine too, with a Golden Swan. What does it all mean patra?"

"I think you had better ask the Mahadevi when you see her next, little one. There are designs on you and the young boy, that's for sure, though I couldn't say what. But be deeply grateful, chicken, there is great honour but hard soul-graft ahead for you both." He came over to where Gita stood at the cooking blocks and offered her a hug, his big arms outstretched to enfold her within his reassuring grasp. Gita moved comfortably into his bear-like embrace feeling about seven cycles young again, the strangeness and confusion of the last few days welling up and threatening to overflow as tears onto her patra's chest. They hugged for a bit while Gita let go of the tremulous fear that had been building up.

"What would you do without your old patra, eh?" said Viriya, trying to cheer up his daughter. "You know we're always here for you if you need us, yes? Go wash your salty face and let's get this dinner done before matra returns. She'll be starving as usual." Gita left her father to calm herself just as Mudita appeared at the door.

"Sorry, the food isn't ready matra. I feel all these changes are getting to me more than I realise but I've just had a huge hug from patra and I feel better. I'll wash my face." Mudita watched her daughter head for the washroom looking after her with concern and sympathy.

"Is she really all right, Viriya?" She asked her consort while walking towards him with open arms offering a loving embrace.

"I don't really know Mudita. She needed a hug but there's much ahead for her. Ask her to tell you about the communication from Nekhamma today. This is a deeply auspicious time for our whole Clan and it would appear that Gita and Khanti are going to be central to it."

73

All this was said as he returned the embrace and the two adults began to snuggle into each others neck, becoming aroused by the familiar closeness of their mutual concern and love for their daughter, which always accentuated the sensuality that they shared.

"What happened to our food this evening, we'll never get to eat at this rate?!" exclaimed Gita, as she returned to the eating-place. "You can do that sexy stuff later when I go for my walk to the river," she said, laughing as she spoke. Her parents parted reluctantly and still holding hands laughed in reply as the three of them got on with preparing their food before it became late.

After their meal, Gita filled in the details of the afternoon's events for her matra who immediately appreciated the import and concern at the turn the situation was taking. Mudita said very little except to suggest that both herself and Viriya should discuss events with the Elder women and men at their respective meeting times, and at the Clan Chakra Circle as soon as possible.

Not long after their discussion, Gita readied herself to go to see the Swan feeling much supported by her parents, but nevertheless with a mind full of questions that she could not dispel. With all this exciting initiation talk she had forgotten to ask anyone who might know, about the procession for Shiva. Just as she remembered this she also realised where she had seen the boy Ravi last. It was in that Procession! What was he doing there? And how had Magadhi come to know him so well? Was he the father of her child? Gita realised that an effect of spending so much time at the river was that she wasn't with her friend as much anymore. She had missed something in the last few days that somehow she knew would come back to her. But wasn't meeting the Mahadevi more important?

When Gita reached the river-bank the Swan was there as usual. This time its head was not folded into its wings and Gita could see that the feathers on Kauri's body were now silver to where the neck began. All of its lower body and wings were completely silver! Seeing this Gita realised how soon the Swan would have to leave. It made her remember that it would not just leave, but die. This realisation brought back the message from Speaking Woman and also some of Nekkhamma's words from the talk this afternoon. Hadn't he said that death did not make an appointment? How come Kauri knew that she would die in two days time? Wasn't that like having an appointment with death? Every question just seemed to lead to another.

While Gita's mind was whirling with thoughts and deliberations, the Swan silently rested its gaze on Gita and gradually she began to feel an emptying. Her thoughts seemed to pour out like a gentle stream of no-thought. Falling and disappearing, simply vanishing as they arose. This made her feel as if she had just awakened from sleep. Gita felt refreshed and clear and heard the Swan's voice say;

"Always keep the centre of the diamond in sight. For the ten thousand aspects will dazzle and confuse. It is such a beautiful treasure that you might focus on the reflection and not its source. Try to maintain clarity of the vital essence which is innermost and from where your purpose, all life's purpose emanates." The Swan continued to gaze at Gita but had not opened its mouth to speak while the words were conveyed. Gita returned the Swan's regard with a new twinkle of clarity and humour and was now ready to listen.

"Namaste Gita." said the Swan in a quieter register than usual. The tone of her words vibrated at a clear low note but it was apparent that her energy was waning.

"Namaste Kauri," replied Gita and bowed deeply, kneeling and offering the Diamond Mind mudra to the Mahadevi.

"Welcome, to the Ground of Being and Luminosity," and as the Swan said this, the river and the trees and the bird disappeared and all that Gita was aware of was a deep, all - encompassing glow of the clearest light, which did not dazzle but penetrated the darkest recesses of being. The voice of the Swan continued,

"You, who shall be called Nagna. Tell no-one this name. It shall be sacred as the innermost quality that will be your greatest strength and your greatest weakness. You will be given one that all will know you by, but not until it is time for the public unveiling after your Flower Bearing Ceremony and retreat is over."

The glow dissipated and Gita and the Swan were once again surrounded by the dark green vegetation, the sun setting haze and the flowing river nearby, as before. Feeling a deep calm and astute alertness, Gita listened without effort as Kauri began her further teaching.

"By meditation and proper breathing, each adept must seek to awaken the power of Shakti through the Kundalini coiled inside the yoni yantra at the first lotus centre. You must learn to draw her up through the intertwined lunar and solar channels, which form a double helix around each lotus centre. You felt sensations and emotions associated with each centre at our last meeting and you will learn the symbols and qualities of each centre when you have completed your initiation. One can become trapped or static at any level. Remember to keep the core of the Diamond in sight. Return at the next rising of the sun at first light. There is much to absorb before my passing …Till Dawn…."

Gita thought she saw the Swan begin to shimmer and fade as she carefully got up to leave, bowing deeply from her waist. All questions had left her for now. Presently, she reached home and slept.

Gita awoke while it was still dark and cool. Rising from her bed with a shiver, she dressed quickly after washing herself briskly in the water generated by the wheel at the back of the house. Gita left a note saying that she had to attend the Mahadevi, and a freshly picked flower for her parents, setting off while munching some of yesterday's bread to stifle the groans of hunger that her belly sounded. She still felt the stillness of the session with Kauri from the evening before and enjoyed the ripples of light that began to reach into the early morning sky. The morning star was still visible, a far off sparkle sharing its last twinkle before subsiding into invisibility as the sunlight gained in strength. A beautiful reddish glow was cast over everything that she passed and Gita marvelled at the glory of earthly life, immediately understanding it as one of the more alluring facets of the Diamond. Yet, as a reflection it was not such a bad one.

Gita reached the riverbank to find that the Swan was not there and was taken aback by this, for it had never been so before. Just as she realised her surprise, she heard the sound of wind rushing back and forth and felt waves of cool air blow over her, making her hair stream across her face. The flapping came from above and as she looked up, saw the Swan soaring down to the water, its wings spread and working powerfully to balance its body, landing magnificently on the water before gliding towards her.

"*Good Dawn, Nagna,*" said the Swan and bowed its head towards Gita. There were white feathers left only on the head and upper part of Kauri's neck now, which looked a little strange. The rest of her body shimmered brightly and took on the warm glow of the rising sun as it reflected the pinkish hue.

"Good Dawn, Kauri," replied Gita, unsure how to respond to her new name. She hadn't had time to absorb it, not knowing its meaning or symbolism.

"*I only, will call you by this Goddess-Given title,*" the Swan began. "*Even when I am gone, if there is a need to*

77

communicate with you, you will hear me call. The name means 'Naked', for you are yet unclothed by many of the layers of conditioned living at your present cycle. I will transmit to you the Dakini Teachings this evening, so that you will be able to bring them forth to enhance the knowledge and experience you will need for what is to come. On the morrow ahead of your Ceremony, we will talk of the crux of your task. This is connected to the matter we must discuss now. Your friend Khanti," she continued, "will join you as High Priest when the correct cycle has been completed. He has been meeting with Sthanu in dream, and like yourself with me, in physical manifestation at this moment elsewhere. I understand that you shall meet each other later on this morn. This is well and good, for you both must accept each other as equals in this undertaking that will move, not only your own Clan, further up the spherical helix to the integral light, but all humankind. You will be the parents of a new aeon without any physical birthing.

"You will join and consort together but not until you are both ready. This knowledge will be transmitted when the time is right. The Holy Birthing that you will both experience is profound and exacting in nature, but it will enable you to partake of sublime bliss. Both aspects require a complete emptying of self by strengthening the spiritual container to withstand the onslaught of sorrow and joy.

"You both must empty the cup of sorrow to fill the fountain of joy and lead others to that fountain, which is the birthright of all humankind. Khanti will be given a new God-given name from Sthanu. When you are joined you may share your names with each other, until then let it be silent for the most Sacred to call on you.

"Spend the rest of your day today with Khanti, visiting the Elders and tell them of the Mahadevi's design for you both. Some will have been forewarned, others not. Accept the gifts of celebration for your Moon Change time and enjoy. Return this evening for further Dakini Teachings."

78

The Swan shimmered, faded then reappeared before taking flight on her powerful silver wings. Gita held her hands to her heart, which ached with deep awe, and rested awhile on the riverbank. She tried to assimilate the teachings that she'd received in the last two meetings from Kauri. This was difficult because there was nothing in her life with which she could compare any of her new experiences. And what of her joining with Khanti? Had he been told of this event to come? How could she look at him; what would she say? Their lives were inextricably bound together now at the decree of those most Sacred. Would Khanti object or resist?

Despite her circling thoughts, Gita still felt the clarity she had received from the Silver Swan, albeit a little frazzled around the edges. She sat quietly and focussed on visualising the beautiful jewel that she and Khanti had brought forth the day before. She rested her attention at its centre allowing the light of luminosity to envelop her. The frazzled edges of her clarity were smoothed and the luminous glow permeated her whole being. Along with this experience came a sublime sense of reverence for all that was unfolding around and within her. Kauri's words from an earlier teaching floated into the light and resonated like the deepest notes of a flute…

"Do not be afraid of the unknown in my words, but let go of the known in your heart-mind. Prepare yourself for what is ahead by remaining in the moment. Stand under these utterances and let them become you."

Just before Gita reluctantly brought her meditation to a close, she saw in her mind, Khanti approaching the place further down the Indus River where they had arranged to meet. As she watched his approach from above and ahead of him, he looked up as if he knew he was being watched. His expression was one of bewilderment and she knew she must now go to him and help confirm their situation and so setting in motion their life together, if he would acquiesce.

"*Namaste*, Lady." Khanti called out and strangely, to her, joined his hands and bowed his head as she moved towards him. He looked older than he had the day before. It was a very subtle change, as if his face had thinned, losing its child-time look. Contours were apparent that had not been there before but the golden lights in his brown eyes, were as they always had been, yet deeper. To Gita's surprise, before she could return his greeting, Khanti spoke again exclaiming,

"Lady, you have changed overnight! Where is that baby face? What has happened to you? You're glowing!" Khanti gave a characteristic blush after saying this, having blurted it out in his astonishment at the sure but equally subtle change he could see in Gita's countenance.

"I was just about to say the same to you or almost the same. You too look different, less baby-cheeked!" Gita offered by way of reply with a deep chuckle.

"I think it's yourself who has a cheek. Cherub indeed! All that aside - how are you? Much has happened in the last day cycle. There is much that we must discuss between us and offer to the Elders later today."

"Yes. Can we walk by the trees on the shore and find the old shelter there, so that we can sit and talk?" asked Gita. She wished to be in a sheltered place the better to discuss what was ahead of them. They walked without speaking, each absorbing the other's presence and when they reached the edge of the canopy of trees and plants, felt in tune enough to reach spontaneously for the other's hand.

They still felt the affection that they shared as child time friends but it had an added dimension now, which neither of them knew how to put into words. They both very much had a sense that speaking unnecessarily would diminish the fragile quality of their time together, before they had to part for their respective Initiation ceremonies the next day.

Once settled in the makeshift shelter, Gita spoke first to fill Khanti in on what she had been told by the Silver Swan about her connection with Khanti himself. She talked openly and honestly about her thoughts and fears and questions but while speaking sounded very clear and purposeful, even to herself. At one point as she described feelings of fear she almost slipped into the state of fear again. Khanti, all the while having listened attentively, raised his right hand, palm forwards in the mudra of dispelling fear. Immediately Gita relaxed once more and noted the natural and commanding eloquence that Khanti had conveyed in this small but powerful gesture. When she had finished, her face flushed with the telling, Khanti remained silent.

The song of the birds sounded much louder and closer in the silence that hung now between the two young people. Shafts of sunlight broke dramatically through spaces between the branches of the trees, directing spotlights on particular plants or gnarled roots at the base of tree trunks. Watching the dust particles play and dance in the sunlight and noticing their immediate disappearance from sight when they floated beyond the rays of sunshine, created a flash of insight for Khanti. He immediately perceived that this shaft of light was like the ground of being, in which all creatures; human or otherwise were contained within, just like the particles of dust.

The living of life was a performance of and participation in, the same dance also. When he had been with the Golden Swan this morning, he had been told that it was a manifestation of Shiva, Lord of the Dance joined with and consort to Kali, creatrix of the Dance of Life. Now he understood! Dying was, as when the particles moved out of the light to be seen no more. Not gone forever, but moving into another dimension where they couldn't be seen with the eye. Dancing to another tune, perhaps?

The priest Nekhamma had illustrated this exact happening when he disappeared beside the palm tree in the

Lotus Garden, at the end of their instruction the day cycle before. This awareness gave him the clarity to form the thoughts passing through his mind, after Gita had finished speaking.

"At my meeting with the Golden Swan this morning, it told me much of what you have said about the roles that we have been given for the near future cycle. He gave me a new name also, which I can't reveal to you or any other. I have yet to begin my teachings with the Golden Swan, as he will return at specific times in the next seven years as my main influence, though I have much learning to do with the other priests at the Temple.

"I am unsure what to say about the prospect of our joining. I feel joyful that if I am to accept joining at all, then the fact that we have been chosen to do this together does not sadden me. I feel great affection and friendship with you and we have a connection, which strengthens each time we are together. I feel anticipation and excitement but there is much growing and learning for us to do before that can happen.

"I feel honoured that I have been chosen by those most Sacred to take up the office of High Priest. It's more than a little daunting to be honest, but it feels inspiring too. I have discussed it with my matra and patra last evening and they seem to understand the importance of what has occurred and what is to come. They have told me they will support these events, for they are mentioned in the Clan Prophesies.

"What is most on my mind now, is the initiation ceremony of the morrow. It is very clearly an important day for us both even without the added dimensions that have been shown to us. Speaking of that, I suppose we should rouse ourselves and go speak to the Elders."

"Thank you for sharing your thoughts and feelings with me Khanti, I appreciate that it's not easy for either of us. Let's get going then," Gita said when Khanti had finished speaking. They held out their hands to each other, holding lightly as a

82

charge of energy seemed to flow between them and settle in their heart area and remain there after they let go, still looking directly into each other's eyes and seeing the same expression reflected back. Gita felt she would never forget the colour of and expression in Khanti's eyes from this moment on.

Gita returned home only once that day, after she and Khanti had spent most of the afternoon with the Clan Elders. They told them as much as they were able and were surprised when the situation became heated and conflictual. There was one Elder who had voiced resistance to the events that were narrated to the circle. This was Magadhi's patra. Kumar had deep set eyes below a thinning hairline. His features were sharp and angular, unusual in the Clan, and his long nose made him appear to look down on others. His tone of voice matched the sharpness of his countenance as he addressed the other Elders.

"How do we know these are not some childish imaginings? We Priests of the Temple are aware that there are changes coming, but my information tells me that it is not that, which these children say is decreed by their Swans."

"So what is it, if not this?!" asked one of the oldest female Elders. "We have waited for this for some time, and it is as we were foretold. What changes do the priests anticipate? Tell us now, so that we can compare it to The Prophesies, as we can this."

"The changes hoped for and sought by some of the priests, are those happening in the lands we trade with. Those lands are moving into the future where they are not ruled by women. The Egyptians and the Sumerians have expressed concern in their dealings with us in trade. They are worried by the power women hold in Sarrappo, for this is not the way elsewhere anymore." Kumar pronounced.

"Our people are not ruled by women." Sarwasati countered. "Men and women have equal say here on all aspects

83

of our society and how else should it be? Women give life as men help nurture. Women work and provide as men do. Women create and trade as men do. There is equal division of all labour, for when we work we work for the benefit of all. What need or purpose is there in men making decisions for us all, when each of us contributes?" Sarwasati's voice was tinged with anger at her clansman's dismissal of the way of life that created a peaceful existence and had done for many hundreds of years.

"But we are living in the past and this way holds us back from making more trade, from claiming more land. We cannot defend ourselves!" Kumar shot back.

"Defend ourselves from who and what? We have enough land and enough trade so that none go without. What more do we need?" Viriya asked wonderingly.

"This is what I mean," Kumar said with contempt, gesticulating with accusing fingers, pointing at Virya.

"There is no ambition, no desire to be seen as a great nation who leads others, be it in trade and commerce or in pride for our sons."

When these objections were voiced by the Elder, it brought back to mind the feeling of unease that Gita had experienced with her friend the day before, and reminded her of the procession to Shiva that she had witnessed. Gita noticed too, that the Elder Kumar wore a gold ring on which there was some creature, red in colour, engraved there. She was afraid for Magadhi now. How would Kumar react when she told him of her pregnancy?

Nevertheless, several of the Elders revealed important dreams of their own, which had forewarned them of the significance of the initiations of their two young clans-people. So, they took a vote based on the detailed events related by the young people and the mostly, groundless objections from Kumar. The heated discussion had now ended and Magadhi's patra had reluctantly accepted the Elders majority decision. Gita still did not understand the motivation for Kumar's objections but it gave her a clue about the procession because as Kumar left the circle, he was muttering angrily to himself about waiting for more omens concerning Shiva's arising. Gita recognised this was no time to be naïve. Wasn't her strength also her weakness and vice versa. She was learning to heed her intuition whilst accepting that there was little action she could take until it all became clearer. Her parents and Khanti's had remained with the other Elders in council discussing the possible implications of events for the whole community and the future of the Clan. Meanwhile, she bade goodbye to Khanti with a short embrace, neither of them knowing when they would see each other again and made her way home to make herself something to eat, change her robe and prepare to meet the Silver Swan.

There was a late afternoon breeze, which lightened the stifling heaviness of the day's heat. Gita breathed slowly and deliberately as she walked the path now becoming visible, to the spot at the river where the Swan normally waited for her. The river was running low and she could hear the water trickling over stones that had lain aeons in its bed. As she moved into the thick reeds, she noticed that there was no sign of the Silver Swan in the shallow river.

Looking around her, she heard a quiet almost imperceptible voice to her left calling, *"Nagna...Nagna..."* Gita quickly moved towards the sound and found the Swan curled up on a bed of reeds resting. It did not attempt to move as she came closer and she sat close by its almost completely silver head. Only its crown remained white feathered now, and she realised how soon it would be that Swan would disappear from her life. Gita was filled with a deep compassion for the suffering that the Swan was experiencing and felt waves of longing to relieve the creature's pain. Whilst understanding that it was a manifestation of the Sacred Spirit, she recognised that it still suffered not less than humankind, but more.

85

Kauri communicated to Gita that she would not last until the morrow and that the significance of The Shiva Adoration must be communicated now before the Dakini Teachings.

"Nagna, you are in danger!" the Swan exclaimed. *"The negative energy of Shiva's followers has drained my life force. They want to subdue all reverence for the Great Mother and shift the focus to male energy as King. What fools! Don't they realise that all life begins with the feminine principle. There is much conflict coming. The world will shift on its axis and the ego will prevail. Life will become about the survival of the strongest, the most calculating and wars will spill the blood of many generations!"*

"And why not, bird?!"

Gita swung round to see who had spoken. Who had disrespected the Mahadevi in this way? She saw only a dark figure that seemed somehow familiar but was hidden by low hanging tree branches. The voice exclaimed again,

"Are we to be told how to live by a bird? Are we to continue to be controlled by women? We have learned that the making of children cannot happen without the seed of man. No longer are we awed by the women's ability to bear children. This makes them weak not strong. The female cycle makes all women weak and we men are of the mighty Sun god, not the moon Goddess who is fickle and indecisive, whose light is naught but the reflection of the Great King and father of us all. Yes, the world will shift from this day forth and men will take their rightful place as rulers of the world in the next aeons. Listen well, Kauri..," he spat the word out with contempt and stepped out from behind the branches, a bow and arrow in his hands as if aiming directly at the swan.

"You have kept our sons from us for too long. We will take back responsibility for all of their growing, not just what is decreed by the so-called Great Mother".

Gita was in shock and watched the man, feeling numb and unable to move. It was Kumar, the Elder from the council who had raised objections. She saw him release the arrow. Gita reached across to protect Kauri, not realising that the arrow was meant for her and not the Swan.

"And neither will we begin a new era with another High Priestess in control. The great Sun God has shown me, that a High Priest must sit alone without deferring to a female."

The arrow found its mark, plunging into Gita's chest. The Silver Swan stretched its head to the night sky and looked towards the stars. She sung her first and last song and then there was silence. The pure note carried into and beyond the dark night and was heard across the city by all, who felt it resonate within their depths. The Elder stepped back under the cover of the tree and Kauri heard his footsteps move quickly away.

The Swan murmured and squawked, barely understanding what had just taken place but feeling Gita's limp and heavy body spread lifeless across her back. After waddling some to get from underneath the weight and using her beak to cover Gita's body with reeds, she eventually forced herself to leave the dead child's side. Kauri moved slowly feeling a great sense of grief, deep confusion and much fear. What would happen now?

She had only begun to raise her wings when she heard the reeds behind her rustling and turned, hopefully thinking to see Gita lift her head. What she encountered was a dark figure moving towards her at some speed and then the impact and pain of a blow. Kauri toppled dead into the river without knowing who or what had hit her. The only sound was echoing laughter and then nothing.

Words that Point the Way - Glasgow-1991

I awoke sobbing with tears running down my face leaving a pool. Lifting my head, I slowly shook myself, realising after a few moments that I was still sitting at the desk. My heart thumped wildly in my chest and I took deep breaths to slow that, and the heaving sobs. The magnifying glass had fallen to the floor and the glass was cracked. I could hear Paula crying in her cot, shouting for me, so I went to settle her, grabbing a handkerchief to blow my nose.

"It's okay, love. Sh…sh.. do you want a drink?"

"Yes, mummy. Juice."

After dispensing a drink and cuddles to settle Paula, I checked the time, astonished on discovering only an hour had passed. I kept shaking my head in disbelief, trying to clear the confusion I felt. I picked up the leaf and recognised the illustration was that of the young girl in my dream. Was it just a dream? It had seemed too detailed, too much like a memory and she'd had the same birthmark as I did. Maybe I would telephone that woman tomorrow after all.

I sat at the phone the next morning after returning from dropping Jane at school and putting Paula down for a nap.

Despite my nervous hesitance, I slowly punched in the number the woman had written down for me.

"Hello, I'm not sure you'll remember me? We spoke at the…"

"Of course I do. Morag MacAulay wasn't it? The woman interrupted before I could finish. Immediately I felt on the back foot and was already almost regretting the call.

"Well, it's just that I would like to ask you a couple of questions, if that's okay?" I spoke quickly to stem my urge to put down the phone but I had to get some answers.

"I've been hoping…waiting really, for your call. Would it be possible to call round to see you sometime today? You can ask me anything you like when I'm there." Mhairi asked with some insistence.

"Yes, about 1 o'clock. Just ring the buzzer. Bye." I rang off quickly losing my nerve.

Before the buzzer rang at the arranged time, it occurred to me that I hadn't given the woman Mhairi my address, so only half expected it to be her when it did. It was Mhairi. I let her in, feeling puzzled. She must have noticed my expression.

"Yes, you're wondering how I knew where you stayed? Well, I have seen you around and we do have a mutual friend. I know Maggie as well."

"Come in, come in. Can I get you something to drink, tea or coffee?" I avoided responding immediately under cover of politeness and showed the woman into the study. Paula was sleeping and Jane still at school, so we had an hour to chat, hopefully uninterrupted.

"No thanks, we'll get right into things if you don't mind. Can we start with your questions?" Mhairi perched herself on the seat opposite me looking eager and for the moment settled herself.

"Oh, well as to our mutual friend, I didn't know you knew Maggie. She's never mentioned knowing a clair...sentient. Is that what you called yourself?" I asked quickly to avoid having to relive last night's experience immediately. This morning I doubted that it had happened at all, except that the images were still so clear.

"Yes, it just means I feel and get impressions of things from other realms rather than see or hear them, but it's no less powerful and Maggie doesn't know that I am. I only share that with those whom I'm instructed to tell or convey messages to." As Mhairi spoke she appeared to be becoming more and more restless, jerking her shoulders and rubbing her hands as she continued till on finishing, quickly stood up and began to pace around the room, muttering as if to herself.

"Are you alright, Mhairi?" I said, startled by the sudden movement but realising the mannerism was not totally unfamiliar.

"Yes, Yes. It's just someone trying to get through. I'm being directed to your desk." She moved, still jerking and murmuring but now I could see she was gesticulating as if someone was besides her, nodding or shaking her head as if in discussion.

"Your magnifying glass? Oh, it's cracked! Yes, yes. They say it's started already. Something to do with this, I believe. Seeing clearer, the bigger picture?" She held up the glass by its handle in front of her face, hugely magnifying her own spectacles and the blue eye behind them, looking unnervingly straight at me.

"Yes, I had what seemed like a dream last night while reading an inscription I was looking at, through that magnifying glass. It seemed less like dreaming of the events and more like entering an alternative world where it was all waiting for me, if it was me? That's what I wanted to talk to you about." I replied in a hesitant voice, still not sure what had actually happened.

Mhairi returned to her chair, shushing whoever or whatever was trying to get her attention.

"Start at the beginning dear, tell me what happened." She encouraged me gently with only an occasional question now and then. When I had finished relaying what I could remember about the vision last night, Mhairi asked to see the leaf and the verse on the paper. She didn't use the cracked magnifying glass to make out the writing, instead read the copy I'd made of it.

> *'Begin at the beginning to see your goal*
> *Look deeper into the path of the Soul.*
> *What came before remains instead,*
> *to guide when passed away; left for dead.*
> *Arise and continue the spiral journey.*
> *Take heed of the signs lest you worry*
> *that you are alone.*
> *Find courage to finish business undone,*
> *in heart and mind for union to come.'*

"You're right it wasn't just a dream. You were able to enter a past life realm by using the reflective surface of the magnifying glass and reciting the verse concurrently. I'm being told there is more to come but not until you finish the process related to you by the swan." Mhairi said at length. Her talk of past lives made sense to me in theory because of my interest and study of Buddhism, but was this for real?

"If that's what I experienced last night, a p...previous life? Didn't I complete it then as I was supposed to?" Morag's voice was more than a little shaky.

"No." Mhairi slowly shook her head as she related the outcome with great sadness in her voice.

"You remember that Gita was attacked and shot with an arrow. She died and Kauri died soon after. Well, it seems the killings were to prevent Gita becoming the High Priestess as was ordained. Many things changed after these events in

Sarrappo. From what Spirit says, the Priests and Male Elders rose up against the veneration of the Great Mother and eventually a High Priest alone was entrusted with the spiritual care of the people."

"Khanti?" Morag asked expectantly, seeing his face again in her mind's eye.

"No, a young man named Ravi, who had many of the Priests as his supporters for the turning of devotions to Shiva alone." The older woman was becoming agitated once more, rising to her feet to resume pacing again. But I had to ask her the question forming in my mind since she had begun her restless pacing.

"You were there weren't you? In that dream or remembrance or whatever you call it?"

"Well, it wasn't exactly me, the same as it wasn't exactly you. Yes, we've shared other lives. I've probably been your mother; father, brother, sister, and friend in other lives that you don't remember. As you have for me and we all have for each other. That's how Karma and rebirth works. It's not the personality that returns but the consciousness and with it the seeds of positive and negative actions from each past life. When the conditions are appropriate the seeds will ripen. Awareness of the process of cause and effect and behaving accordingly, is the only way of changing the patterns built up over aeons... Yes, Yes. Your father is saying that you can help redress the balance. There is another much older spirit here as well. She calls herself Speaking Woman."

"I've been told of her presence before but haven't felt her around for some time until last night. She was in the remembrance too." I recalled this as we spoke of her now.

"She has always been with you. She is whispering that you must fulfil the Teachings by practising what you were instructed. Your friend abroad is waiting to continue the process with you."

"Enrique!? But I haven't seen him for a couple of years! What's he or my father got to do with any of this? Why can't Dad stay out of it? He's always tried to tell me what to do. I don't appreciate it anymore now than I did when he was alive, and he's been dead for the last six years!" I was angry at my father's intervention again!

"He means well, Morag. He's learned from his mistakes since passing over and he will always be connected to you. You will meet him again, even if not in the form you might expect." Mhairi tried to console me by encouraging me to consider what needed done but she did not insist. Soon we could hear Paula calling and I had to breathe deeply to soften my annoyance before going to her.

"Well, thank-you Mhairi. I'll have to give this a lot of thought. Can I call you again?"

"Of course, dear. Anytime. Why don't I walk round to the school with you to collect your other little girl?"

A Moor in Mallorca - 1998

I spent the next seven years living out the directions given in the last remembrance: from Mhairi, from my dead father and other spirit guides that came through my dreams. Mhairi's gifts helped me greatly over the following months as I prepared for the move to Spain. Would Dad always be around watching, commenting, criticising even from the grave? Yes, the instructions did correlate to the remembrance of the Indus Valley and yes, I did have someone; that someone who had been lingering in the background of my life then and who had come to share the learning that had been predestined. It had been deep, exciting and sensual and I felt prepared now. More integrated and centred than ever before.

I had kept in contact with Enrique during those dark days in Glasgow and told him of what had occurred to me; the meetings with Mhairi, of which there were many in those first few months, the remembrance too. Enrique had gasped in shock when I mentioned on the phone, my apparent passing into a past life realm. Not as I initially thought, because he'd found it hard to believe but because he had had a remembrance too and hadn't yet shared it with anyone for fear of being ridiculed.

Until of course I shared mine with him. I remembered landing at Palma airport that morning seven years ago where Enrique was waiting, as he'd waited since I'd called him to say I would be coming some months before I arrived.

"*Hola, qué tal* Mora? I've been expecting your call. I dreamt of you last night. I dreamt of the days we will share and the journey we must take with one another." 'Mora' was what Enrique always called me, never Morag but I liked its softer sound, especially with his Spanish accent.

When we finally arrived he had helped me to find a home for myself and the girls in the old town not far from the La Seu, in Calle Estudié General. He spent most nights and many days at the house with me. I had tried to write down everything that I could remember from the Teachings given to me and had researched the philosophy of all schools of Hinduism and Buddhism. To my surprise much of the Dakini Teachings were already in print. I also found books and references to the *Tantra* and the *Yab-Yum* ceremonies and practices.

When I called Mhairi every month, she filled me in on the gossip at her evening services. She was not, in this life anyway, of the Buddhist persuasion. She was a believer in God and Spirit wholeheartedly, but not a great church goer or fan of organised religion. Her services were those where mediums would take to the platform and convey messages from the Other Side to members of the audience. She appreciated not always having to be the one giving all the time. On some occasions there were sessions of Spiritual Healing. Most of her days though, were spent visiting elderly friends, taking care of them, keeping the lonelier ones' company and going for lunch every Monday at the Swan & Half Moon Bar in Glasgow with some of her clairvoyant-sentient-audient cronies. She still had a mischievous sense of curiosity even though she was getting close to seventy. She also continued to give me communications over the telephone.

"I've got someone here. He seems to be rocking back and forth. Skull cap on his head. He's wearing a long cassock or habit. I think he's a Rabbi. Says to tell you that: "All Paths lead to Rome." Speaking Woman whispers that you are developing as was ordained and it will be time to remember soon."

"What? Again! How many lives do I have to remember?"

"As many as it takes till full awareness, she says."

"Ok, how will I know when it's going to happen?"

"You won't. It will happen when you're ready but look and listen for the sign from the wind?"

That sharing Enrique had talked of sealed our fate for the next seven years. We found a few others to help consecrate these now, mainly Buddhist rituals and we both knew their origin was deeper and required our devotion to the Mother of all Buddhas, *Prajnaparamita* not just Siddhartha Gautama, the historical Buddha, or Buddha *Shakyamuni* as he became known.

Siddhartha Gautama too, was a man of his time and took on the patriarchal conventions of his day until persuaded otherwise by his disciple Ashanti. Women were considered secondary and initially a negative influence by him, but many female spiritual practitioners who became Dakinis proved this assumption wrong, as have many women in most religious philosophies across the ages.

I knew my work was not yet done and Mhairi had confirmed that in the last telephone conversation. I had had many glimpses of other realms in my couplings with Enrique. We had ascended on the wings of Kama in desire and its satisfaction. We had dived deeply to the depths of our being, especially when retreating in Valldemosa outside the city, not always liking what we found buried inside.

In the early days many of the practices were at a foundation level.

"Enrique, we need to make a commitment here about being honest and open with each other. I realise this seems obvious, but it's about learning to have a level of communication that can transcend the petty games that couples often play with each other."

"*Lo entiendo,* I understand. We want to be playing games of love, learning respect and admiration for each other, *Si?*"

"*Si caro,* we want to encourage and build each other up so that I can be strong when you feel weak and vice versa, and have a way of coming together again when there is disagreement between us. Shall we try the nurturing meditation?" I stroked Enrique's face and he laid his hand over mine before we moved to lie on the bed.

"This feels familiar. We're kind of lying the way we usually do before we go to sleep or make love, aren't we?" He asked as we got comfortable in a spooning embrace.

"Yes, the main differences are that neither of us should remain in the position if we're not comfortable as we might normally do, and we need to lie only on our left side to allow the energy to flow properly. We can take turns depending on how we feel about who lies to the back or front."

"*Bien*, didn't you say it's best to do this twice a day? If that's true we can try in the morning and evening and both have been in the two positions."

"Yes, so when you're behind me as you are now, your right hand comes to rest on my belly or my genitals and your left arm can slip under the crook of my neck."

"Do you need a pillow Mora? Is my arm hurting your neck?"

"No, only if it's comfier for you? You can rest that hand on my forehead or my chest."

We were already feeling quite affectionate and Enrique began to stroke my belly with his right hand, clearly feeling the beginnings of arousal.

"Mmm…that's really nice but if you keep doing that we'll never learn this today."

"*Lo siento.* Sorry, but you feel very lovely. *Vale,* what's next?" He murmured into my ear but stopped stroking my belly. "We can get to that later, *si?*"

"*Si caro,* for now we just need to lie and relax and focus on deep breathing. Inhaling together, holding the breath and then exhaling. Let's try with three whole breaths and you're the giver, so try to emphasize your out-breath projecting the energy from your heart chakra to mine. Then move your focus to the brow and then the base chakras."

We lay like this practising the harmonising breath for about five minutes and then moved on to the reciprocal charging breath so that I breathed in as Enrique breathed out and in between, one holding and one letting out. We were both trying to be conscious of the energy we were imparting to the other. We continued for about another five minutes. By now we were communicating on three different levels, and most subtly, chakra to chakra.

We finished off by turning face to face and looking into each other's eyes. It was when we did this that I knew this man as I'd always known him. It was his eyes and the expression there. We both had a soft, twinkling gaze which conveyed gentle strength, support and above all, love.

We were reluctant to get up straight away and I began to stroke Enrique with my fingertips gently down the front and sides of his body.

"That tickles Mora?" Enrique said, jumping slightly.

"Do you want me to stop?" I murmured breathing into and licking his neck.

"No, but just move your hand over here and a little more pressure there, mm…yes that's very …mmm…." The sessions were full of delights but sometimes made us feel very vulnerable. But we could always slow down and come back to the nurturing position when we felt that way.

I was feeling vulnerable now that I had gradually acknowledged our time together in Mallorca was coming to an end, but slowly, slowly. The thought of Enrique's reaction then, was scarier. We'd been through a deep journey in the last seven years.

We travelled up to Valldemossa from the city, for a weekend every month at the new moon and stayed for a full week twice each year in May and October. These retreats were a combination of lengthy periods of meditation and Tantric Practice which at times combined exercises on physical, emotional and mental levels.

The Sant Bartomeu tower would become visible as we came up the steep hill towards the town of Valldemossa. Although, one of the most well known villages on the island of Mallorca, it wasn't greatly populated and looked today as it always has. Though it's probably in better condition now since there's a concerted effort to maintain the original buildings, with few new properties built, unless in the old style.

We rented a small house in the village and kept a room upstairs for our more intimate and therefore private practices. The street where the house stood had, in summer particularly, a picture postcard, almost idyllic look with its green shuttered windows set into buildings of original blond stone work. The cobbled street below was lined with container pots filled to overflowing with greenery and colourful blooming flowers.

We had arranged to use space in the old Carthusian convent, *La Cartoixa,* for group meditation practice with others who joined us on occasional weekends. The view looking over the village was spectacular. Small blond brick houses with their sloping tiled roofs, huddled on the hill at varying levels on the incline, interspersed with deep green topped pine and palm trees and bush foliage, set against the forest in the background. From the highest view point in the village, it was so unchanged that I often had the impression of looking back through time. Ever resting, being as it always had.

Tantra on the physical level is the Art of Conscious Loving but has the dimension of emotional and spiritual integration as its purpose. It always begins with focusing the mind using Yogic Breath techniques.

"Enrique, can you go and buy some scented flowers? I'm just going to set the room up for our session later." I smiled and looked directly into his eyes when he turned to me, eyebrows raised and I held his gaze for a few moments. His face broke out in a corresponding grin.

"Is it tonight?" he asked expectantly with excitement in his voice.

"*Si caro,* it's tonight." I replied softly and he practically skipped out the door. I laughed out loud at his boyish excitement and began to prepare the room as one or other of us always did. The walls were painted a deep golden yellow and the floor had at its centre a beautifully woven thick wool circular rug with traditional Arabic designs of birds and climbing plants in deep rich reds and gold with fringing around its edge. I let down the wooden blinds seeing the sun set across the rooftops of the village houses in a reddish glow.

I laid out round cushions on which to sit while we meditated in front of the shrine presided over by Padmasambhava, the Precious One and Green Tara, a female Bodhisattva. I laid the Tantric texts out with our malas or rosaries. Enrique's made with amethysts and mine with green Malachite. I lit scented candles and incense of lotus and cinnamon to fill the room with fragrance. At the other side of the room I heaped up large and small, soft silk and velvet cushions on a slim mattress covered with brushed cotton sheets of the deepest burgundy and pulled around it the fine mesh cotton curtains woven with golden threads that hung from a dais on the ceiling, for later.

"*Gracias* Enrique, they're beautiful and they smell heavenly. I'll just put them in some water. Do you want to bathe now while I finish off in here?" I asked when he got back.

"*Si Cara*, but first…" and he pulled me towards him wrapping his arms around me and I felt the warmth of his firm body pressed against me with urgency that was also in the long slow kiss we shared. He released me and I let go reluctantly, but not before feeling the hardness of his sex grow as we kissed.

"*Vale*, how I can go for my bath now?" He looked down at his bulge and then at me, holding his groin and moaning softly. "Do you want to join me Mora? No, no we need to have pure thoughts for this, don't we. The wicked stuff's for later, *Si?*"

"*Si*, Enrique my love. Maybe you should have a cold shower instead? I'm only kidding, but don't be too long in the bath, I still have to bathe too. Remember, get focussed!" I teased him, going into the kitchen to find vases for the flowers. Tonight we would practice the Yab -Yum, in meditation first and then physically, although each practice had elements of the other. It was the culmination of all our practices these last few years.

"It looks and smells wonderful in here, Mora." Enrique came into the room carrying two glasses of water. I was sitting on my meditation cushion after my bath, wearing my new kaftan of Mallorca's traditional *Roba Llengues* cloth of white hand-woven cotton, patterned with emerald green diamonds and felt good and ready for this.

" Mmm…you look and smell wonderful too." I said as I leaned into Enrique's shoulder when he'd lowered himself onto a cushion beside me.

"Now, Now! None of that Señorita. Remember, focus!" he kidded me, chuckling as he gave me a brief embrace and then sat up waiting expectantly. I pushed him gently and then we began.

"*Vale,* I'm not going to explain all this before we do it. I'll talk us through as we go, *Si?* So, assume the position! Not that position!" I quickly said as I heard him laugh quietly.

"We're meditating right?"

"*Claro!* Sh..sh…So back straight, lifting up through the spine… Shoulders dropping down and chest open…Releasing any tension, letting it go on the out-breath… Begin to be aware of your breath…Let the mind rest on the subtle sensations of the breath as it moves in and out through your nose. Begin now to visualise yourself in sexual union with your consort…See your consort and yourself as God and Goddess…Buddha and Dakini…Shiva and Shakti…focus intensely and clearly. See you and your consort as transparent radiant divinities making love…Actually allow yourself to become sexually aroused…co-ordinating the feelings with your breathing…on the in-breath, breathe light down the front of your body to the genitals, seat of Life…on the out-breath, you breathe Life up the spine into light at and above the crown of the head…any pleasure you experience is directly up the spine and released into the Light at the top of the head, home of infinite Light and Release…on the in-breath, keep breathing Light directly down and into the body…as your body-mind begins to feel bliss, take it directly to meditate on Emptiness …Compassion and Wisdom in every breath you take. When you are in the state of spacious bliss of I AMness and full to infinity with no desires and wants, allow a gentle, small ripple of a thought to arise…'I vow to liberate all sentient beings into this free and open space'…allow a ripple of compassion to arise out of this vast ocean of bliss…allow waves of compassion to flow out to all beings… 'May they be Well, May they be Happy and free from suffering'…rest in Infinite empty bliss…"

We continued the practice for about an hour feeling the intensity and clarity of the transformation of sexual energy into radiant bliss and compassionate embrace, at the most deeply subtle levels.

102

On spontaneously rising together in deep silence, Enrique and I reached out for each other and moved under the curtains and onto the bed. Enrique removed his white dhoti with some help from me and then reciprocated by unbuttoning my kaftan and pushing it slowly over my shoulders caressing my breasts as it fell away. He then sat on the bed with his back straight and his legs crossed to support my weight and I sat astride him, lowering myself onto his erect lingam, as he slid deeply into my yoni, with sensations that took my breath away. My legs were open and around his back, the soles of my feet touching behind him. Then we rocked and circled sometimes slowly, sometimes faster to explosive and exquisite orgasmic heights, touching, stroking, moaning and gasping and bringing to the dance all that we had learned together, mostly looking into each other's eyes the whole time. We continued to dance for several hours. Making love until sated, pleasurably exhausted and hungry enough to stop and eat the food I had prepared that afternoon.

And many afternoons had followed. Both the practices became regular after that, at home and in Valldemossa but sometimes when we did a retreat, there was no lovemaking at all; just intense meditation. These sessions had a powerful effect on our relationship at many levels.

I took off to visit my mother on the coast in Puerto Pollensa. I needed to create a space between Enrique and me so that I could be sure the realisation I felt about the future or lack of, for our relationship, was a genuine response to a deeper calling rather than a reaction of some kind.

"Hi, mum. How're ye doing?" I gave her a big hug trying to make up for not having visited for a few weeks. I was always a bit taken aback after not seeing good old Grace for a while. She was visibly and too rapidly ageing but always bright and talkative. The children affectionately called her 'Granny Ripples', which just makes her laugh now, even if the first time she heard it she had looked just a wee bit shocked, not to say offended.

"Hello Morag. I haven't seen you for a while. What's been happening? How're my two granddaughters? Do they still remember me?" She just couldn't resist having a dig but admittedly I deserved it.

"Of course they do! They keep asking me when they can come and see you."

"Yes, so....?" She waited.

"Ok, Ok. I promise I'll bring them over next week. Next Saturday. How's that?"

"That's fine. I've nothing planned that day. So, what's been keeping you away?"

"Well, my aromatherapy practice has been quite busy. My appointment book's pretty full."

"So how did you manage to pry yourself away today? What is it? Has something happened with you and Enrique?"

"It's not Enrique, mum. It's me. I think it's time to go to back to Glasgow. Something's calling me back."

"Oh, the river Clyde, the wonderful Clyde. The name of it thrills me and fills...."

"Very funny! You're getting a bit facetious in your old age Mum, aren't ye?"

"What do you expect Morag? You want to go back to that?! You've got a great life here and the girls are settled. Why do ye want to go and wrench them away from everything they've got here, school, friends, *and family*?"

"Well, you know me, Mum, if I feel that it's the right thing, I'll do it and it'll work out even though it might not be easy."

"Yes, I do know you Morag. Are ye sure this is not you just being impulsive? It has been known. If I remember rightly there was that time....."

"Please don't Mum. I'm not doing it just out of a whim. I do know I've got work to do back there and I need to go and find out what it is."

"So, you've already decided then? You better bloody bring those kids to visit *a lot* before ye go. What does Enrique have to say about it all then? Mmm… You haven't told him yet have you?" She was searching my face, reading it like a book.

"No, but I will when I get back to Palma. I'm planning to go home in January. I need time to wind my business down here, give the tenants notice at the house in Glasgow and sort things out at school for the girls."

"There's not much I can say then. When you get something into your head…Are ye staying for dinner?"

"Yes, I was going to stay the night if that's ok? But I'm just going for a walk on the beach just now. I won't be long." I closed the door behind me with a sigh of relief. That was the first hurdle over. Not the hardest though. Those were still to come.

The glistening, emerald green water lapped against the shore, shedding debris as it flowed with an almost imperceptible rhythm, in and out, mirroring the breath of life. The deep golden, fiery sun was beginning to set. Its rays were bouncing in sparkling array across the water on this warm and still summer evening. I loosened the shawl I was wearing against an imagined evening chill, expected but unrealised. The tide's movement was calming, its rushing sound washing through my soul, cleansing and invigorating me. The choices sitting poised before me, for the moment, fell away leaving peace of mind. This Spanish island was beautiful; bright and heady, stirring dreams and a wish that I could stay forever. But nothing lasts forever. Impermanence seemed an indelible mark on the manuscript of life. Often, too often for lasting tranquillity, came the sagest saying; 'Change is the only constant in the universe.'

The words reminded me that what happened in life was a natural and universal phenomenon, even if not everyone was aware that it was so. Not too long ago though, it had seemed like things, events, feelings were spinning the globe of my world and my reality, a little out of control. If only life would slow down or at least stay the same for a while! In the past, this was the thought that had penetrated many times in my fugue of fear and uncertainty. Hoping someone, some power would clear my confusion and acquiesce to my demand.

In treasured freedom and aloneness I wandered, seeing the daily goings-on of the golden-skinned people of the island. The houses of the more affluent had white stucco walls that glimmered in the hot afternoon sun. Each one bore its own character. Stamped with touches of originality, built on different levels, balconies jutting out, patios closed in for intimate family meals held traditionally late in the evening. The slow, languid pace of Spanish life attracted me strongly, as too did the other more passionate face of Spain, like the sounds that moved and stirred my gypsy soul. Its music, loud and rapturous with their custom of hand-clapping and castanets, together with the strumming of a classically romantic 'riff' on the guitar, inspired and excited me.

Puerto Pollensa was the place where I'd first met Enrique. He had been working as a chef in one of the restaurants along the seafront, but was off duty sitting smoking and drinking his ubiquitous café solo. I sat at a table nearby to also smoke and have my ubiquitous café con leche. I was very aware of him sitting there, though he had only briefly glanced in my direction as I sat down. But I knew he was as aware of me as I was of him, and that he would speak to me.

"Perdone, do you have the time?" I told him and five minutes later he left saying *"Gracias, Adios!"* on his way past. Mmm…nice, I thought and saw again in my mind his fine

featured face and chocolate brown skin and most significantly a flash of those deep brown eyes with golden lights when he dazzled me with a grin. Where had I seen those eyes before? I finished my coffee not long after and headed round to the bookshop not in the least surprised when: there he was. We bumped into each other again a few days later, which wasn't hard to do, since he worked ten minutes away from my mother's flat. This time we had our coffees at the same table; again his black, mine white.

Enrique was originally from Andalucía in the south of mainland Spain. He'd have been known centuries before, like all his people, as a Moor, from the Spanish *moros* meaning dark coloured. He was of African descent and so his heritage was ancestral slavery.

We found we had much in common. He was a dancer by profession and I loved to dance, it had been one of my unrealised childhood dreams. I was an aromatherapist by profession and he loved being massaged. He had been meditating for a few years and I, for over a decade. Many synchronicities appeared, and the undeniable attraction was only a surface reflection of an equally undeniable depth of connection, but from where?

I recognised him the moment I saw his eyes. Khanti. What kept us apart then was because when we met he had been in a relationship, though this didn't prevent me carrying home from that holiday, the notion that he was my 'could-be lover'. We had kissed and what a kiss!? But it was not a safe place I could enter comfortably after the history with men I had! We kept in contact by phone and knew that the connection merited, at the very least, an attempt at friendship.

So, Spain has contrasted, no, clashed deeply with the reality of dullness and the grey of northern city life that I had in Scotland with its hardness and apparently shallow music. I seemed to feel more affinity with the Bolero than with my own long-forgotten Celtic roots, of which in Glasgow there had been little evidence. In that city, I had felt rootless and carried a nagging doubt as to where my home really was. My centre had crumbled in the daily grind and loneliness of Glaswegian existence until I met Maggie. Her friendship had supported me in many ways.

I had met Maggie at the cash-desk of the Co-op supermarket where she worked part-time. She recognised me from the school gates where the children were picked up daily. Her daughter Claire was in the same class as my eldest, Jane.

"Hiya, I'm Maggie. Your wee lassie's in ma Claire's class, is she no?"

"Primary two? Does Claire have red curly hair? A wee dancing dynamo?" I asked, picturing the little girl dancing and whirling to Michael Jackson alongside Jane at the class party the previous week.

"Aye, ye're right there hen. She's non-stop that one. Keeps me on ma toes! Are ye goin tae that parent's social next weekend?" Maggie was waiting for an answer and I was procrastinating as I hadn't been out for a while and wasn't too keen on school parents' events.

"Em…I'm not sure if I can get a babysitter." I said doubtfully.

"No worries, I'll ask ma man, Martin if he'll look after the weans. Is it jist the wan ye've got?" I shook my head and mentioned Paula hoping that would put an end to it but Maggie said how Martin loved kids and she'd ask him, sure there'd be no problem. We swapped phone numbers and she called me that night to say it was all arranged. That was the beginning of a long friendship.

I had managed to fulfil my dream of studying aromatherapy while living on the island. I found, in Palma, an organisation that helped me learn in detail over four years, about the properties and use of natural substances like flowers. These were distilled to their essence and added to carrier oils for massaging the body and improving people's quality of life on emotional and physical levels. I had since managed to build a small private practice from my home in the old town.

But really, when had things begun to transform? When had everything I'd seen and experienced, begun to fall into place, the coincidences beginning to resemble connections? A shift in consciousness had occurred after that remembrance and my perception of the world had changed drastically. My life had taken a turn. As if I was upside down and back to front but now topside was up and the delusions of my happenstance had begun to fade into shadows.

What of the people of uncanny and uncommon wisdom like Eva Moon or Mhairi, who had appeared in my life just when I'd been suspended on the knife-edge of meaninglessness? Theirs had been the sharpness that had cut through the darkness of despair like a diamond on dirty glass.

In that synchronistic second of linking the chain of lives, I'd been able to hear the words I needed to hear. Certainly not in the time of my anger before which was like fireworks exploding without pattern and with unguided force. All around me I had, at times in the early days with the children and with family members, let fly missiles sure to destroy the contact and support with those I needed most. Its effect was to blow up the bridge of human need and exchange.

In those years, I dealt my children an uneven hand of roller coaster rages and tender affection. They, never quite knew which to expect, and me, never quite sure how to deal with their development or mine. I wanted to remain true to my belief that children were the most sensitive of human beings, relying on sensation, instinct and intuition to make sense of their chaotic world. There was an unwillingness to stifle the girls' spontaneity coupled with a sometimes, confusing inability to create a healthy boundary for their behaviour. My resultant grappling with guilt began to cloud their lives, and I now and then, wallowed in the mud of misery or got wired on the unpredictable shocks of anger, sparking the girls' already enfolded terror of violence. My contact with the family web became limited by defensiveness and the hard edge of poverty. Friends then, were shunned, ignored or tolerated until I met Maggie. She wouldn't let me stay enclosed in the prison of self-imposed exile I'd built. She climbed over the wall I was trying to build, bringing it down. Maggie stopped me closing out the light and laughter that we needed to know. Even now when I called her every few weeks she still had me bursting my guts with laughter. Like yesterday morning,

"How're ye doin' hen? Whit ye up tae noo? Are you and that man still doin that acrobatic shaggin?" That's Maggs, straight to the point.

"Do I detect a note of jealousy there Maggs? Besides it's none of your business."

"Ooooh! Excuse me! Since when did you get so hoighty toighty? C'mon 'fess up. Maybe I could learn a thing or three. Here, do you do threesomes?"

"Now that would be telling. Anyway how're you? How are ye getting on with those sticks?"

"Mo, It's no bloody laughin matter when ye cannae feel yir legs or anythin else for that matter. Jist think whit its done tae ma sex life. In fact, have ye got any tips on how tae shag a tree? Martin could use a few. I feel sorry for him sleepin wae a wummin whose body feels like a big lumpae wood." Not an ounce of self-pity in the woman. She was awesome.

"Is that what it really feels like, Maggs? How's your balance? Have ye had any falls?" I wasn't kidding anymore. Maggie had been diagnosed with M.S. three years before and it seemed to get worse as the years went on, but mercifully was taking its time.

"Well, I mostly feel numb all over, and I have been stumblin around a bit. But ye know whit it's like aroon here. People jist think I've been on the booze when they see me totterin about. The other day at the school, I saw that uppity cow, whit's hir face? Aye, Charlene. She says, "I think its disgusting being in that state when you've got children." I nearly slapped her intae the morra or I would if I had the energy. So I says tae her, 'I think you're disgusting in any state, ya cheeky cow!' "

"Good for you. Don't let the bastards get to you, Maggs. Listen, I'm coming back to Glasgow in January. So we can have a good chinwag and catch up on the gossip when I get back, eh?"

"That's brilliant Mo! I miss ye even though ye can be moany faced besom. Ye jist canny manage wae oot me can ye?" I could feel my eyes filling up. She was lonely and having a hard time.

"Ye're right Maggie. I would probably have topped myself if it wasn't for you and your pathetic jokes. But then again, too many of your jokes could have me looking for a length of rope. Maybe I'm making a mistake here?"

"Seriously though, are ye really coming home Mo? Dae ye want me tae let the tenants at the house know?"

"Aye Maggie, if ye can manage, but don't worry about it 'cause I'll have to write to them anyway." Home? Yes, I was going home.

"Listen Mo, make sure and find me some secret positions for trees like I said, right?"

"Yes, and if I can't find any info on the Sacred Art of Tree Shagging, well, you seem like an expert, so you'll just have to write the book. Here, we could make a fortune! But I'll do my best. You take care, Maggs. Love you. I'll call you next week okay. Bye."

Beginning my slow walk back along the beach at the water's edge, taking leave of my short-lived peace of mind, forsaking the gentle waves behind, my thoughts began to race again. My affair with Spain would end soon and on my return, could I keep with me the seeds of contentment to sow amidst the daily responsibilities? I'd have to forfeit the bittersweet delusion that thoughts of death, at times, had tempted me into wanting that sweet repose, leaving the constant earthquake of emotions and guarded relationships behind. To slip into the bed of the long night, where dreams it would seem, are lives lived over and over. But it's not my time yet. There are many more futures than we can possibly imagine even in our wildest, wish-fulfilling fantasies. Parallel worlds that reflect other lives; recognisable but profoundly different.

Starting to climb the hill back up to my mother's apartment, insight resonated and I visualised the long foreboding journey of life. I thought of the many mortar bricks that had stood in my way. The lengthy frightening journey of myself had only just begun to unravel itself, but the barriers were beginning to slip away. Brick by awful brick, the wall that had seemed so ancient and everlasting, began to feel surmountable. As the plaster cracked, crumbled and fell, each day brought the sweet smell of beckoning pleasures and a world full of chances. Dark and dusty corners of myself that had been hidden away so long, began to feel warmth and light. The wall was crumbling, and I had always it seemed, been waiting agonisingly for it to fall. My stone protection, my cold outer shell, was melting. It was washing away the dust and debris from my heart and the cobwebs from my soul.

Half way up the hill, I came across the numerous stray, but well-fed cats and their litters of kittens. Unlike city cats, they had no fear of people. They crept forward hoping to be offered some small morsel to fill their always hungry bellies. A tiny jet-black kitten followed me playfully for some distance, hiding, now jumping out for a game of peek-a-boo. It reminded me of the dream I'd had during my siesta earlier in the day. I recalled finding, in the dream, a small green kitten with a white-tipped tail. Having decided to keep the creature, it had fallen into and been swimming in deep water. In my effort to care for the wet kitten and dry it out, I put it under the grill, but instead of warming it, the tiny thing had been grilled, shrivelled into a small ball and was dead. I felt sorry. I hadn't meant to hurt, much less, kill it.

The dream seemed symbolic of my need to return to Glasgow, to care properly for my own sensitivity and that of my children. It was time to get out from under the burning heat of the sun and find cool calmness and comforting creativity, in our own natural habitat. There was a deep compassion in my heart that burned to be expressed towards those who needed it.

It's time to go home, they're waiting for you.

Speaking woman was back whispering in my ear and that was the final confirmation.

I travelled back to Palma the next day promising my mum, that not only would I bring the girls on Saturday, but they could also come and stay for a week over the festive break.

I started packing soon after I got back to Palma. Little things here and there that helped me feel the change of direction: a box for my books, a bag to take the gifts of shells, jewellery and other accumulations. The girls would have to be taken out of school, but not before the holidays. At least they were older and bi-lingual now. It would help them see the world in other ways, make them less narrow minded. The people of Glasgow and Scotland could be very blunt and judgemental, not always open or kind to those perceived as different for any reason. This much gave me second thoughts about moving, but only fleetingly. The girls had settled well here eventually, and would do so again in their birth country. They were returning more confident and secure in themselves, and I had been able to transform some of that early anger into creativity, but not alone. My coupling with Enrique had helped me make great inroads in this respect. My anger had become constructively directed passion. Meditation of course, helping to calm and soften; helping to smooth the sharp edges sculpted from granite and poverty of spirit.

"It's not fair!" Jane shouted, stomping out of the room as she had done many times, not just today, slamming the door behind her. But today was the day I had told her that I was thinking about going back to Scotland. She echoed what my mother had kindly pointed out,

"But that means I won't be able to see my friends or Granny, ever again!" At thirteen years old, this young girl naturally believed herself to be the centre of the universe. She needed to be at the forefront of everyone's thoughts and felt their actions should always follow this course too. No doubt, giving her all their attention first, especially her mother.

"You're just being selfish, mum!" So she thought the same of me as I did of her. Like mother, like daughter. Mmm...Well, isn't that what you're there for, she seemed to express, as she proceeded to throw herself on the bed and lie there sulking heavily about the unfairness, the injustice of the world. I often wondered if all children her age were like this or was it a consequence of her circumstances. She appeared to be, at times, a powerfully negative child, who pushed boundaries to the edge of patience and beyond. She had been conceived and born amidst a violent struggle between her parents. Her father resenting the pregnant presence, but also resenting that I knew this pain and made plans without him for the life I would have on my own with the child. An irresolvable dilemma that was to cause many disputes before and after the child's incarnation into the world, until, when she was seven months old, her father left to go abroad for some months.

For the first three years of her life as a toddler; the bright, intelligent, blue-eyed girl was desperately let down by the brief and inconsistent visits of her father, Gareth, and while I tried to play both roles, was fraught with my own ghosts of the past, as I still was sometimes now. My daughter was more accurate than I was giving her credit for. It wasn't fair.

I left my angry daughter in her sulk, to go meet with Enrique for the evening. He was chatting to a young woman at the door of *el estanco* when I came round the corner at our arranged place.

"*Hola, Que tal, Enrique?*" I greeted him. The young woman smiled, blushing before she turned and went inside the shop. Enrique seemed a little uncomfortable at being seen talking to the woman, unsure and turning towards the door of the shop then back to me, which made me frown slightly and gave me strong sense of déjà vu. I felt puzzled, for we had always had other friends of both sexes. Especially him, since he had lived on the island for longer than I had.

"*¿Va bien todo?* Is everything okay?" I asked as I reached the shop.

"*Si, claro.* Of course! Why wouldn't it be?" Enrique replied a little on the defence.

"*De nada!* Can you suggest a bar where we can get something to eat?" I hadn't eaten today and was feeling grumpy, so let the awkward moment pass as being my own over-sensitivity.

We went further along the street and found one of the many tapas bars dotted all over the old town, and ate in silence after ordering and being served our food. I realised that some of what I was feeling was my own guilt about knowing I would be leaving in a few months, and I had yet to tell Enrique. He would lose the girls too. This was not going to be easy. I felt a bit better after my tapas, and made an effort to fill the silence with talk of the performance at the Cathedral tonight.

Palma Cathedral had drawn me inside many years ago on my visits to my mother, but since living here my practice was centred in the beautiful building once a month. I had joined the Gregorian choir there and loved to sing, lifting my voice with the others in deep harmony. It filled me with awe and joy on these occasions, and my heart felt like it would burst with the intensity of emotion. This had also been an inspiring way to express my passionate nature, which was in evidence even as I talked excitedly about the performance tonight, my hands gesticulating wildly.

"*Si Cara*, but you are not even singing tonight!" Enrique tried to calm me somewhat before we made our way there. Then he reached into his pocket.

"What's that?" I asked, surprised as he smiled and handed me a small package wrapped in colourful tissue paper. I unwrapped it to find a small clay figure, about three inches high, painted white with red and green markings on it. It was a bearded man with a wide-brimmed hat and long cloak, his hands held in front of him. To the back was an unpainted protrusion with a small hole.

"It is *el Siurell*. A Mallorquine whistle. It has been handmade here for many hundreds of years, mostly by women and children. Its origins are shrouded in mystery, but it is said to be associated with the old Spirits; those of the elements like earth, water and fire, but especially air and so, the Wind Spirits." I blew softly at the back of the figure and heard a high pitched note on the air.

"*Muchas Gracias caro!* It's beautiful Enrique." I reached out to him and kissed him softly on the lips.

"*No hay de que!* Don't mention it! *Cara.* Now shouldn't we get going?" he said as he stood. I put the beautiful gift in my pocket, vaguely remembering Mhairi saying something about a sign from the wind. Then I remembered the concert and started enthusing once again.

116

"It's '*Los Claveles y Las Rosas*' tonight and I've been waiting for this for such a long time. I admire them so much!" I could hardly contain myself, but just about managed whilst we paid the bill and made our way along Carrera Almudaína, under the arch and then down Calle de Zanglada towards the Cathedral.

The night was better than I could have imagined and I had to stop myself from singing quite so loud on the harmonies I knew, but didn't hold back, like many others, as the choir sang the *Ave Maria*. I drifted home forgetting for now my need to talk to Enrique about leaving, and that doubt or shadow, which I had picked up on meeting him earlier in the evening.

We made exquisite love that night using the Yab-Yum practice, all awkwardness forgotten in the memories of the music in the Cathedral. As I drifted off to sleep, I could still hear the voices of the choir giving their superb rendition of the *Ave Maria*. But my sleep, rather than become peaceful from memories of the choir's harmonies, was more disturbed by the shadow created at my meeting with Enrique earlier in the evening. Speaking Woman stirred bringing long forgotten happenings from another place and another age once again.

SECOND CHRONICLE

"The Divine is both within and yet beyond everything."
Bernard Simon
'The Essence of the Gnostics'

The Lilac Dove - Mallorca 1575

A flock of gulls were screeching and diving in the bright blue sky, fighting for any scraps they could find around the ships huddled in the port. Those just arrived were unloading cargo and spilling people down the gangplank and onto the dock. Xavier had come to the port to survey the variety and amount of goods coming in on a typical day. The types of vessels carrying cargo were also of interest to him. He noticed that there were still many more of the carvel-built ships than the newer carracks, but as the former were fishing vessels this wasn't surprising.

Fishing was one of Mallorca's most lasting and lucrative trades and these three or four-mast ships were known to be agile and reliable as worthy vessels that sailed well into the wind. They were fast and had a shallow draft that made them suitable for coastal and ocean travel. A deck hand on the nearest ship saw Xavier watching and shouted to him,

"*Buenas tardes, Señor*! Are you looking for someone?"

He had his hands make a funnel so that the sailor could hear him over the gulls, the water and the cacophony of noise from people meeting and greeting each other. *"No, Señor,* I was just admiring your ship. She's a beauty!"

"Si, she is a beauty. You have a good eye, Señor. *"* The sailor stroked the side of the boat gently, as if stroking a lover.

"What's the news from the mainland Señor? Anything new?"

"Only bad news, Señor. I heard that the King has declared the country bankrupt again!"

"Isn't that the third time? I don't know how, for he taxes his people hard. On the island we are feeling the effects of his *"millones"* tax, even on bread and milk. The people are struggling to eat. Maybe we are paying off the King's debts for him, eh?" Xavier smiled grimly.

"Si, Señor. I think you're right. He is like a bully who cannot support the country to feed her own people."

"You are right Señor. How was the voyage? Any sign of pirates?"

"Not this voyage. They must be lying low. We were lucky this day. It would have been a disaster. The ship was loaded with fifty passengers and bales of cotton, spices and many other goods."

"Cotton! No wonder we are ruined. The traders keep importing Dutch cloth, whilst we have our own hand woven cloth here and in many other places in Spain. It is a bitter blow to the weavers and their families." He shook his head concerned about the state of trade, his hoped for area of future work. "I must go. *Muchas gracias,* for your news, *mi amigo.* Even though it is not happy, it is helpful."

Xavier waved goodbye to the deckhand and turned towards the city. On the horizon he could see the spires of the Cathedral and the Almudaína Palace to the left of it. The Cathedral's upward-reaching lines seemed to rise endlessly as one got closer, until they merged into a protective shield of palm trees at the front. It was completed only seventy-five years before and the golden limestone hewn from the Santanyi quarries still shone in the sunlight. They were both enduring icons of the city's multi-faith history.

He caught sight, through the crowd of home-coming voyagers, of a Dominican priest making his way slowly down the gangplank. One of the last to disembark, he appeared to be struggling with his bag, though it did not look large. Seeing the priest reminded Xavier of the other change that was being felt in Le Cuitat. There was a new puritanical atmosphere emanating from the Catholic Church since the Council of Trent three years before, and the Holy Order of the Spanish Inquisition had continued to promote and police the Catholic faith under the leadership of the Dominican Order. He wondered what had brought this priest now, at this time, from the mainland. He felt an inexplicable sense of danger reverberate in his belly as soon as he spotted the priest's robes. He continued to watch him move with difficulty in the direction of a waving Fray Villalonga, the Franciscan Brother who was the Choir Master at La Seu. Xavier loved the Gregorian Chants of the Cathedral choir and loved the old monk who was a kindly man, trusted by the people of the City. Most people lived a devout and ascetic life, which was as much down to the daily struggle with taxes and making a living rather than the Edicts of the Church.

His alerted senses urged him to find a way to let his mother, Sige, know about the arrival of the priest, his mind rushing as he fought his way through the noisy crowd of sailors and carts and seagulls.

Padre Josep had indeed been sent by the Inquisitor Generale. He had been ordered to investigate rumours; strong rumours about a group of possible *Alumbrados*: those heretics diverging from the Faith and indulging in the mystical practices of the Gnostics.

He had not enjoyed the relatively short voyage from the mainland. During it he had been sicker than usual, able to eat little food, and what he could eat returned soon after swallowing. That and the flux had left him in bad humour and exhausted, making him all the more determined to find the culprits he sought and deal with them harshly, if need be. If they were here, he would find them.

It had been some years since the Inquisition had had to deal with *Alumbrados*, among other heretics on Mallorca. They had been thought to have all been dealt with when they were exiled. If the information in that letter he'd received from some loyal parishioners was accurate then it had been too lenient a sentence.

He spotted Fray Villalonga some distance away, waving at him while he struggled with the weight of the Bible in the bag he carried. He was not partial to Franciscans, thinking them too tolerant by half for his liking. Padre Josep was tall and looked almost cadaveric; his nose perched on a gaunt, deathly pale face. It was but February and he felt the chill of the sea air. He pushed and jostled his way through the laughing people shouting to each other in order to reach the monk in his brown robes. He would not have recognised him but for those robes.

Fray Villalonga reached up to kiss the priest on both cheeks with a "Bless You Padre. Welcome to the City of Mallorca." Padre Josep suppressed a shiver of distaste as he leaned down to accept the greeting. *Why doesn't he just kiss my hand and show me the proper respect that I deserve as a Dominican Priest,* he thought irritably.

Fray Villalonga had the creased and kind face of a man of three score years. He had a smile that always reached his eyes unless he was stirred to anger, which wasn't often. He felt uncomfortable with this tall priest, who looked down on him with mean searching eyes as he stooped to take his blessing.

"*Que tal, Padre?* The trip seems to have tired you somewhat. Why don't we hail a carriage and get you settled at

The Bishop's House? It's not too far." Fray Villalonga tried to take the priest's arm to help support him, but it was rigid and only made the gesture superfluous and uncomfortable. Padre Josep had stiffened at the monk's touch, trying not to pull away and offered his bag to hide his reaction. "*Gracias,* Fray Villalonga. If you would be so kind?" he said, his voice scratching the air. The monk took the bag.

"I will have a siesta when we get there. I still feel a little ill from the journey. Then, I can get down to work and proceed with my investigation, *Si?*" The priest's tone was clipped.

"*Si,* Padre. Is there anyone you would particularly like to speak to? I can arrange to have them brought to the house for you." Fray Villalonga asked helpfully. He had no wish to arouse any suspicion about his own aversion to the practices of the Inquisition or his contact with some of the *Alumbrados* on the Island. He would be in very serious trouble if that were known. He did not practice their ways, but understood that they meant no harm. They were believers in Christ too but also revered his feminine counterpart Sophia or Wisdom. Fray Villalonga felt that 'All paths led to Rome.' For didn't the title Catholic, literally mean 'Universal', taking all ways, all people into consideration, rather than judging and punishing?

"Not at the moment Brother. I will make some enquiries tomorrow and draw up a list. I would welcome such an offer of help when I am ready. *Gracias.*"

"*Claro!* Of course Padre!*"* The monk bowed and called to the driver of a passing carriage.

Sige, Xavier's mother, lived in the country with an aging couple who between themselves managed to eke out a reasonable living by harvesting her modest almond and orange orchards when the weather was on their side. Marissa kept house and Fernando traded their goods in Le Cuitat and managed the stable. Sige was afraid of the Grand Inquisitor, Cardinal Don

Fernando Nino Guevara, hearing of the meetings of the *Alumbrados* at the Hub in Bellver Castle. Those involved had a spiritual practice that was founded, not in Christianity, but in Gnostic philosophy that came before the Catechism and gospels written by the Holy See. So they were always concerned about their practices being uncovered. Sige had been intuiting a sense of danger recently, but was not sure about the source until Leon had come to visit last evening and confessed his betrayal.

Since Leon had left, she could feel only the churning in her gut like thick black treacle. It weighed her down, pulling her under its heavy blanket. It had made her bend to accommodate the weight of the burden of knowing something she didn't want to know.

As if from a distance she heard a sound, a shriek escaping into the air, a disembodied, "No... – it can't be true!" Sige heard the words and realised they had escaped from the hell of her own pain, searing like hot knives through her. Slowly she'd felt her spirit shatter like a glass bauble dropping on the floor as if from some great height. Hitting the floor in a slump, she'd lay there unable to move, paralysed by disbelief. The emptiness inside her had felt cold and hollow. No tears yet. Her body had begun to heave from the depths, wanting to rid itself of this knowledge. Not of a betrayal to the Inquisition as she had feared after receiving word from Xavier about the Dominican priest's arrival, but of her lover's infidelity. As it was, she'd mostly gagged and shivered with fear, her body shaking and heaving while the sense of being outside watching the pathetic scene prevailed.

Then there'd been no more words; no more thoughts and the tears came in waves as she'd wailed wordlessly. The unbelievable wrenching at her heart pulled gasps and gulps of grief from deeper than the darkest ocean. Stumbling towards her bedroom and falling onto the bed she'd continued to sob and wail as if from an endless nadir. The ache like an open wound had emptied through her nose and eyes, pouring faster than she'd cared to wipe. Gradually, as exhaustion triumphed over weeping, sleep laid a comforting veil on the corpse of her love.

The room was in virtual darkness when Sige had wakened several hours later. Marissa must have come in and closed the shutters. She'd gradually surfaced from distressing dreams and within a moment felt the stab of reality. Her eyes had swollen and felt as if bulging from her head. Sige had tried to get off the bed to stand but felt a little dizzy and unsteady on her feet. Abruptly she'd slumped down again. When her vision had cleared and she warded off another threatening tear storm, she'd tried again and managed to make her way through to the kitchen for some herbal tea.

Marissa had been preparing supper for later in the evening and tried unsuccessfully to ignore the Señora's puffy face and sniffles as she put the pot on to boil.

"Señora, *perdona*...excuse me if I speak out of turn, but he was no good for you. I never thought well of him, but I did not say. You cared for him so," she gently remarked.

"*Si*, Marissa, it would seem that you were right. *Muchas Gracias,* for your concern and for the tea." Sige had gratefully taken the clay bowl of Chamomile tea from the old woman's outstretched hand.

Marissa and Fernando, her husband, were natives of the island and spoke the local Mallorquine dialect. They had been with Sige since Christos, her late husband, had died and she could no longer manage the farmhouse alone. A widow living alone with her two children would not pass unremarked upon, especially in a small village like Santa Eugenia.

Sige had become very fond of them both and trusting them with the knowledge that she no longer followed the Catholic faith as she was expected, like everyone else, to do.

Marissa herself was prone to visions and prophecy and was often heard muttering to herself around the house. Since the couple had first come to stay she had observed Marissa's strange behaviour. On confronting her, Sige was told by Marissa that the old spirits whispered to her, spoke through her; the spirits of the wind, *Le Siurell.*

"*Si us plau,* Señora! Do not tell anyone, for I will be burned as a witch!" Marissa had pleaded with a terror stricken face after admitting her truth.

"*Vale*, Marissa. I know of these things. I will not breathe a word to anyone for I have my own secrets that I do not wish the Inquisition to hear about. We must say only that you are getting old and a little confused. But you must be careful when there are others around. *Si?*"

"*Si, Gracias* Señora, *Muchas Gracias!*" Marissa said, thanking her profusely while Fernando stood nearby letting out a long breath and looking greatly relieved.

The memory of Leon confessing came back to Sige then and immediately thoughts began jumping in her head again. Veering between madness and sanity, challenging each other to see which one would gain the upper hand and send her in its wake. She couldn't keep the thoughts to herself and blurted them out to her housekeeper.

"I'll never manage without him, Marissa!"

"You don't need him. You have us and your children, Señora!" Marissa consoled.

"I can't live without his love," Sige insisted.

"He couldn't have loved you very much anyway?" Marissa replied, knowing she sounded heartless.

"*Si, Claro*, I'll get by, I have before… But not like this, how can I live with this pain?"

"Señora, it will pass. You must have patience like you had after Señor Christos passed away. He was a man worthy of your grief but not this one. You also have other things you must think about. What if he reports you and the other *Alumbrados* to the Inquisitor Generale?" But Sige couldn't yet let it go. She tried, in vain, to find a way to slow the fractious thoughts.

As she sat at the window looking out onto her now dark, daytime beautiful garden, all she could see were black shadows and creeping corners that snaked and curved their way around the bushes, mirroring her soul. What would her next step be? Sige knew she had to talk to someone to help extinguish the anguish and anxiety sending little shocks to her brain.

She'd have to go the House of Silence at the Hub in the Castle. Maybe Rosita would be attending this evening. She could spend some time there and try to recover some of the perspective that eluded her for now. Her decision made, Sige gathered herself up out of the slouch she had dissolved into while sitting at the table. She dragged herself along to the bathroom with some effort, where Marissa had prepared a hot tub.

Just as she was stepping out from the cloak of warm bathwater into the chilly air, there was loud knock at her dressing room door and she started, almost losing her balance in mid-reach for a towel. Sige steadied herself, quickly grabbed it to dry herself and threw on a chemisette before hurrying to the door. She was breathless from the rush and anticipation and she spoke too loudly from the other side of the door.

"*Si, que pasa?*"

"There is a letter for you, Señora," the deep voice of Fernando boomed.

"*Si?* I'll get it after I'm dressed. Leave it in my bedchamber, *Si us plau.*"

"Señora, they are waiting for a reply," Fernando insisted.

"*Vale,* Fernando. Tell them to wait in the kitchen. I will answer it directly. Could you saddle my horse Fernando? I will be going to the city soon." On moving through to her bedchamber, both the letter and Marissa were waiting for her.

"Damn you!" she said out loud, fighting to hold back the imminent grief as she realised it was from Leon. She would recognise that writing and seal anywhere. Leon always used the engraved dragon on the gold ring that he wore for his seals. There was no mistaking it. Marissa had readied quill, ink and paper at Sige's writing desk. But first she insisted on helping Sige to dress. Marissa had laid out a full set of dress robes but Sige wanted a suit for riding. She didn't want to take time for the layers of *verdue* and *vasquina,* those bulky undergarments required for gowns.

"Marissa, I need clothes for riding not for a ball, can you change these quickly? I must go soon." Marissa hurriedly went to look out some slops: the straight, close-fitting breeches with a waistcoat for under the doublet or *jubón* that the Señora requested and then Sige changed her mind.

"Just a plain dress and *vasquina, si us plau* Marissa, *ho sento*...I'm sorry, it's just that wearing breeches, even though they are better for riding, will cause idle chatter that I'd rather avoid just now. *Gracias*" she said as Marissa put back the slops and handed her the dress: a plain blue damask which she wore with her waistcoat and the high collared doublet. It would have to do. She reluctantly attached bands and ruffs but nothing lacy, just simple lawn. Absence of these fripperies, as she considered them, would have her dubbed as practically undressed. She didn't want to attract more attention than necessary.

As much as Sige wanted more than anything to be with her lover, she needed the distance to recover her footing again. Her balance had been knocked way off and knowing she was unable to make any clear assessment or decision about what to do next, needed support. Determined to stick to the one decision she had made, and despite the inviting bed covers under which she could easily hide, Sige finished dressing and prepared to meet the world, which had gone more than a little askew since last night. She quickly read the letter from Leon with distaste.

12 Carrera de la Puresa
Cuitat de Mallorca
Febrero 1575

My Dearest Sige,

       May I call on you tomorrow evening, for mustn't we try to make peace? I did not wish to hurt you and I beg your forgiveness. Please reply as soon as possible,
   Your Everloving Leon.

Her reply was brief, stating in the affirmative and including a time for the late afternoon the next day, signing off with no flourishes or declarations of love. Sige gave the letter to the messenger waiting in the kitchen, who left immediately. She made her way out to the courtyard, pulling on her kid gloves, where Fernando awaited her with the horse. She stroked its nose and whispered greetings in the horse's ear before mounting, while Fernando opened the gate to let her through.

On reaching the chapel just below the castle, Sige dismounted and tethered her horse, giving its nose a rub and a little water to drink in gratitude for their speedy ride. She then walked slowly up the steps looking out at the view towards the city and the bay, reflecting that the castle deserved its proper name: *Castrum de Pulcro Viso*, Castle of the Beautiful View; justified even in the late afternoon sun and the gathering mist, for she could still see hazy points of light among the huddled buildings of the overcrowded city streets and the masts of fishing boats anchored at the port. She moved under the square arch at the entrance and walked towards the main building crossing the wooden moat bridge and into the huge circular courtyard.

    The Meeting House was located downstairs in the lower castle away from prying ears and eyes. But so too, was the prison. She pulled her hood over her head, only briefly nodding to the apathetic guards who merely nodded back with a quiet '*Gracias',* when she handed them some silver Reales, paying for their silence, as each member did on arrival. On entering she saw a few people that she knew but didn't stop to talk, scared that if they asked her how she was, she might just breakdown. Everything was too close to the surface and she knew her eyes still looked puffy and red. There was no way of saying *"Muy Bien!"* and being believed.

Sige moved quickly through to the back room to locate her friend Rosita, who was also Matron to apprentices like herself. As she knocked unusually timidly on the door, Rosita answered immediately reaching out and gently drawing her into the room and a hug. They said nothing for a while. The only sounds, as they made their way to the chairs on the other side of the room, were those of Rosita crooning and sadly muffled sobs coming from Sige.

Rosita was the same age as Sige but somewhat shorter in height. They were both in their late forties, though often mistaken for being ten years younger. Rosita still had much of her dark curly hair even if now mingled with silver strands. She had a warm creamy complexion with clear though gently wrinkled skin. Most noticeable, were her laughter lines and the twinkle that seemed ever present in her chocolate brown eyes.

Alternatively, although Sige shared a similar eye colour, hers were more hazel with speckled grey lights and her hair had by now, turned silver with streaks of snowy white. Her skin was unusually pale and translucent. It's only dark patch was a diamond shaped birthmark on her neck. She was also much taller than her friend by at least a head. Rosita was rounder and still curvy whilst Sige was tall and slim, not counting her well-earned belly from surviving the births of her two children, the last almost twenty years before, in a time when the death of women in childbirth was terrifyingly frequent. The help of doctors was not to be trusted, but her own knowledge of herbs to prevent complications like sepsis, had got her through without harm to her or the children.

132

As Sige's weeping subsided, the two friends sat quietly reflecting on their fortune. No matter what else had gone on in their varied lives in the last ten years, they had always had each other for support. In fact, there was often no need for letters. They had become so attuned to the other that it seemed unnecessary much of the time, knowing as they did, the way the other felt before talking or seeing. But they never assumed that the physical contact was unnecessary and relished the time they could spend together. Though there had been many long breaks of distance over the duration of their friendship.

"Sige, *cara,* all will be well for you. It may not seem so for now but the universe is unfolding as it should; as it always does. I'm not saying niceties to make you feel better. We both have learned these truths, the hard way. The pain will teach you yet again, that which has slipped your mind. Nothing is forever. We must go into the Hub and refocus into this moment. Are you feeling a little better? It's almost time to start." said Rosita in mellow tones of solace.

"*Si*, Thank-you Rosa. If you could just give me a minute to wash my face I'll follow you. And thank-you again for understanding what I needed without asking." Rosita smiled gently and left her study, closing the door quietly behind her. She shook her head and breathed deeply into her diaphragm, aching for her friend but having to shift the empathy into a wider feeling of compassion for their session this evening. This would include not only her friend Sige, but was pre-arranged to involve all the other Matrons and Patrons in the House of Silence. In fact, Sige had never attended a session with these others before tonight. Synchronicity often gave an ironic twist to the paths of humans. Rosita shook her head with quiet amazement at the workings of Providence, not for the first or last time she supposed.

The others were waiting in the Hub as she entered with Sige following close behind. The room they moved into was circular with a high ceiling. Arcs of gold painted stone drew the eye to a beautiful stained glass window in the shape of a rose. The coloured glass of pink and blue was subdued in the night sky to deeper shades of red and sapphire, the silver coloured leading glimmering in the glow of countless scented candles. Their perfume was heady and calming like the bouquets of blue flowering Rosemary and Rose buds that the essential oils had originated from. Some bunches of each, were represented in gold vases at points around the room.

A deep silence began to pervade the Hub, becoming more noticeable than the strong odour of the candles and flowers. Everyone had eyes lightly closed and was breathing to their own rhythm. Sige looked once at Rosita with a questioning expression. She had immediately realised on entering the Hub, that this was not a session she had attended before. Rosita returned her look with a reassuring nod and closed her eyes. Sige did the same not quite sure what to expect. But wasn't her life turning out to be much like that anyway. There were no coincidences. She must be patient and try to remain in the moment that she now found herself.

A slow and emphatic deep bass hum began to emanate from the Patrons in the room. Sige could feel a very subtle vibration in her body, moving from her feet up towards her pelvis. Then a hum at a higher note issued from the Matrons and blended in harmony. The vibrations continued to travel upwards but seemed to spiral around her spine from opposite sides, high and low separating then crossing again harmoniously. The sensation was new, strange and fascinating, if not a little disconcerting to Sige. As it moved through her stomach and chest area and up into her head as she sang, she had to breathe deeply, for the ache of her new found but unpleasant knowledge surfaced and throbbed with the vibrating hum moving around and within her.

She began to feel and see colours although her eyes were still closed. Sige allowed her mind to float on the mingling shades of rosy hues, calming blues and greens. A golden yellow throbbed intermittently and a vibrant lilac became bright and luminous as the volume and intensity of the hum increased. As her grief was carried up to a crescendo without tears, a shape emerged in her vision for a moment before the hum abruptly stopped.

"*A dove, it's a lilac dove!!*" Sige exclaimed silently. The silence that had begun to deepen when the session had started was now rich and profound, palpable in its strength. Everyone sat for a long time surrounded by this fathomless quietude.

Gradually and in their own time, people began to rise and leave the room. Sige and Rosita were last and walked side by side, maintaining the silence, towards the mutual space where people ate, drank and talked if they felt the need. Without speaking, Rosita offered Sige some herbal tea, which she accepted. They moved to a couch in a corner to talk some more before Sige had to leave.

"How do you feel now, Sige?" asked Rosita, in a concerned tone.

"Mmm, a bit strange but much calmer than when I arrived. That was quite amazing!" Sige answered, unable to keep the surprise out of her voice.

"*Si*, it's as well you get used to it now for you will need to spend more time with the Silent Moment practice from here now on."

"Really? I kind of thought it was a lucky coincidence my being here?!" Sige said this with a disbelieving look that matched Rosita's raised eyebrows, on hearing her say it.

"We both know better than that, eh?!" They both laughed and hugged each other. Sige raised herself from the comfort of the cosy couch and Rosita's warm presence with reluctance and readied herself to go home. Despite the lighter sense of herself both in perspective and mood, she was not looking forward to being alone with the sickening, oily treacle still lodged in her gut. She had much still to work through. Many confused feelings about her relationship with her lover, indeed if there remained a relationship at all. Rosita watched her expression droop a little and squeezed Sige's hand as she stood to see her to the door.

"You of all people have the strength and courage to turn this around and make it a positive learning experience. You're one of the wisest women I have ever met. Don't lose the light you are, before you've even uncovered it properly. Do what you have to, to make this part of your radiance. That includes expressing the shadow side. Don't get too afraid to be what you are when the wrath comes. It is your passion and it can become the Holy Fire. Blessed Be, *mi amiga*." Sige leaned into her friend only half understanding the words but welcoming the care shown her. Rosita turned to go back inside and Sige started the walk back down to the chapel where her horse waited patiently, then mounted and set off for home. Luckily the night was dry though cold and she huddled into her thick woollen cloak to keep in the warm affection and keep out the cold shivering fear that ever waited at the edge of her awareness.

Sige brushed off the dust from her clothes after dismounting, letting Fernando stable the horse. She was glad that it hadn't rained for some days or the ride there and back would have been much more difficult and dirty. Sige's house was built traditionally from local stone and was a fair sized *finca*. Its walls were two feet thick with roughhewn, blond limestone like the few other homes dotted along this long winding track, alongside fields of almond and orange orchards or grape fields which continued onto the next village of Biniali. The gate pushed open easily into a wide courtyard paved with irregular stones and large pebbles sunk into plaster. The stable was off to the left behind the open gate, and under a square stone arch with pretty daytime yellow flowers winding their way round it, whose scent she could smell in the darkness.

All around the far edge were the dark outlines of trees of several varieties like olive, dates, a false pepper tree and a huge cactus with prickly paddled segments. The land to the back held an almond orchard like others in the neighbouring fields; the trees coming into blossom with their creamy coloured petals drifting in the cool evening breeze. The orange trees to the east were ripe with fruit, heavy to falling, calling to be picked which Sige did, lifting them from the ground where several had already fallen in a hurry to fruit and took them inside. The entrance of the house was also arched over double doors sectioned with glass and behind them a second set made of thick wood. Sige locked and bolted the doors behind her, stepping into the main living area of the house. The walls were of blond stone enclosing a wide, spacious area. Hung around them were the brightly coloured clay plates and plant pots of the traditional Mallorquine 'Majolica' type that she loved. The room was warm after the early evening chill outside. Fernando had kept the fire in the right hand corner built up and blazing for cooking, the logs stored in baskets close to the hearth. Marissa had also set one end of the large wooden dining table on the far side of the room for the three of them. Sige had just taken off her riding boots as Fernando came in the side door after closing the gate and stabling the horse. Marissa served their evening meal of *pa am Boli,* a typical dish of home-made dark Mallorquine bread, olive oil, salt and tomatoes accompanied with the spicy *sobrasada* sausage and stuffed aubergines on white glazed plates with blue patterned motifs of floral and geometric designs. They ate quietly, talking intermittently of the work needing done in the orchard now that it was time to harvest the ripe oranges.

That night while sleeping Sige's images were of shifting shapes and puzzling pieces that didn't quite fit together. There were the faces of her lover and an as yet, faceless woman in whose company he had been spending time, while saying he was elsewhere to Sige. The images now rushed towards her, then away and back again, huge and looming or small and laughing. Sige was sitting rocking in a chair holding her head and feeling like she was about to slip into madness, while behind her two figures fought with swords of rage to cut each other down. She saw herself slipping into a whirlpool of thick, treacle blackness. A bottomless hell, from where she would not return if she didn't stop herself from being pulled under. With a terrifying jolt Sige found herself awake and tried to calm her breathing. She was so paralysed with fear that at first she could not move. She lay still and gradually relaxed though the images remained disturbingly vivid. Soon, exhausted from the turmoil of her emotional day, she fell into a dreamless sleep.

The morning was bright and sunny. Sige, though tempted to stay curled up in bed with her tears and burgeoning sense of injustice, got up instead to do some work in the garden. She carried the heavy ache with her as she prepared some breakfast and sat eating. It was difficult to swallow past the lump of sorrow in her throat but she knew she had to try. Looking out the window onto the garden, Sige cast her learned gaze over the flowering plants and shrubs but couldn't see her small patch of herbs from where she sat.

Finishing her paltry efforts at eating, she put on her outdoor clothes, this time wearing an old cotton ankle length skirt without the vasquina, and a waistcoat over her chemisette. Both were washed out and fraying, but useful for working in the garden. Once outside she breathed deeply, taking in the scent of her favourite plants and the almond flowers in the cold and refreshing morning air. There had been a slight frost these last few nights, so she wandered around the garden to survey any damage and made a plan of what needed to be done. Sige had created this garden and sown most of the plants, herbs and shrubs from seedlings, beginning about seventeen years ago.

While her children lived with her, wherever they had stayed, she had had at least some small space to nurture plant life; as she nurtured them. Since they'd moved to Santa Eugenia, it had been a struggle getting to grips with the land and planting the orchard, but then, Christos had been there to help her in the first few years. It was both her personal passion and had given her a means of supporting her family with their father. During those happy years, Sige had trained herself by the trial and error of maintaining plant life through the seasons, but had also relied on visits to neighbouring orchards to glean information from those land owners who had been here long before she had. The children had loved having the garden and orchards to play hide and seek in, and as they grew, learned to help with the harvest. She eventually became well known from those visits and by eventually learning how and where to sell their crop.

In the last seven years this occupation had taken on another dimension. She had met and begun her friendship with Rosita ten years ago and this led to contact with The House of Silence. During that time, she had become the apprentice to an apothecary and herbalist with whom she had made acquaintance and who had eventually taught her the art of extracting and blending the essential oils from plants and other substances. She had also been trained in the art of preparing herbal remedies.

While repairing and pruning the damage done by the frost to the herb garden, Sige reminisced on the days spent with her children, Xavier and his sister Anna. She had loved the closeness of their soft cuddliness and the sometimes hilarious, other times frightening antics of the early years when they struggled, as children do, to get on their feet; to grapple with language and to meet the world in their own unique way.

She had been married for some twenty years before her husband died. Sige still missed Christos. They had been the closest of friends and enduring lovers. His death almost ten years ago had left a huge gap in her life for a long time that even her love for her children couldn't fill. They had missed him greatly too. His death had been sudden and apparently 'out of the blue', but she had since realised that he had been letting go of his attachments to the physical world for all of the time she had known him. In hindsight, what other final way is there, than the death of the physical body to relinquish attachment to all things material? He had taught her much about connecting with the mystic soul of the universe and always encouraged her in her passion for gardening. He used to tell her that she worked in the Garden of the Beloved and was blessed. Sige felt blessed by sharing the gifts of their offspring together.

She saw the children much less now. They had begun to choose their own paths and sought the space to test their new-found independence that young adults need, so no longer lived with Sige. She had been able to buy them a small house in Le Cuitat, in one of the streets not far from the port. The narrow streets and small houses were very crowded and Sige didn't feel it was the most pleasant place for them to live, compared to the country. The lack of any sewage system brought the danger of disease and meant there was a constant stench, but her children were attracted by the potential for working and making money as well as the excitement of city life.

Sige had only agreed to buy the house in Carrer Estudi General because both Xavier and Anna had agreed to share. It was unusual for a young woman of nineteen to be unmarried never mind live alone, which was unthinkable in the city. As long as Anna had Xavier there, Sige was placated somewhat but still had Fernando visit most days to check that they were managing. So far, Anna had managed to secure some employment with Catalina Zaforteza Togores as a governess to her young daughter, a few streets away in Carrer de Portella, while Xavier had made contacts at the port and was hoping to start as a clerk in La Llotja de Le Cuitat de Mallorca. The Commodity Exchange Market was close to the seafront and was the meeting place for shipping merchants and commercial traders alike, who gathered in the city to discuss exchange rates, availability of products and levels of demand in various markets for trade in Mallorca's traditional diamond patterned cloth of cotton, linen or silk, or as it was known locally; '*Roba de Llengues*', or Tongues of Flame. There was also trade in fish and pearls among other goods like the oranges, almonds and olives that many farmers like Sige produced across the island.

Xavier was keen to enter this world. He found it exciting, sensing the cut throat atmosphere with insider deals being struck on the stone benches and watching hard-done-by merchants gazing up in despair at the palm-like pillars supporting the vaulted roof. For despite the kindly guardian angel hovering over its entrance, trade had waned in the last few years resulting in dropping prices. This combined with regular pirate attacks meant that some of Mallorca city's main traders from the Maghreb, Italian domains and the Turkish Empire were now more reluctant to dock at the port.

Xavier was clever and good-looking and had a persuasive charm. His enchanting smile also captivated the young women of Mallorca city, who were constantly on the look-out for a husband. But he had chosen his bride to be. Isabella was a young woman from Santa Maria del Cami whom he'd met at a social gathering. But Xavier had never been short of invitations to socialise with his peers. This gave his sister Anna, less visible in society, the opportunity to make friends only because her brother would accompany her to various gatherings and parties in the homes of some of the more well-respected families in the city.

"Xavier, what am I going to wear? I mean what *does* one wear to a birthday party when you're twenty? *Socorro!* Help!" Xavier was busy looking at trade route maps and navigation charts, sitting at his desk poring over them with a magnifier, checking the spaced measurements, marking the depth of the waters that the carracks and caravels traversed. The charts had been lent to him by Isabella's father and were made from the best parchment, attached to first rate linen backings. His thick, dark hair had fallen over his handsome face and he pushed it back and looked up in exasperation at the sound of his sister's wail.

"*Que pasa* Anna? Clothes? I don't know. You can wear one of my suits if you like. The green damask one would look good on you." He smiled to himself and waited.

"You're impossible Xavier and no help at all. Where's your fiancée when I need her?" Anna was predictably storming into the study, hairbrush in her hand ready to launch it at her brother. At the last moment she thought the better of it, reminding herself she was twenty and a young lady.

"She'll be here at the end of the week. I'm going to Santa Maria later today to meet her parents and we'll come back together on Friday. The party's not until Saturday." Xavier replied, suppressing a smile at his sister's expression. Anna's sulk made her look about twelve years old, as she turned, flouncing out of the study throwing her long wavy her behind her as she went.

"I should tell Fernando to ask Mama to come and help me." She muttered to herself.

"I heard that! I thought you wanted to be independent?" Xavier stood up to stretch, all six feet of him, lithe and fit, his thigh muscles visibly rippling under the black hose, below the mid-thigh length breeches he wore. "But now you mention it, maybe you should go back to the farm with Fernando when he comes later. I don't think you should stay here on your own, Anna."

"No! I *am* independent and I'm old enough to manage on my own for three days. Besides Fernando does come almost every day doesn't he, so I'll be fine."

"Are you sure? You know Mama will worry when she finds out and I'll get a tongue lashing for leaving you. Couldn't she help you decide what to wear? Won't you at least think about it before Fernando gets here and I leave?" Xavier had actually begun to feel hesitant the more he thought about Anna being here alone.

"One minute you are telling me I should be independent and the next saying I should run home to Mama. I think you are just worried she'll box your ears, brother of mine." She came into the study again as she spoke, her hair now up in a chignon looking much more like the proper young lady she thought herself to be. She was wearing a day dress of rust coloured damask with a cream lace partlet across her chest. The dress had full sleeves and a fitted waist. It was one of Anna's favourite dresses but she didn't consider it grand enough to wear to a party. The colour of the dress set off the golden tones of her skin and the darkness of her hair, very well.

"*Vale, mi hermana*, but I feel uncomfortable about it and wish you would reconsider. I think I will talk to Mama about getting a *dueña* to live in with us. She would be company for you."

"Don't you dare Xavier! I don't need a chaperone. I have to do this sometime; be on my own." Xavier did not disagree further with his sister. She would only become more stubborn, but he still didn't like leaving her and resolved to write to his Mama about the *dueña* as soon as he got to Santa Maria.

Alone in the garden while dead-heading flowers, Sige realised she was putting off decisions about the situation between herself and the man who had been her lover for the last four years. Leon had been good for her. He had brought sensual love back into her life at a time, when although she had mostly let go of the sense of loss concerning Christos, she had forgotten, or rather submerged, her needs as a woman to support her children through their own grief and growth after their father had died.

Leon had seduced her with attention and romance and concern. Through his admission of infidelity, she now felt that he had betrayed the trust and respect that she thought they shared. As she mulled over his words of yesterday morning, relating to her the extent of his deceit in the last few months, her stomach began to heave again. What, she wondered, was his reason for telling her now? She felt a fire in her belly that flared and ignited further. Sige's nearest neighbour was some way down the road, so she let out a roar of indignation that shook her body from head to toe.

"How could you? How *could* you?!..." she ranted. Another tear storm descended and Sige allowed it to pour through and out of her. She rested on the garden seat and asked the universe to accept her pain for the benefit of all. There was surely some purpose to this suffering. She knew it would pass in time and she had also learned that creation can be born out of destruction. From her experience of Christos' death and her own soul searching, and since being supported at the House of Silence, she realised that emotions negative and positive, needed to be expressed without harm to others.

Her pain, her anger and her loss could resonate like the energy of the healing oils she prepared, with others pain, anger and loss. The secret was to be able to allow the emotions to move through her so that she became less attached to the specific memories. She needed to transform her anger and sense of betrayal into compassion and forgiveness for not only the one, but the many. There was quite a way to go yet. Experience told her to take her time and ride out the storm. To be prepared to accept the unexpected gifts that were thrown out of the tornado, as the true meaning of her circumstances.

Sige allowed the intense emotions to subside some, but did not lose the first gift of clarity that the fire of anger had bestowed. This would enable her to meet Leon, maybe for the last time, with a sense of discernment that would be useful to cut through the projections and outdated needs they would each use to defend themselves against the other. She did not want to go over old ground, but they needed, at least, to talk. Whatever happened: events, feelings, couldn't be left hanging in limbo indefinitely. She tidied up her gardening tools feeling subdued but clear. After washing up, she reminded herself that she also had the orange harvest to complete as soon as possible, so could not afford time for further self-pity.

Leon arrived sometime later in the afternoon. His dark curly hair, chiselled features and blue eyes, though handsome, had a set expression. Sige had seen it before. He had made up his mind about something and would not be budged. She almost melted as he brushed past her into the sitting room. His scent was quite overpowering but she recognised her vulnerable state and didn't cave in. Following him into the room, she sat in the chair opposite, the better to have a clearer view of his beautiful lying face. She realised how little she knew this man. How many of the moments that they had shared had been true? Lies have such a destructive quality. How did you ever after believe anything that person has said or will say? For a moment Sige almost felt dizzy as the last fours years of their relationship seemed to disappear before the reality of the situation. She waited in silence to let him speak. Presently, he began to defend his actions in a short clipped tone, as if to brook no argument.

"Look, Sige. I apologise for hurting you as I said in my letter yesterday, and I meant it, but I don't see why we can't see other people as well as each other. I know I shouldn't have told lies but I couldn't bring myself to tell you. I knew you wouldn't understand but I'm telling you now because this woman is a good friend to me, and I don't want to have to choose between you both. I didn't mean it to go as far as it did, but we just got carried away. It's not a problem really, you know. It was just the once. I still love you but I won't cut her off. So, let's work it out from there."

Leon finished speaking abruptly, with a hard defiant glint in his eye as he stared at her, waiting for her reaction. While he had been saying these words, Sige had felt her anger and disbelief rise at the sheer self-centredness of the man's chosen position. Her eyes had gone wide at his temerity and for a moment everything had a reddish hue. Fuelled by indignation and hurt, she felt an explosion mounting.

"How dare you! *How Dare You!"* She raised her voice in red hot anger. "I can hear that you believe that you're right, but it's not for me. Only cowards tell such lies, to themselves more than anyone else. I'm too old and have come too far to want to fight with you over the right and wrong of what you say. I feel betrayed and angry about the way you have behaved but I'll survive. In fact, I'll do better than that. It's clear to me there's no future in continuing our relationship. How would I know when you're telling the truth? Why should I accept your selfish arrangement? This is not what I want or need. Let's not prolong the misery. At least you managed to be honest eventually, but it's finished. We're done."

Sige's voice had become quieter but stronger as she had responded to Leon's terms. She was in no doubt now. She had to remain true to herself and not allow it to be violated by deceit and revengeful thoughts or actions. She stood and walked towards the door, not without noting both the flash of uncertainty passing over Leon's face, as he realised his strategy hadn't worked, then an unexpected but momentary sneer that chilled her insides. He followed Sige to the door saying,

"But I still love you, Sige."

"I'm sure you think this is love Leon, but it's not the kind of love I need. *Adios."*

Sige only managed to get the door closed behind Leon before the tears welled up, but they didn't spill yet. She still felt as if numb all over and went to make herself some herbal tea. It helped but warmed her inside and out so that she melted into a torrent of tears that though intense, did not submerge her. She breathed a sigh of relief and thought determinedly to herself, *I'm not playing these games anymore. I have a rich life that fulfils me deeply on many levels. I'm going to be forty-nine soon. It's time to leave behind the realm of sex and its politics and focus on my spiritual path.*

Sige's thoughts were clearer and she felt the truth of her understanding as a glow in her chest. Joy in the life she had and for how much more she had to give. It was going to be sometime before her pain subsided and she knew some of her resolve was an attempt to rationalise the pain away. But, because she followed the Gnostic philosophy of the *Alumbrados*, she knew that her practice would prevent this knowledge becoming only an intellectual exercise. It could bring her to redemption and liberation, helping her to break free of this bondage to the world. Meantime she had her business, her garden; there was her healing work with others, there were her friendships and her children. She did not forget either, that somehow she had given permission for this situation to arise. She had a responsibility for her own betrayal. There were many lessons to be absorbed with the loss of her lover.

Noticing the time, Sige called Marissa to help her dress quickly and asked Fernando to saddle her horse so that she could leave as soon as possible. She had heard the sound of Leon's horse receding into the distance and hoped he was far enough ahead of her that she wouldn't come across him on the road. Fernando knocked on the front door,

"*Si*, Fernando. Is she ready? I won't be long."

"*Ho sento, Señora*. Would it not be better to tether her to the buggy and I can accompany you to le Cuitat? I could also call in to check on Señorita Anna and Senor Xavier." Fernando 's voice sounded concerned as he came into the sitting area.

"Are you worried about them?" She queried, her eyes narrowing as she watched him.

"No, Señora, I am worried about you meeting Señor Leon on the road, if you don't mind me saying. He is an evil man Señora, and I don't know what he might do if you met him alone in the middle of the countryside," he said quickly,

147

averting his eyes and dipping his head in fear of being thought presumptuous.

"*Si*, Fernando, you are right. That's a good idea. I did consider that that might happen, and I would not welcome being on my own if it did. Thank-you for offering and Si, could you do that and I'll be ready by the time you've finished."

She had arranged to meet her Teacher. The man who had taught her all she knew so far about herbs and plants and oils. If she didn't get a move on, she'd be very late. Sige was looking forward to seeing him. It had been some time since their last meeting and they were to arrange the final set of lessons that they would share.

Looking back to the happenstance of her first encounter with Aluzzo, even then he'd seemed old and wizened. She had been at a lecture on the healing power of plants and had heard him talk about the spiritually energetic nature of every substance on earth. Some of the ideas and concepts he had presented seemed outlandish and almost heretical to her, but she was fascinated and excited by the sense that, even if half of what he said was true, just think of what she could do with the plants and herbs in her garden in the courtyard at home. He had consistently, during the lecture, directed his gaze towards her as if he was willing her to accept what he was saying. His eyes were pale blue and twinkling and she felt somewhat embarrassed by the attention. Sige had been so new to this side of plant nature that she had been too frightened to ask any questions at the time. She soon made up for that once their association was established. It was as if Aluzzo had, during that lecture, chosen her to be his apprentice.

Their second meeting had been even stranger than the first because they had apparently just bumped into each other the very next day. It was unusual for Sige to be in Mallorca city two days in a row, but she had needed to visit the trader who had agreed to buy some of that year's orange harvest.

Sige had been quite thrown by the encounter in more ways than one. Aluzzo seemed so out of context on a busy street in the centre of Le Ciutat with his wide brimmed black felt hat, long red cloak and white beard. He had shown no more than a nod at surprise over their coincidental collision and had immediately taken her arm, apologizing profusely and led her to a nearby bar offering to make amends for almost knocking her over. Sige had allowed herself to be led, despite her bewilderment and once ensconced in a corner of the bar with wine and a small *ensaimada* that he'd recommended, in front of her, she managed to catch her breath and ask what was going on.

"*Bien*, my dear. First things first. *Me llamo* Aluzzo. As you may remember, I gave a lecture at the conference yesterday. And you are…mmm…Sige, *Si*?"

"*Si*. How did you know my name?"

"I know much about you from several sources which I will reveal in time."

His eyes were twinkling with amusement as he watched her surprise at the turn of events.

"But, who are you? I mean, what do you want?"

"All in good time, *cara*. Have your wine," he countered.

Sige took a sip of her wine realising being addressed as 'my dear' made her feel like a very young girl again. This, even though she had just turned forty-two only days before.

"*Asi*, you were going to tell me…?" She tried again but he interrupted before she could finish her sentence.

"You eat your pastry and I'll talk, *vale*. You see, my dear…" He was doing it again, calling her 'my dear'. "I'm looking for an apprentice for my apothecary. What that is …"

"I know what an apothecary is!" Sige interrupted him this time.

149

"*Claro*...Of course you do. Anyway, what *I* do there is distil plant and mineral essences as well as prepare and dispense herbal remedies, and I need an assistant to help me with my research work." Aluzzo didn't explain any further but looked directly at her with the same intense gaze he had directed at her the previous day during the lecture.

"*Por que?* Why do you keep looking at me like that? You want me to be your assistant...apprentice? Why me? You don't even know me or me, you. And besides, don't you think I'm a little old to be an apprentice?" Sige fired at him. Unperturbed, he replied with a slow smile spreading across his face.

"*Si y no*. S*i*, I'd like you to be my assistant *y no*, forty-two is not too old to become an apprentice. *Así*, it is decided then?"

"*No!* It certainly is not. I only set eyes on you for the first time yesterday and today I'm to become your assistant?! I need to think about this. Where is your apothecary anyway?"

"You've passed it many times but you may not have realised it and really, what is there to think about?" Aluzzo replied with that smile still on his face, his gaze still directed unflinchingly, into her eyes. This man was infuriating! He answered every question with another, often leaving no room for argument. Sige was just about to tell him so, when he quickly spoke first while rising from his seat,

"*Bien*, all right, *cara*. You have your think and let me know. But don't take too long." With these remarks he started to walk off, out of the bar.

"But how can I let you know?" she asked quickly before he was out the door.

"*No se preocupe.* Don't worry *cara!* We'll probably bump into each other again soon. *Buenas tardes!*" He threw this back at her as he disappeared through the door. As she stared after his vanishing cloak she heard him laugh loudly to himself. A luscious laugh, deep and throaty as if he'd thoroughly enjoyed some great joke. I think the joke's on me, Sige thought,

150

as she sat alone, amazed and more than a little incensed at being accosted and propositioned by a near total stranger who called her '*cara*' and looked at her in a baffling manner.

And so, here was Sige, almost seven years later going to meet Aluzzo, having studied with him all this time. It had been a course of study that had completely turned around her every preconception and assumption about life and the world. In fact, upside down, back to front and inside out was nearer to the truth.

She hurried down Carrer Sant Michel, turning from the main thoroughfare into the narrow Carrer Arabi, which immediately felt like slipping into another world. The street was populated with many people as most streets were, shopping or watching the artisans at work in the patios or courtyards of homes. These patios were based on the Catalan model with full central arches at the entrance and Coróneles windows inside.

She took in the Muslim influence of several centuries before, which still held sway in Mallorca through the smells of the spices they used to cook food; saw it also in the traditional utensils for sale and how visible it was in the architecture of the buildings, the design of pottery, carpets and especially the manner of haggling for goods.

The market-like shops had striped canopies flapping in a warmish breeze that she was sure had a scent of the sea, smelt even above the usual city stench. The seller's wares were piled on stalls inside on gaily-covered trestles and they were shouting from stall to stall. Although it was getting late the shoppers and proprietors were still haggling endlessly to get and give the best prices. Some stalls had fresh fruit and vegetables, others herbs and flowers, while others sold clothing, sandals, carpets and pottery.

She had passed by this street many times before Aluzzo had indicated that she need only turn that particular corner and she would find it. She squeezed in between two stalls and waved a greeting to the sellers on each side, who both knew her well after all the years of her attendance to Aluzzo at his little apothecary shop upstairs above the patio.

From downstairs it couldn't be seen, the stairs almost hidden behind the stalls and it still looked tiny even when at the door or attempting to glimpse anyone at home through the small dusty windows. On entering, the attention was caught by the light and gentle melodious tinkling of chimes above the door.

Moving into the shop, dim from lack of light and despite the often noisy haggling outside, there was an immediate hush as the door closed behind her. Sige had been rather scared the first time she'd been there but then, as always, Aluzzo appeared quietly and held out his hands, saying, "*Mi venir con.* Come with me."

The greatest surprises and adventures had always begun when she acquiesced and followed him beyond the counter and into the workrooms. Inside it was dark and gloomy except for the rosy glow from the furnaces. There were strange sounds of hissing and bubbling, which she later discovered were from diverse concoctions of smelted and melting substances in different stages of the alchemical process. The place looked like a laboratory of some eccentric magician.

Today, unlike the first day she had arrived, Aluzzo embraced her in a warm hug and as he pulled away, she saw that his eyes were moist.

"*Que tal?* I am aware of your troubles the past day or so, Sige. But you have made the right decision, my dear. Though you needed the presence of Leon for more purpose than you can yet imagine, it is right that you move forwards without him. Don't think that you will not encounter him again, that you will; but in a very different way from what has come before. Preparation for that time, which will be soon, is of the utmost importance."

"*Que quiere usted decir*...what do you mean Aluzzo?" she asked, surprised at this uncharacteristic, though brief, display of emotion and his warning, which seemed to portend something not wholly pleasant.

"I asked you to come today knowing that the lessons we will broach would be of a different order from much of what we have covered in the past seven years. All of that has its significance in the areas of sowing; planting, harvesting, distilling, blending, diluting and potentising both herbs, minerals, metals and other substances, but these processes also have their significance in The Hidden Work."

"Do you mean the deeper energetic work that we've done with vibration and resonance?" Sige asked, as yet not too concerned about where this lesson was leading.

"*Si cara*, I do, but at yet more esoteric and significant levels. Let's get started properly," Aluzzo replied, with an expression of both excitement and concern on his greatly wrinkled face, the twinkling blue eyes having lost none of their intensity over the years.

They both sat down at a great counter which was covered with many clay and metal pestles, mortars: glass bottles and tubes used for trituration of herbs and minerals in the making of remedies. Herbs and medicinal plants were stored in narrow-waisted jars, their shape again derived from the Muslim world and its Arabic pharmacies. At one end of the counter stood a distilling machine, which he had told her was an original. Not that ascribed to Avicenna, the eleventh century Arabian doctor and philosopher, who was credited with inventing the first distilling apparatus. But one much older based on an illustration from a sacred text in the possession of Aluzzo himself, with his own adjustments of course, and was the invention of one 'Maria the Jewess'.

Around them in the surprisingly large room, were shelves and shelves lining three walls, full of books and scrolls and codices, many of which Sige had never even looked at. Aluzzo was very protective of the scrolls in particular, and some of the oldest and most sacred were kept in sealed caskets so as not to disintegrate. Sige shared, to some degree, Aluzzo's great respect and awe of these papyri but was never quite convinced of their authenticity. They did look old, but how had Aluzzo come to be in possession of them?

"Let us begin this lesson with a review of the planetary influences. In particular, *la Luna*." Aluzzo's quiet but clear voice drew her attention back to the table and the subject in hand.

"Remember when you first began studying the proper cultivation and care of plants with me? I taught you about the necessity of being guided by the phases of the moon as to the best times to apply appropriate activities. Then, I told you that the phase of the waxing moon favours the growth above the soil and the nutritious sap in plants has a tendency to rise. In this first quarter, the human body is also especially receptive to growth and regeneration. These are the days also when, if we are distilling or blending, we do so with herbs and substances which promote growth and regeneration of tissues and nerves. We also prescribe that they also be used according to this influence."

"*Pero* Aluzzo. What is it I have to do differently? Isn't this what we've been doing all this time?

"Be patient and let me finish Sige. For our present study, the crucial point is that you must concentrate on the growth and regeneration of your own internal powers during this phase, which has just begun.

"By means of meditation: using Intuition, Imagination and Inspiration, you must develop your energy to greater heights than has ever been possible before. I will support you with essences and oils, remedies and reading matter. You must attend the House of Silence each midday and midnight for the next thirteen days, and be nurtured by the support of the Matrons and Patrons there. They will teach you to use vibration and resonance to the deepest and highest levels, some of which you experienced last night. Do not miss one day Sige! Your life

154

depends on this, my dear." Sige had been listening intently to this discourse but was startled by Aluzzo's last remark.

"What do you mean my life depends on it!? What aren't you telling me Aluzzo?"

Aluzzo sighed deeply; he was not enjoying the necessary prospect of compounding the pain of separation that Sige was still coming to terms with over Leon. "Take yourself back to four years ago, *cara*. Close your eyes and remember meeting Leon."

Sige cast her mind back and saw Leon standing on his own in the meeting space in the House of Silence. She had never seen him before, but thought then that he was somehow familiar to her. His chiselled looks and distinctive eyes made him stand out. There was something about him both attractive and repulsive at the same time. She had felt a sensation of being watched and *this* was what had made her turn round, whereupon she had noticed his unusual presence and approached him, drawn by his gaze. Aluzzo continued,

"At the time our work was coming to an important juncture and we were just at the crux of completing the potentisation and transmutation of a particular substance. I didn't tell you at the time what that substance was, in case any feelings or reactions you may have had to this knowledge would affect the outcome of the work."

"So what was it? Can you tell me now?" Sige asked, coming out of her reverie.

"*Si*, it was the blood of Christos." He replied without preamble, sitting a little farther back awaiting the understandable and expected outburst.

"*Como dice?* Ch...Christos! My husband...Christos!?" Sige was astounded. She couldn't believe what she was hearing.

"S*i cara, That* Christos." Aluzzo regarded her closely.

"*Como*...How did you get his blood; how did you know him...? He died six years before that." Sige held her head in her hands and the tears began to flow as much from confusion, as

155

from the thought that she had been working with a part of her beloved Christos without knowing.

"How could you not tell me? Oh, I know all about your 'objectivity', but that was unfair Aluzzo." Sige struggled with the ensuing sobs.

"*No cara*, it was not. It was the fairest course of action in the circumstances and necessary. Its necessity is now apparently justified. When you met Leon that first time, of what did you speak?" he asked quietly.

"Leon, Leon??? What has he to do with this?" Her distress was acute. Sige couldn't yet make the connections.

"*Por favor,* Sige, what did he say to you? Aluzzo insisted. Sige took several deep breaths to calm herself.

"*Bien*, he thought I was someone else. When I went over to him he said '*Hola* Sophia, so we meet again.' But I told him he was mistaken, that my name was Sige but that he *was* familiar to me. Then he asked me how long I'd been coming to the House of Silence, and we talked about my gardening work...just general conversation." Sige looked at Aluzzo blankly.

"Sige, what do you know about Leon? Where does he come from? How old is he? What does he do when he is not with you? Sorry, my dear. I know how his admittance of lying abed with other women has cut you to the core, but I have to say that this is only a minor aspect of his deceit and artifice towards you."

"*Que quiere decir mujeres*? He only mentioned one woman to me!" Sige exclaimed.

"More lies, my dear. I know this is painful beyond measure but you must strip yourself of all affection for this man and soon, for otherwise he will use it to destroy you and much more besides. Leon is the 'Son of Darkness'. If we can overcome the satanic influences that are working through him, we can save you and The Hidden Work. Both of which, are inextricably bound together." Aluzzo's face was dark and beseeching. He meant every word he was saying and Sige was suspended in disbelief yet again. The thick, black treacle began to churn and threatened to pull her down into madness. She gagged and tried to stand but staggered immediately and was caught by Aluzzo. He made a quick gesture of his hand towards the end of the room and Rosita came swiftly through the curtained doorway and helped lay Sige on the bed in the corner, which Aluzzo often used when working through the night. Sige had begun to moan and pray, babbling snatches of long-forgotten prayers from her childhood religion and clasping her hands in devotion and twitching violently. Aluzzo quickly moved to his medicine cabinet and extracted a tiny white tablet.

"*Stramonium,* Datura. She needs this in high potency or she will become violent and turn to the darkness. We must harness this fire so that she can use it against Leon, for he senses her vulnerability." He quickly slipped the tablet between her praying hands and placed a crystal vase on the floor between the three of them. Both he and Rosita clasped their hands in invocation, the opposite gesture from Sige, their palms touching at the sides and open.

They began to invoke the Spirit of Christos and the Light of Sophia. They continued their invocation while Sige prayed with devotion to every god or goddess that she could wrest from her subconscious. Presently there was a flash of blue, which initiated a stream of light moving from one pair of hands to the other in a circular motion, its speed increasing and decreasing and then funnelling into a downward spiral into and around the inside of the vase. The crystal began to sing a high clear note of such purity that it brought Sige out of her madness and she sat up. As she rose from the bed her hands dropped downwards and the stream of light ceased moving between the three and was directed between only Sige and the *Vas Spirituale*. It travelled from her hands, up her arms and around her whole body. Sige glowed with electric blue streams and sparks of light. Her eyes were now wide open but she was smiling calmly, as she willingly received the lightning wisdom.

Aluzzo and Rosita were now on their knees and began in earnest devotion, their palms together and pointing upwards to honour the Great Mother standing, no, floating in front of them. They began…

"Does not Sophia cry? And understanding put forth her voice? She stands in the top of high places, by the way in the places and the paths. She cries at the gates, at the entry of the city, at the coming in of the doors…."

Now Sige opened her mouth and in harmony with the singing of the crystal, spoke:

"Unto you, O people, I call: and my voice is to the sons and daughters of the world.

O ye simple, understand Sophia: and ye fools, be ye of an understanding heart. Hear! For I will speak of excellent things; and the opening of my lips shall be for the right things…. Sophia is better than rubies and all the things that may be desired are not to be compared to her. I, Sophia dwell with prudence, and find out knowledge of witty inventions…. Counsel is mine, and sound wisdom. I am Understanding; I have Strength!"

Sige stopped speaking and the streams of blue light ceased flowing through her body and spiralled solely into the vase and gradually slowed. The light stream diminished and all that remained was the glowing crystal vase. She slowly slumped down onto the bed and slipped into a deep sleep. Aluzzo and Rosita breathed a deep sigh of relief knowing that they had almost lost her to the Darkness. They had not expected Leon to attack so quickly, but he had clearly outdone himself in his duplicity. He knew Sige well and had lost no time in preparing and carrying out his strike on her mental faculties. Aluzzo wrapped the Vas Spirituale in a length of the bluest silk and then in a bag of purple velvet and put it safely away under lock and key, in the thick wood cabinet that also housed his most potent medicines. Both protectors to Sige were also surprised at how quickly she had found the strength to embody the light of her true being. They had thought that there was much more work to be covered. Leon had clearly been trying to undermine Sige's burgeoning powers by playing on her present weakness, but he had also underestimated that those same areas were also her strengths.

Rosita and Aluzzo continued to discuss the next course of action concerning Sige's welfare, and the inevitable attacks from Leon that would probably increase as soon as this moon quarter was complete. They took this evening's assault as a warning, but it also assured them of Sige's ability to overcome his attempt to malign her spirit. They felt optimistic about her progress and awaited her wakening to complete their difficult, though important tale of past, present and future and other realms besides.

Leon had left Sige's finca that afternoon feeling that his rather large ego had been dented some, though to him the interpretation was slightly different. He was annoyed that he hadn't been able to talk her into accepting his reasonable idea. Why shouldn't he sleep with more than one person? Why, maybe they could have gotten a little ménage-a-trois together sometime? He smiled at the image of old Sige, the pure of heart, in bed with the lecherous and craven Jade. It would have shocked the pants off Sige; not such an unpleasant outcome. But it would also have begun the necessary slide into decadence and weakened her self-righteous defence. It could have started to make some cracks in the power he could feel building up. She was too well supported by that ancient, decrepit old shyster Aluzzo and that little Rose, who was ever hovering around Sige, including around her astral body when asleep.

It had been a long four years, and the Master of Darkness was none too pleased at his progress. Surely, he was allowed some little diversion from playing the loving, romantic partner that apparently, Sige couldn't do without. It was too boring! He was kind of relieved he didn't have to woo Sige anymore, yet already he missed her lovely laugh and gentle ways. Who cares, anyway! Who did she think she was, ordering him out? He would show her! Now, is when the real fun starts, he thought.

Leon chuckled to himself and rubbed his hands together with gleeful malice. He had to surpass himself this time. He had sent a warning this evening, one that had come close to breaking her spirit. Using his inverted cross and backward invocations, he had called up Sata, the Great Dragon King, asking him to direct the power of the Black Sun, bringing decimation to the security of Sige's certainty that she already knew the worst. That she had already experienced her worst nightmare. Her ensuing madness came from her own sense of pride. This Lucifer within had brought her to the edge of insanity, but she had been stronger than he'd realised. He would have to send some other demons; those of her own making.

Ever since he had discovered Le Dragon Rouge Codicil, he understood that according to its text, he only had to spend some time with someone to discover their personal demons then evoke the circumstances that would cause them to rise. Which devil would he test her with next? He had seven principal ones to choose from. He mused thoughtfully over them. Lucifer had been useful for he had vibrated well with Sige's inflated sense of pride. He would call on his help again. What about Mammon? Naaa…Leon hadn't detected much in the way of greed in the last few years but, there was still time. Asmodeus? Her lecherous energy had resonated perfectly with Jade, providing Leon with some wonderfully obscene evenings in the last few months. 'Got carried away?' Leon laughed out loud at the memories. They certainly had and not just once either but several times day and night and in a variety of interesting positions. He and Jade would have been real contenders for the 'Karma' Sutra awards. Alas, Sige still believed that she could ascend the heights and depths of spirituality...with love!! Ah! Now here was one he could use. Satan himself. The fire of old Nick. That all-consuming blaze of anger. He had to come up with a plan to get her anger roused to volcanic proportions. That's it!

Leon almost jumped with jubilance but he hadn't won yet, so settled down to contrive a way to see to it that he could catch Sige alone and send a visitor. A certain Jade; who would relish telling the details of her nocturnal encounters with Leon. It might also get a reaction from a little demon lying not so dormant in Sige called Leviathan, better known as envy or more accurately in Sige, jealousy, its first cousin. She has more of a protective than covetous streak. Yes, he could do some real damage there and have some fun too. Beelzebub and his gluttony, Belphegor and her sloth could wait. They might come in handy for some of the others and loosen their grip on Sige long enough to raise the Dragon that would take her in one bite. Of course, he must not forget the *Vas Spirituale,* also known as the Womb of the Great Mother or the Magic Papyri. They must be destroyed along with she, who is set once again to embody the essence of Wisdom – Sophia

Sige had begun to waken from her healing sleep. She was aware of the presence of friends around her, but still expressed surprise at seeing Rosita sitting by the bed.

"Rosita, what are you doing here? I'm so glad to see you!" exclaimed Sige as she reached over to hug her friend. She felt a little strange and looking around for Aluzzo saw him coming towards her with a steaming bowl of broth laced with chunky vegetables and reviving herbs.

"When was the last time you ate anything, *cara*?" he said as he approached the bed, handing her the bowl and a spoon on a plate with some fresh wholemeal bread.

"*Gracias,* Aluzzo", she was feeling ravenous now that she could smell the delicious savoury aroma. "I was having the strangest dream. *Que pasa*? I remember becoming distressed at what you were telling me about Leon and then it's as if I passed out. After that, I remember a vibrant blue light all around me, and seeing the dove that emerged yesterday during the meditation." Then Rosita said,

"Tell us about the part of the dream where the dove appeared,Sige."

"*Bien*, there was a glowing lilac dove, the same one I remember seeing at the Hub last night when I attended with the other Matrons and Patrons. It was flying over a city of shining gold with a tall minaret sitting on pink clouds! The sky was dark as midnight. At one point I felt that I *was* the dove, looking down on the city below. There was a huge, luminous full moon and a glittering star to the right of my vision. Its silver blue light was shimmering and flashing and I could feel it pulsing through me. I only remember one sentence, it was something like: 'I am Sophia, I have strength; I have wisdom'." Sige said these last words with quiet power, while watching the faces of her friend and protector. They both exchanged a glance before Aluzzo said,

"Finish your soup *cara*, and then we'll tell you the whole story, that is, the parts we know of." They all sat, eating silently while each person's mind clattered with their own thoughts and unanswered questions. Aluzzo collected the bowls and set them aside before beginning to talk.

"I will recap something I told you way back when we began the deeper work. I told you then, that nature is so careful and exact in her creation that she cannot be used without great skill, for she does not produce anything that is perfect in itself. Humans must bring everything to perfection. This work is called 'Alchemy.' One is an alchemist who carries what nature grows and provides for the use of humanity to its destined end. What the eye perceives in herbs or stones or trees is not yet the

162

remedy. The eyes see only the non-essential exterior. Inside however, beneath this the remedy lies hidden. After it is cleansed of the dross, the essence is there." Then Rosita continued the lecture smoothly where Aluzzo left off.

"This is Alchemy relating to physical substance including the human body. This can be sublimated to give body to the spiritual energies that are released through transubstantiation. Like the essential oils we produce, or the remedies that are dynamised by potentisation, we have, like many before us, sought to capture the essential spark of divinity. Even the oils we produce have long been thought to contain the Holy Spirit and are known as the Holy Chrism." Rosita looked at Aluzzo and nodded for him to continue.

"My place in this century and many before, is a matter of the most high and subtle practices of Alchemy. Fourteen hundred years ago in the late first century A.D., I was known as a philosopher called *Origenes Adamantius,* who hailed from Egypt and lived for some sixty-nine years. There are still surviving writings in Greek attributed to the person I was then. As a defender of the Church I was imprisoned for heresy, but I came to appreciate the doctrines of the Gnostics. Obviously more than I realised at the time; for here I am leading the way now.

"It is also why I have been able in this life to recover many of the Magic Papyri that I use for our hermetic work. Including the one called 'The Gold-Making of Cleopatra', which concerns secret processes discovered by a Seeress involved in mystical gnosis during a time of much alchemical research carried out in Alexandria, a northern port of Egypt around the third century. The work over the last two millennia has never quite come to completion and I have returned in several ages to continue its progress.

"We are close to that point now and can fulfil and initiate new archetypal energies. These will herald the continuance of the most subtle evolution yet to be embodied by humanity."

"This is why the Inquisitors would burn us as heretics, isn't it?" Sige commented.

"*Si, cara.* So we must be very careful from now on. A new priest from the Dominican Order has been given a mission in Le Cuitat at Sant Michel Chapel. The Dominicans are extremely orthodox Catholics who are strongly opposed to any superstitious aspects of religion and have previously banished *Alumbrado* practitioners in Valliodad and elsewhere some years ago. They were lucky to escape with their lives."

"But Sant Michel is not far from here!" Sige looked at Rosita, who nodded in confirmation and added,

"That's true. So we can tell no-one of our plans, but we cannot stop now!" Rosita exclaimed. Aluzzo agreed and continued,

"You are a crucial factor in this process and this is why Leon, who was your son in a past life, has returned to try to destroy this process. It is not in the interests of the Luciferic and Ahrimanic Forces that prevail in many humans to see the race become essentially creative and optimistic. This is abhorrent to those of such an ilk. They prefer to bring us to destruction and pessimism, to ugliness and cynicism. I have spoken with Fray Villalonga to ask if it is possible to use one of the smaller chapels at La Seu and he wanted to know why, if we believe in the Christ, we could not make peace with the Church. I had tried to explain when I met him at the Cathedral.

"Fray Villalonga, it is not so simple. We *Alumbrados*, feel that the Supreme God of Truth is so remote from human affairs that he is unknowable and undetectable. Not the creator god, which you believe it to be." They stood talking quietly inside the vast and striking interior at the Royal Chapel to the rear of the Cathedral which is almost as large as a church in its own right with interior features like the three naves resting on forty-four-metre-high octagonal pillars and eight chapels to each side of those naves.

"But of course he is the Creator of all life!" Fray Villalonga objected. He looked confused as he listened to Aluzzo, feeling a sense of danger, for he already recognised the heresy that the old man standing with him would be accused of should they be overheard. He checked surreptitiously around the church seeing only empty pews then led Aluzzo to the first one in front of the main altar. "So who created life in your view?" he asked his voice a notch quieter than before.

"Ialdaboath is the name by whom we know him to be. He is also known as Jehovah in the Hebrew Scriptures. Sophia gave birth to him thinking she could be in control, a prideful mistake on her part which resulted in this defective, inferior Demiurge. Gnostics regard him as fundamentally evil, jealous, rigid and lacking in compassion, made worse by the fact that he thinks he is supreme. His pride and incompetence have resulted in the sorry state of the world as we know it and the blind and ignorant condition of most of humankind."

"But what of Original Sin? Was it not the first humans who became evil because they ate from the Tree of the Knowledge of Good and Evil, and being seduced by Satan in serpent form?"

"Gnosticism gives responsibility to Ialdaboath for creating an inferior world. We do not believe all began in perfection and that humans, 'missed the mark' but rather that in choosing to learn of Good and Evil, they became fully human and could then attain salvation by learning secret knowledge of their spiritual essence: the divine spark of light or spirit." Aluzzo meantime could not help admiring the one hundred and ten breath-taking walnut choir stalls behind the altar carved in flaming Gothic style; thinking how useful they would be for the Matrons and Patrons. With the acoustics within the interior's large-scale harmonious proportions, their melodies would be incredibly powerful.

"*Así,* what is the place of the Christ in your philosophy?" Fray Villalonga asked, while scratching his head, trying to make sense of what Aluzzo told him. He was still aware that he should end the conversation, but was too intrigued to stop just yet.

"*Bien, Le Christos* is much more of a Liberator or Revealer rather than a saviour or judge to us. His gospels help spread knowledge that can free individuals from the bondage to the world by actively understanding and ultimately transcending the intellectual; by actualising their spirituality. Remember Christ said, 'The Kingdom of God is Within.' We *Alumbrados* seek to experience that fully as men and women who are equals as human beings." Aluzzo looked at the monk seeing his expression of almost shock and some part recognition. Fray Villalonga stood up quickly, realising that he had begun to understand what Aluzzo was explaining to him and that he was beginning to recognise it to be more appealing than some of his own doctrine. This made him nervous and he coughed, putting his hand to his face in an effort to conceal any expression that might give any doubts about his faith away.

"*Vale,* Senor Aluzzo, there seems much to consider in your doctrine, but I am not at liberty to go further with you for it would mean grave punishment according to the edicts of my Church. This brings me to your request. I feel that it would bring much trouble for both myself and others here, who would need to be involved if we were to allow use of La Seu for your practices. I understand that your main wish is to accommodate your own choir, but by your own admission your harmonies produce effects of a different order from what myself and the choir here aspire to. It would not be possible to be discreet and people would wonder at the Cathedral being closed to them when it is not normally so. I'm sorry Senor, but let me think on it. There are many churches in the city, many of them hardly used. I will let you know at the first opportunity."

"*Muchas gracias,* Brother. Both for your consideration and for your ear. It is rare indeed for one of your faith to hear such things without offence. I understand that you are expecting a visitor from Seville on behalf of the Inquisitor Genérale?" Aluzzo asked as he stood up, making ready to leave.

"*Si, mi amigo.* You will understand my reluctance all the more if you know of this. I thank you for trusting me with your confidences and would ask of you the same discretion, Senor." The old monk looked tired and far from enthusiastic about the impending visit from his superior.

"*Claro,* Fray. We will speak again but not here, for I fear as you do, the echoes and shadows of your magnificent Cathedral that carries sounds so well when it is the last thing that we would wish at the moment. *Adios!*"

Aluzzo took a last look up at the ceiling and vaults of this sacred space, seeing with wonder the red and blue light shining amidst the golden yellow of the stained glass in the huge east rose window above them, glowing vibrantly with the light of the sun passing through. He easily appreciated the dedication and craftsmanship that had gone into the creation of La Seu and made a short bow of respect to the monk before he was let out through the port-side entrance at Le Portal de Mirador.

"I must go to dispense alms now Senor. The poor will always need fed and our talk of harmonies pales in importance sometimes when our fellow humans are in such need. Bless You. *Adios.*" The monk closed the great heavy wooden door behind Aluzzo.

Aluzzo brought Sige and Rosita back to the matter at hand, which seemed to have become more urgent as they spoke.

"*Así,* there is much more I could tell you Sige and I will as the days go on, but it is extremely important that we are able to defend and parry the assault of the man who presently heads the attempts at sabotage. One Ialdaboath or 'Leon', as you know him."

Sige had been much more able this time to hear Aluzzo's words without reacting. The energy of Leon and his minions had been diminished somewhat by the corresponding but stronger force of the *Vas Spirituale*. Sige was still trying to take in all that she had heard and experienced during the last twenty-four hours, not to mention the couple of days prior to that. And she hadn't heard Rosa's story yet. Sige slapped her hand to her forehead with an astonished but exhausted smile. Tomorrow would bring more enlightening activities and she could feel the pieces of those puzzling images of her dreams beginning to fall into place.

Rosita and Aluzzo would not let her return home to her own house alone that night. Neither did they feel she was sufficiently recovered from her brush with madness to travel to the House of Silence at midnight, so they had a session of 'Silence in Moment' upstairs in Aluzzo's own meditation hub. The quality of the vibrations did not seem to be lessened by the dearth in quantity of voices. Sige knew then that she was in the presence of a venerable Patron and a formidable Matron. Their hum was pure and clear and resonated in the perfect harmonies of tenor and alto. There was not a vibration out of sync. The energy that cascaded and swirled over and around them was of a warm golden light which massaged their spiritual web, making it pliant and strong.

At the midday session the next day, Sige would be expected to add her soprano hum, so they decided to suspend all conversation and maintain silence until just before the session when they would choose the appropriate notes that would produce certain colours of energy. In this case it would be gold again, for 'The Gold-Making of Cleopatra.' Their attempt would be to produce the alchemy of sound.

When the three people left the apothecary the next morning, Rosita stopped at the flower stall to buy some beautiful pink carnations and a bouquet of tuberose. Sige recognised them as *Dianthus carophyllus* and *Polianthes tuberosa*. The creamy-white flowers of the tuberose were known in Asia, as those that were made into garlands to be hung around the statues of various deities originating in India, like Krishna, Shiva and the Buddha. Sige had distilled and blended the absolute oils of both varieties of flowers many times for some of the people who came for healing. The first helped those who needed to open up to receive spiritual insight, clarity and compassion and the second, to assist in the understanding of life's purpose and to better give love.

They managed to hail a horse-drawn cart to get them to the castle, which was situated at the top of what was formerly known as '*Puig de sa Mesquita*' or hill of the mosque. It had stood on the land before the castle was built some 200 years before. The castle was used both as a palace and a prison and was soon to revert back to its original purpose of being a military complex. Its unique circular structure was what made it so useful for the meetings of the *Alumbrados* who, despite the effort required, welcomed its long climb and the cover of the pine woods framing it. This meant few people wandered around or undertook the climb to the castle itself unless with some specific purpose. The *Alumbrados* had had enough of the right friends in society and the castle enough space for them to meet monthly, until recently.

The influx of military personnel to adapt the castle for artillery and the increased activities of the Dominican Order, who were becoming more suspicious and insistent in their mission, confirmed by the recent arrival of the priest, meant that soon the friends would need to locate elsewhere. As here, having been under the nose of the occasionally visiting royalty without being noticed, they had sought the support of Fray Villalonga, knowing he was risking his life to do so. The

169

Franciscan Order was more open to and interested in unorthodox events and practices. Some of the Brothers were avid collectors of those reports of seemingly supernatural events and keenly interested in anyone who showed prophetic gifts, not immediately suspecting heresy. This is why the *Alumbrados* had approached him. What the result would be of their discussions about relocating to an unused church was not yet clear. They must await word from Fray Villalonga.

On arriving at the House of Silence, Rosita led Sige and Aluzzo into the Hub where they, still maintaining their silence, began to prepare the room for the Midday session. Sige was sent off with the flowers to find four gold vases in which to place the mingled bouquets, which she did so gladly, deeply inhaling their wonderfully sweet scents. Aluzzo meanwhile set up oil-burners, diluting the absolute oils of both varieties of the chosen flowers that he had brought with him, adding some water and lighting the candles inside the beautifully ornate copper bowls. Sige returned to the Hub with two of the vases and placed them on high plant tables just as the other Matrons and Patrons were beginning to take their seats on the circular benches. The benches were raised in ascending levels of seven heights and each held seven people with space to kneel or sit cross-legged, still allowing for each person to see everyone else.

As the men and women seated themselves, most of whom Sige had come to know over the last ten years, they acknowledged her presence with a slight bow of the head and a reassuring smile of acceptance. Sige nodded, smiling in response and went to fetch the remaining two vases. While Aluzzo lit the forty-nine candles set up around the outside of the circular bench, Rosita started to encourage the choir, for that's effectively what the company was, to stretch their voices to the notes she wished them to use.

At last the silence was broken. Aluzzo then lifted his hand and it repaired. In the quiet with spring sunlight shining through the rose window, its pink and blue glass throwing coloured shadows onto the walls, Sige had an image of some heavenly choir tuning up to sing its praises to the most Holy. Aluzzo's voice dispelled the image momentarily as he began to speak to everyone present.

"*Buenas Tardes* to you all and thank-you for lending your support. It is not often that I get to stand out front here to talk to you, but we have an unusual but critical situation that requires your most learned and practised selves. Today as you hum the notes that Rosita has offered you, please keep in mind the specific focus.

"Normally, I know that the humming would be done without the meaning and focus being explained, but today all awareness must be directed to this task. Rosita has given those of the bass tone, the note B in the second octave and for those in treble tone the note F in the fourth octave. These notes are connected with the flowers you see and the fragrances you smell. The B is for the carnations and an F for the Tuberose.

"Today, I ask that rather than humming, you open your throat and allow the pure note to flow unless conducted otherwise. Stay in tune but feel free to raise and lower the pitch and intensity of your notes. Our focus with the archetypal carnation is to soothe the soul. With your music, rejoice in the rebirth of the spirit. It can allow long forgotten memories to merge into a symphony of being, in one with the universe. Let even the shyest aspects of the self be brought into the sunlight. Rejoice in the glory of heavenliness. Luxuriate in knowing the experience of being. Feel the joy and gladness in reaching the higher realms." As Aluzzo finished relating the necessary focus of the carnation vibration, there sounded a quiet rumble in the background that was only just discernible. Aluzzo and Rosita glanced at each other and he swiftly moved onto the Tuberose archetype.

"The tuberose embodies forgiveness and helps us once again find love for the self when we feel lost and the spirit is low," Aluzzo directed his look to Sige with compassion and the

171

rumble became a little louder, the flower tables rocking slightly with the tremor. He continued quickly,

"This scented note helps transport the spirit to unknown places, where it will dwell long enough to find comfort and knowing. Find truth in truths long forgotten; bring hopes, dreams and prayers to their rightful place. Integrate the highest elements of the ego within spiritual wonderment."

Rosita lifted her hand as soon as he stopped speaking and directed the singing of the notes to begin. The timing of the onset of pure sound was perfect. The background rumbling continued for some time trying to increase, but as the notes lifted into the air and soared from the open mouths of the choir, it began to dissolve under the pure vibrations.

Rosita indicated that everyone singing the F note should become quiet and as the B note resounded around the circular Hub, colours began to appear. First, a deep pink light became observable but quickly turned to mauve then blue. As it further changed to gold and silver Rosita indicated that those on the treble note F should join in, while the others hold the pitch and intensity. On the treble note more coloured light became visible, moving from orange to red to yellow and then gold. Here Rosita had those singing the F to hold the pitch and intensity as the bass were doing. The effect was quite astounding. The predominantly gold coloured light formed into a spiral at the centre of the room resembling a tornado and moved in a circular motion across to where Sige sat on the front row at the end of the bench. It completely surrounded her and Rosita conducted the choir in lowering to a hum then take a breath and lift the notes again into circular chorus. The golden whirlwind spun around Sige slowly but picked up speed as the choir lifted the notes. She heard her late husband's voice quietly but clearly in the bass tone saying,

"*Sige, my love. You, whose name means Silence; out of Silence, Sophia is born. Take your place by my side as infinite wisdom to the infinite love of Christos. Defeat the hatred,*

extinguish the fear, and forgive the wrongs that are also right."
While the voice faded, the gold coloured light began to fleck with green, Sige saw brown eyes with flashes of gold glinting in them. It was her beloved's face gazing at her with profound yearning.

The choir had dropped to hum exclusively in the bass note and the light was a fresh spring green. The scent of carnation and tuberose filled the Hub and Rosita brought the singers of the F note into the hum to bring the meditation to a close on a high. The rumbling had completely dissolved and the faces of the choir were wreathed in smiles. Everyone let out a deep breath. As well as the astounding play of light that had taken aback most of the choir, though they were too practised to have let it interfere, everyone had a sense that something not too pleasant had been avoided by being able to counteract the destructive rumbling that had almost taken hold just as they had got started.

Sige was sitting quietly, noticeably not smiling, with tears streaming down her face as she silently sobbed. She felt wonderfully loved but confused. Aluzzo and Rosita had not told Sige about her embodiment of Sophia the night before, so she had been still unaware of the need to accept the destiny that was right in front of her, until now.

The rest of the Matrons and Patrons filed out of the Hub still filled with the joy of their singing. They hadn't heard the words of Christos but felt their own joyful reconnection of ego to spirit and were close to ecstatic. They went to relax and enjoy the sense of resonance with their friends in the lounge before heading out into the early afternoon sunshine. Rosita and Aluzzo stayed in the Hub with Sige, but left her in silence to continue to complete the connections that were now clear, while they doused the burners and blew out the candles.

When they had finished, Sige was waiting with an expression that seemed to convey conflicting emotions. She felt both apprehensive of the role she had inherited and also a deep

173

sense of calm within herself. This contradictory, though not unpleasant state, resulted in many questions that she only now realised she had to ask.

"Let's find a quiet café somewhere to talk," said Rosita, taking Sige's left arm whilst Aluzzo linked his through her right one. They wandered solemnly out into the bright spring sun, shining in a clear blue sky. The air was still fresh as the new season had yet to begin, so they pulled capes close in and headed down the few hundred steps from the castle to find an open air café on the streets below the pine wood. The traffic was quiet, it being Sunday and they managed to skip across the road, free of the usual cart dodging that took place mid-week. The silence continued as their internal thoughts rolled thick and fast.

After ordering their drinks and Aluzzo's usual *ensaimada*, Sige began to ask questions about what they needed to do next.

"I mean, what are we going to do about Leon? I feel such a fool about him. Why didn't I recognise what he was like?"

"Didn't you? Are you sure you didn't realise you were playing with fire? Desire of the kind that Leon offers and incites is that of lust. Did you really love him or did you only love his body, his sex?" Rosita gave Sige a searching look.

"*Si*, I did love his body and I enjoyed the sex we had together," Sige was blushing, for Rosita and she never had these kinds of conversations in front of Aluzzo. "But, I did think we had learned to love and trust each other too!" She replied with indignation.

"*Si*, we were all fooled to some degree, *Cara*. He has such a pleasant manner and could seem so helpful," contributed Aluzzo.

"*Si*, obviously when he wants something. I was never quite wholly convinced about him. You both know that," continued Rosita. And this, in fact, was true. She had warned Sige way back, close to his first appearing at the Hub. It was not accepted that visitors should be judged as to their motives for coming to the House of Silence. Rather it was hoped that if they found it was not for them, as had often happened over the years, they would just stop coming. Or, if their behaviour became unbalanced in some way, they would be offered appropriate support. But Leon had never done either. He had seemed to be very interested in the philosophy and practice there, though seldom participated and this was what had made him suspect to Rosita all these years. He had immediately zoomed in on Sige and that seemed his main interest in being around The House.

Rosita had also felt twinges of jealousy then because he was taking up time that the women would normally have spent together, so she had dismissed much of her feeling as being immature. Later on, she had suspected Leon was seeing other women but had never had any concrete knowledge that this was so. Nevertheless, her intuition kept her wary of him and concerned for Sige, so was not surprised when several months ago Aluzzo had contacted her with his own recently learned knowledge of Leon's distinctly shady past.

Aluzzo told Sige then that while he had been working with her the last seven years he had begun to realise his hopes for the culmination of his long millennia of labour. She retained information surprisingly quickly, as if she had only needed reminding. She had amazed him on many occasions with her profound observations concerning the healing of patients who had come to see him, and had allowed her as time moved on, to sit in with and demonstrate her learning in a practical way. She had an understanding that came from her own life experiences, yet there was, in the beginning, occasional and then increasingly more frequent observations that heralded some opening of a sense of timeless and ancient knowledge, which could not have come from her present life.

"I chose you as my apprentice Sige, because I had an inkling of your potential as a healer of some distinction. I sensed that your contribution to my work would be of great significance."

"You talk about me as if I'm special but I'm not!"

"Ah, but it has only been in the few months after we potentised the blood of Christos, and I had taken the medicine, that it was revealed to me what your true role would be!" Aluzzo answered. In proving the remedy, he had been gifted with foreknowledge about events in the coming months.

"*Lo siento.* I'm sorry, Sige. But although I then realised what Leon's true motive was, I could not interfere with events that had still to happen. I could only prepare myself and to some extent Rosita, for the consequences of Leon's revelation to you; that your relationship was not what it seemed".

Aluzzo had seen Leon find Le Dragon Rouge, in fact they had fought over its possession five hundred years ago while both were in different incarnations. Aluzzo had managed to hold onto the document then, but lost it between his next two incarnations and could not recall its location until well into this one. When he did, he realised that Leon had already found it before him and so waited for him to make his move, while feeling Leon's power, or rather arrogance, growing.

Rosita laid her hand on Sige's shoulder, "It was unfortunate but necessary that you have been caught in the middle of this shifting swell of murky forces. *Así*, now we can deal with it together." Having listened to the unfolding of events and feelings described by her friend and her mentor, Sige felt the stark reality of the conflict yet to come. The Holy Adversary! The realisation sent a terrible shivering chill through her from head to toe and she recollected a verse from the bible in Revelations 12.

"Is it the same Satan as in Revelations, we battle?" she asked, quoting the verse from the bible. '*There appeared ...a great red dragon ...*' and '*...the great Dragon was cast out, that old serpent called the devil, and Satan, which deceiveth the world.*' Sige shivered, recollecting that same chill on seeing the

176

sneering expression on Leon's face when he left her yesterday. Had it only been yesterday?

As they paid their bill and turned to leave the café they noticed a Dominican priest, recognisable in his black houndschoot habit, watching them from under his hood at a table beside the entrance to the café. He was frowning with narrowed eyes as if he'd overheard their conversation. They wished him *'Buenas tardes.'* as they passed him by on the way out the door. But he was not so easily dismissed.

"Siento molestarle. Sorry to trouble you, *Señor y señoras?"* He said smoothly to their retreating backs.

"Si, Padre. ¿Le puedo ayudar? May I help you?" Sige asked as she slowly turned back to face the priest, finding herself looking up at the sharp featured face into eyes bright, black and penetrating. He had stood as he spoke, and now pulled himself up to his full height. The priest's emaciated frame towered above all three of them. His hood had fallen back to reveal a skull-like head and sunken face with skin an unhealthy grey. There was a sheen of sweat on his brow.

"Me llamo Padre Josep. I am with the Inquisitor Generale's office. May I see your Tizón de España? I don't recall having seen any of you at Mass today and it is my duty to make sure that all the citizens of the city of Mallorca can be assured that there are none among us who are losing faith in the Holy Mother Church. *Si?"*

"Claro, Padre," they each replied, searching under their cloaks for their documentation.

"Rápido!" he suddenly demanded with some menace. Startled by his command Sige dropped her papers on the ground. *"Deprisa Señora!* Is there something wrong?"

"Que quiere usted decir, Padre - What do you mean, Father?"* Sige asked, trying to keep the tremor from her voice as she bent to pick up her papers.

"You seem a little nervous Señora, *no*?" the priest said in a rather sarcastic tone, smiling thinly as he examined Aluzzo's papers thoroughly with keen eyes.

"*Aquí tiene.* Here you are*, Padre.*" Rosita managed, handing her papers to the priest while Sige steadied herself, also placing her document in the priest's pale and grasping palm.

He handed them back after taking a note of their details in a small book hanging from the rope belt at his waist. On finishing this, he looked searchingly at their faces as if committing them to memory, then nodded his head abruptly before walking away. They looked at each other, eyes wide with shock, unable for a moment to say anything.

"That's all we need! Now we have the Inquisitor *and* Leon breathing down our necks. *Vamos!* Let's get this over with as soon as possible." Aluzzo, suggested at length, looking concerned. Rosita insisted they arrange to get together later in the evening. They had no idea when Leon would strike again, but Sige needed to be alone for now, both to come terms with her fate and to ponder on the unexpected confrontation with the Inquisitor's lackey. She left them both and turned onto the road leading to the house and waved to the driver of a carriage before he could pass her by. Rain clouds were gathering to the west when she reached home and the sky was darkening to pencil grey above. Sige heard a rumble but dismissed it as some loose thunder.

The dreary heaviness of the clouds overhead plunged her thoughts in a downward spiral. The sometimes overwhelming feelings of hurt and disbelief cut her to the quick when she thought about the times that Leon had called off from seeing her with some, at the time, reasonable explanation as to why he couldn't be with her. She thought of his last birthday, he'd wanted to be on his own, he said, yet now she knew he had been with someone else, spending the day with them, being late and leaving her sitting, waiting. The knife turned inside her and she faltered on the path. A heavy, cutting ache weighed in her solar plexus. And there were other times too.

She had to stop thinking about Leon the way she had before. He was an enemy of all she held dear. She had to let go of wanting to be with him. There were other events on the horizon which held greater significance for her future. She would have to consign her fantasies to oblivion for that was all they were; fantasies, nothing more. The rumbling became louder as she got to the door of the *finca*. The pain had taken the edge off her awareness and she failed to notice a light dimming quickly as she turned her key in the lock.

As soon as she stepped inside the cottage she drew in her breath. Sige could feel a dark presence; in fact, she could *smell* the malevolence. It reeked of envy and was heavy like a dank swamp. It stank like rotting matter. She felt the hair stand up on the back of her neck and pulled her cloak tighter around her as the icy chill of the intruder pervaded the atmosphere.

"Is that you Marissa?" she called, not quite trembling, but none too steady or secure either. There was a high-pitched laugh in reply to her question, which caused her even more uncertainty. Who was this? It had a familiar tone to it; that laugh. Sige moved further up the hallway following the stench of malice into the front room, where she had last seen Leon. As she came in the doorway her mouth fell open in disbelief at the person who stood before her.

"*Vosotros!* You!" Was all she could manage when first able to speak. Her face had drained and she felt the dizziness of two days ago returning.

"*Vosotros!*" The woman mimicked. "Don't you look a sight? You're a bit pale around the gills, dearest Sige. Here, I brought these for you. I know how much you like flowers," the woman continued in a mocking tone as she thrust out a bedraggled bunch of the strangest flowers Sige had ever seen.

They were bright yellow with scarlet centres, black leaves and stem. They were oozing sticky red fluid that looked like blood. Sige stepped back, away from the dark offering.

"What do you want? How did you get in here? I don't want your disgusting flowers."

"You gave me the key; don't you remember? I just dropped by to fill you in on my latest exploits. I know how much you care, Ha Ha!"

"What are you talking about? I never gave you a key to my home!" Sige shot back at her.

"Not that kind of key, you fool! I thought you were the all-wise and knowledgeable one. I mean the key to getting your man; your lover, your precious Leon!!" Sige's mind was racing. She could barely hold a clear thought in her head, and her stomach and heart were doing somersaults.

"It was you he was with, on his birthday!? On the other days he left me sitting waiting for him?" Sige was stunned and felt the knife in her heart grow to sword-like proportions, feeling slow and searing open-heart surgery begin as she tried to stay standing to take all this in. She shook her head as if in slow motion, her eyes staring at the woman in front of her with abject disbelief.

"I know you thought we were friends, and I suppose we were for a while. So what if you've always been there for me? But what about that time when we were both meeting that advisor at the Hub, but you didn't tell me for months, did you? Betrayal! Ha! You're pretty damned good at it yourself! And after you so kindly once again helped and encouraged me to join with others to start my own practical work, I didn't need you anymore and didn't they tell me a few things. Not everyone thinks you're so goody-goody Sige. It seems they thought you left some nasty vibes there that they didn't like at all, and so they had the space cleansed. Isn't that a surprise for you, eh!?

"And then...you shared all your worries and concerns and insecurities about how things were with your precious Leon and encouraged him to come for herbal treatment from me, Ha! What a fool you are Sige. It didn't take long in that kind of setting to gain his trust. What with him seeming so confused about whether he wanted to keep on being with you, I saw my chance to take him from right under your nose. Why should you get all the breaks, why should you live the life you wanted? Happy being poor, happy thinking you had it all your own way. Are you happy now Sige?"

As much as Sige was feeling like she was being hit with blows from all directions, she was managing to gather some energy and ground herself whilst this venomous tirade went on. She was leaning against the front room wall to steady herself and briefly closed her eyes. She saw in her mind's eye an image of Aluzzo and Christos and the golden whirlwind spiralling around them. She had noticed the manic look in Jade's eyes when she first came into the room. Jade's face was even paler than hers and she had lost a lot of weight since Sige had last seen her. How many weeks, maybe months, had it been since Jade had stopped replying to her letters? What Jade didn't know was that she wasn't the only one that Leon had been seeing, or more accurately using. Jade continued her tirade:

"And then last night, doesn't your precious Leon come and ask me to visit you and tell you all about our little lust nest. How he had better sex with me in one week than he'd had with you in four years. He likes the kinky stuff; didn't you know? We did it everywhere we could think of. We got into all sorts of weird and wonderful positions. Are you jealous yet, Sige? Do you just wish it could have been you? And that day of his birthday, I gave him a special birthday present. Will I tell you what I did for him?" Jade didn't wait for a reply, her rambling story picking up speed, becoming more incoherent.

"Well, I dressed up you see, and had my erotic underwear on and I bought a special whip…and… and…I was supposed to whip him… but…but… he got carried away…and he whipped me…" Jade started to sob. "It was so sore…I had welts and

181

cuts...all...all over. I didn't mean for it to get so out of hand. His face was so cruel and he was enjoying giving me such pain and saying over and over... 'I've got you now, I've got you now...'" Jade trailed off and subsided into sobs as she collapsed into a heap on the nearest chair.

The rumbling had become louder and louder the whole time Sige's former friend had been babbling and it was now at deafening levels. Every free-standing object in the room was shaking and a woodcut of Leon fell from the wall and crashed, splintering to the floor. Sige continued to bring the golden light into her solar plexus and it became tinged with blue. She began to focus on the blue glow at the edge of the golden light until it sizzled and grew outwards warming her with its electric hum as her whole body began to vibrate. Echoing in the rumbling was the sound of Leon's velvet laugh becoming louder and louder as he seemed to be gaining strength from the heap of misery that Jade had been reduced to in the telling of her tale.

Sige could see an aura of sickly green streaked with dirty black around Jade, which was growing by the second. She held her hand palm outwards in the other woman's direction in an attempt to direct the blue lightning energy towards the evil smelling miasma. Sige was standing upright and was completely focused now, her body giving off an eerie blue glow that was travelling down her arm. She felt protected from both Jade's vitriol and Leon's increasingly malevolent power. She could feel its pressure and see the indentations it made in the blue light. She began to hum the treble F note that they had used at the Hub not so long ago, but which now seemed like an eternity away. Soon words came to her and she intoned them with strength not of the physical, but with a potency that seemed to emanate from her soul.

"I am Sophia. By me kings reign, and princes decree justice. By me Queens rule, and nobles, even all the judges of the earth. I love them that love me; and those that seek me early shall find me...I lead in the way of righteousness, in the midst of

182

the paths of judgement. Blessed is the man or woman that hears me, watching daily at my gates, waiting at the posts of my doors. For whoso find me, find life...But he or she that sins against me wrongs their own soul: all they that hate me, love death. I have Strength! I have Wisdom!"

This time Sige was fully conscious of her embodiment of Sophianic power and watched as the blue light streamed across the room, enfolding the sickly aura that surrounded Jade until it was extinguished. Sige saw again the lilac dove briefly flutter its wings above Jade's head and disappear as the blue light diminished. Jade had brought her weeping head up sharply when Sophia had begun to speak through Sige, and her eyes were now wide in astonishment. She had no more words to throw at Sige. They had vanished amid her tears and the realisation that she had been an obscene pawn in a situation that had never in fact, been in her control. Leon's laugh too, had been strangled into silence as the blue energy overpowered his creeping, poisonous spite.

"I think it's time you left Jade," said Sige quietly but firmly and looked on with exhaustion as the woman sloped pathetically towards the door. She locked the door behind Jade, even though it was obviously just to make her feel a little better and clearly wasn't at all effective at keeping anyone out if they really wanted in. She opened the windows to let in some fresh air and blow the remaining stench clear.

Despite being able to take back some purpose and use it to temporarily stay the rising powers of Leon, Sige now felt the hurt of the double betrayal. An aching numbness bruised her inside and out and she walked around the house straightening up objects that had been disturbed or knocked over due to the tremor. The whole time tears streamed down her face and she constantly shook her head in disbelief. She heard then the gate being pushed open and went to see who this was now. Sige saw Fernando stepping back from the gate to let Marissa guide the horse and buggy in. As soon as it was through, Fernando took

183

the reins and Marissa climbed down from the buggy as quickly as she was able and hurried into the house.

"Señora, Señora, where are you? Are you all right!?" she cried, running to Sige and putting her arms around her.

"*Si* Marissa, I'm okay for now. Where have you and Fernando been? There was someone in the house when I got back," she answered wearily, gently moving out of Marissa's urgent embrace.

"We saw a woman along the road. She stopped a cart going towards Le Cuitat. She is gone now, Señora." Fernando answered as he came through the side door. Marissa looked stricken as she said,

"I knew something was wrong! Speaking Woman was whispering so urgently in my ear, telling me to hurry before it was too late! We got here as fast as we could Señora. We had to go to Santa Maria del Cami for supplies today, as we always do on a Sunday, and we had planned to go to the city to check on Anna but the whispering was so urgent! Forgive me, Senora?"

"*Vale*, Marissa. It's okay. It was not your fault or Fernando's. You were not to know Jade would be here or that she could get in. But we must be more careful. Like not mentioning 'Speaking Woman' whoever she may be? There may be more attacks and it is Señor Leon who is behind them. Also, I was stopped by Padre Josep with Rosita and Aluzzo today. He wanted to check our papers. We are not sure if he overheard a conversation where we mentioned Satan."

"Satan, Senora? But why would you be discussing Satan?" asked Fernando looking at Sige suspiciously.

"Because Fernando, he is Señor Leon's Master and we had to make a plan how to defeat the forces of darkness," Sige replied, watching horrified expressions appear on both Fernando and Marissa's faces.

"Oh no! What will we do? I don't want to be burned as a witch. What if they start talking to people, asking around in

Santa Eugenia? There are any number of *las cotillas* and that Luisa at the market, she is such a gossip!" wailed Marissa.

"Enough, Marissa. *Tranquila si us plau, cara.* We'll be fine as long as we don't panic and we go to mass every Sunday from now on. We *Alumbrados* can deal with Leon, *No se preocupe!*" she said earnestly, trying to convince herself as she spoke the words.

"*Bien, Buenas Noches.*" Sige said finally. She was too tired to do very much upstairs, so left the mess till tomorrow and went to lie down a while and sleep away a little of the pain and exhaustion.

Over the next ten days as they approached the full moon Sige continued to attend the House of Silence at midday with the Matrons and Patrons to meditate and strengthen her energy. At times it was difficult for her to receive the vibrations or to participate in the note singing. She became distraught trying to slough off her own sentimentality and attachment to Leon and her former friend Jade. Coupled with this, several times she had the spirit of Christos return during these sessions and this aroused in her old grief, which she thought had passed off over time, in the aftermath of his physical death.

It was strange and perplexing, at first, to relate to this voice as no longer the person she had lived and loved with for twenty years. As she began to accept her own place in the scheme of things it became easier, for some of the energy surges had her feeling rather disembodied herself. In truth, there were times she wished she *could* die. The waves of pain from recent events were slow in fading and often caught her unawares. They left her feeling helpless in their wake, wondering if this life or any were worth the suffering for all concerned. Her lessons with Aluzzo helped her understand just a little bit more. He had begun to remind her of their last meeting with Leon/Ildaboath several aeons previously.

185

Aluzzo took her back into the past using light trance and the use of sweet Marjoram oil, which calmed the senses and stilled Sige's mind long enough to ignite the memories in the warmth of sparks from the cosmos. She felt the need to go with the deeply centred peace that enabled her to tread carefully through images that suggested evil. Sige recognised a need to forgive without judgement or criticism, lest she be judged yet again and have to be turned from the flow of humanity, where all that our evolution had created in the bearing of suffering, could be undone.

She came to remember a sense of herself as Barbelo, feminine and powerful but supported by the co-workers she had requested: Incorruptibility; Foreknowledge; Eternal Life; Intellect and Truth. In that time, she as Barbelo, had conceived the light and brought forth Christos. For Barbelo this wasn't enough and who'd been so arrogant to think herself able to create something without the help of the Universal Void of Silence, resulting in the forming of her offspring Ialdaboath. He had the body of a Serpent and the face of a lion. Soon he had usurped Barbelo's power and withdrew from the fullness of the higher planes and ruled the fallen world.

Rejoicing in his misappropriated power, he proclaimed there were no beings higher than he. As Barbelo, Sige saw herself grow ever darker, her energy shifting and billowing turbulently in repentance at her prideful act of creating this wayward being. She remained in the ninth realm till her power was restored many aeons later when Ialdaboath was undermined by his *own* creation. Only then Barbelo was able to join with Christos to reveal a Saviour that would descend through the seed of life, for all time. Sige recognised that Leon, as descendant of the same spirit of Ialdaboath, would not give up easily. Now the battle was to be fought on the earthly realm in order to put the higher realms to right.

Aluzzo also revised with her the outer manifestations of Alchemy proper, so that she would understand her own process of purification. They began with *calcinations,* where the material is purgated into powder. This Aluzzo explained as Sige's own becoming into material existence once again.

"After the descent into matter, there must be *sublimation* and the removal of the spirit from matter. This has caused the divide of logos or intellect from wisdom and the resultant ability of humanity to divorce themselves from their actions. This creates a loss of heart and therefore a loss of compassion in the acts that are perpetrated on the earth and on each other. They are two sides of the same coin and from whence come the actions of, for example, your former friend, Jade.

"In the stage of *solution* the matter is dissolved, as you know, into water that does not wet the hand. And the Power of Sophia is extracted in a primary way to be used arbitrarily as it was in the last meeting with Ildaboath. Next is *putrefaction,* where matter is subjected to vigorous disintegration by heat and the power of wisdom is subsumed into many different ideologies. This is followed by *distillation* and the vapours given off are condensed and reabsorbed in the vessel. This happened in your first embodiment of the power of Wisdom when the *Vas Spirituale* absorbed the lightning energy. In the material world wisdom works through many paths and disciplines and is reabsorbed.

"We are now at the stage of *coagulation* wherein matter is deprived of humidity and forms a solid. Wisdom is coming into the awareness and perception of many people, not least the adversaries. Now, the importance of our work is to continue to transform the matter into its *tincture*; its holy or primal essence. Only then will Sophia be understood by the many to be of one holy blood and kinship with humanity." Aluzzo ended this short but powerful lecture with an air of gravity but could not keep the excited edge from his voice. Sige interrupted, a quizzical expression on her face, masking her trepidation,

"What more need I do, Aluzzo? I thought Christos coming to me the other day was what it was all about."

"We've been working towards this for so long, Sige. It must not be undone again for a long time. Before the body of light can be attained we must complete the reconciliation and integrate the elements from individual and cosmic spirit. It is no less than the re-sacralisation of matter, resulting in the integration of feminine and masculine. If we can perfect the craft of Sophianic restoration through your prepared being then it will be a living example for all to come. This will mean absorbing the spirit of Christos, your creation and your partner in Hieros Gamos, the Sacred Marriage. There is only one chance of allowing the Saviour to live again in this age. That chance lies with you. Meantime we still have Leon or Ildaboath to deal with. Remember, my dear, even if we overcome his present manifestation, he will ever be the shadow to your light." This then, was her explanation for both the gravity and the excitement.

It would be a full moon in two days time, the turning point between two contrary directions of the waxing and waning of the moon. Sige and her friends had to be on their guard more than usual. The wrong thing could easily happen in this transitional period and they tried to avoid doing anything much, except be prepared. If there was an opportune moment for Leon to do his worst, this would be it.

Rosita stayed at Sige's house for the next few nights, especially after the last visit from Jade and Leon. Sige had eventually sorted out upstairs in the aftermath of Leon's attempts to rock her senseless. Though she had found nothing obvious missing, she knew Jade or someone had rifled carelessly through her drawers and cupboards looking for what, Sige wasn't sure. It had added to her sense of violation in light of the entry to her home without her knowledge but she had heard nothing further from Jade or her dark master. No news is good news? Sige certainly hoped so.

After that last fiasco, Leon had been for a visit to him whose name he bore. Lion-faced Sata, the Dragon King.

"Must I do this myself again!?" roared Sata, "I give you written instructions in Le Dragon Rouge, I let you use my archons and still you can't destabilise this mere mortal enough to fill her heart with darkness?"

Leon had been summoned a day or two after Sige had quashed the malevolent miasma he'd sent with Jade. Leon was sleep in his flat with her curled up at his side with all her apparent remorse. He had thought he was dreaming when he felt his body whizzing at high speed in a downward spiral of searing heat. It was too hot to be a dream! Ouching and cursing as he hit a hard, flat surface, he realised in whose dark, cold shadow and volcanic breath he stood.

"O Great Sata, forgive my weakness. She is more powerful than we anticipated, Lord. You know I'd do anything to please you. In fact, I have another plan. Would you like to hear it, Grand Master?" Leon grovelled under the overbearing, smelly jaws of a once regal lion, whose mane had become matted and singed to jaggy bristles around a scarred face. Its tail flicked furiously as it breathed out sulphurous fumes that turned Leon's insides to bile, threatening to burst from his mouth. He gagged as unobtrusively as possible; swallowing the acidic liquid back down, becoming breathless as he did so.

"No..ooo!" Sata roared again. "Just get on with it! You have one week to darken her heart with irrevocable misery and pathos. She must give up or I am lost. And so are you, little Leon," the Dragon King added in a sickeningly sweet, mocking tone which chilled Leon to the depths and made him catch his breath. The next moment he was back in his bed, hyperventilating and feeling more panicky than he had in a while. Jade had awakened and was worrying over him like an old hen.

"Leave me alone!" he managed to scream at her. "You're useless anyhow. Go on, get out! You're no match for Sige, you never were. She may be my nemesis but she still has my admiration. At least she had some resistance. You're just a lustful bag of envy. Go on, get out, I said." Jade scrambled off the bed, seething with anger and limped off in humiliation. She dressed and left quickly without a word, her head hanging. Leon couldn't get back to sleep when she'd gone, so lay and planned what he was sure would be Sige's undoing this time.

He thought he would go and visit his little, or not so little, 'stepdaughter'. He chuckled and gloated to himself. He was glad he'd got Jade to search Sige's place while he was there. He had Anna's address now, so no problem. He would write to her asking if he could visit. Leon sat down to compose the letter to Anna, putting his most seductive phrasing and sentiment into it, trying to ensure a speedy and sympathetic reply. He hoped for an answer that day.

12 Carrer de Puressa
Cuitat de Mallorca
Febrero 1575

Dear Anna,
It is Leon, your neglectful stepfather writing at last. I hope this letter finds you in good health and humour. How is your dear brother Xavier? I'm spending some time in the city these days and I thought I'd come to visit, if you've no other plans, of course? There's something I must discuss with you that is close to my heart and you have always been such a good listener. I have missed your youthful presence and innocent beauty. I would appreciate a speedy reply so that I can set out tomorrow hoping that you will be at home,

Your Ever Faithful Stepfather, Leon

Leon carried out his ablutions and prepared for his trip anyway, whistling a self-satisfied tune as he went to carefully pick out his attire. A black velvet doublet, breeches and hose with snowy white ruffs and sateen cloak to match. He would melt yet another heart with his flair and flatteringly concerned manner. He needed only to find a carrier to deliver his letter across the city to Anna's house and ask them to wait for a reply. He finished the letter and went onto the street, holding a handkerchief to his nose to dampen the usual stench of rotting food and human waste. He soon saw two young rascals in a doorway stuffing themselves with fruit from a basket by their side. He wondered where they'd got that from; guessing that they had probably stolen it. He wasn't sure he could trust them. He'd have to speak Mallorqine Catalan to these commoners.

"Hola chicos, Cómo estas?"

"Be, i tu Señor?" At least they were polite so far.

"D'on ets chicos...Where are you from boys, le Cuitat?"

"Si, Señor." The boys looked at each other, wondering what this overdressed fop wanted of them. He looked like he had good coin, so they waited for what was coming next.

"I was wondering, could you deliver a letter for me?"

The boys were dressed in ripped chemises, grey with dirt. Their three-quarter breeches sported gaping holes at the knees. They had not a sandal between them. They carried on munching the melon and grapes while he waited for their reply. It was only when Leon looked at them a little more closely he noticed that the boy, who also wore a ragged waistcoat, was holding a knife in his hand. Granted it seemed to be for the melon, but it gave him a start all the same. "

"Esta lluny...Is it far, Senor?"

"No, Just a few streets away at numero dos, Estudi General. Do you know where that is?" The boys straightened up as if he'd challenged them. They were proud of how well they knew the city. They lived on the streets didn't they?

"Claro, of course, Senor!" they chorused indignantly.

191

"Vale, quin pre...how much to take this letter for me? Uno reales?" The grape eater stood up with a look of disappointment.

"Oh Senor, I don't think we can help you with that." He emphasised his regret by shaking his head. His friend stood up to join him, putting the melon down amongst the rubbish and peel on the ground. Hooking his grubby thumbs into the pockets of his waistcoat after wiping his hands on the already filthy breeches he wore, he appeared all business now. His demeanour looked the part, except for the dirty face still wet and slick from the juice of the melon.

"Maybe we can work out something amable Senor, Si? Uno Reales won't go far between dos chicos, no? I think it only fair that we ask for dos Reales. One each, Senor. Si? And we'll have your letter there in a flash."

"But it doesn't take two to carry a letter, does it? I'll give you two Reales if you do it; wait for a reply and bring it back. How about that? Have we got a deal chicos?" The boys knew they'd been outfoxed.

"Vale Senor, you strike a hard bargain. Where shall we bring the reply?" the grape-eater asked, wiping his hands now on equally filthy breeches.

"Just there at numero doce. I'll give you the quarter Piece of Eight when you bring me back the reply." He turned and pointed further along the street and handed the letter to the melon eater, because he had pockets. "Now don't lose it or I'll come looking for you. Someone is waiting for this letter, so I'll know chicos. Vale?"

"Perdona Senor? Can we trust you to look after our fruit basket till we get back? It will disappear if we leave it on the street," the melon eater asked, as he searched and found a place to carry the letter and the knife, hiding it in his scraps of material that passed for clothing.

"Claro, chicos, but don't be too long or I might get hungry myself." Leon teased them, picking up the basket and turning towards the door of his house.

Leon was feeling more pleased with himself than ever, and having received his reply from Anna within the hour yesterday, was anxious to leave in plenty of time for a stroll and a bite to eat on the Passeig Maritime before going to her house. Leon hoped when he arrived at Anna's house that Xavier wouldn't be home, for he needed to secure Anna's sympathy while she was alone. He knew Xavier had rightly never trusted him.

Anna was puzzled as she put down the letter, but a little excited too. He'd never come to visit her in the last six months since she'd moved away from home. She liked Leon. Anna had missed her Papi after he died and eventually became attached to Leon after he seemed to be in her Mama's company regularly. She kind of envied her Mama having such a handsome man as her beau and had flirted harmlessly with him when she was fifteen going on sixteen. Now she was twenty, he'd see how grown up she was.

Anna wondered if she should write to Mama and find out what was going on, but dismissed the thought. She hurried to reply to the letter from Leon, trying to calm her excitement but already she was thinking of what dress to wear when he came. Anna had a moment of doubt before she handed over the reply to the two young boys. They were obviously beggars. She also quickly handed a one Reales coin to each of them before she could change her mind. They glanced at each other with a brief smile, burying the silver in their pockets and took the note from her, running off as fast as their filthy bare feet would carry them.

The next day the cart driver slowed his horse as they came by the corner of Carrera Estudia General and Leon gave him a half Reale piece before he jumped down from the cart and wished him a *"Buenas tardes."* He was glad he'd decided to have that delicious tortillas de patatas and glass of wine. It had made him a little late for his appointment to see Anna, but it was good to keep her waiting. Even if she wasn't here he could give the place a thorough look over. He might find something to his advantage that would make the expense worthwhile.

If Anna was here she would be taken aback by his attendance, since she probably thought he wasn't coming now. The black wrought iron gates were closed over the wooden front door, but were not locked. He was right. She jumped on coming through from the kitchen to find him in the hallway. She had given up waiting for him, thinking something must have happened. So she was thrown by his now unexpected arrival and blushed.

"Leon!! *Como…*? I thought those two little beggars had kept the money and thrown away my reply last night! I did not expect you to come!" She gasped and tried to pull herself together quickly, which wasn't easy since she had gone back to doing some household chores, so was wearing her work clothes. Leon laughed hard,

"Oh, so you gave those rascals silver too. They were well paid then. All power to the greedy little tykes. That's what I say!"

Anna smiled and politely excused herself and went off to get him refreshment, disappointed that she had not had the opportunity to freshen up and look her best but what did it matter. He was her stepfather, not a suitor.

Leon closed and bolted both sets of doors when she had gone, for he didn't want to be disturbed. He hoped this would be a coup d'état for him in the struggle to, once and for all, shatter Sige's spirit and darken her soul. If this didn't work he didn't want to think what the Dragon King would do to him.

"Are you all alone in this big house? How do you manage? Isn't Xavier here? When will he return?" he asked Anna on her return from the kitchen.

"Let me get those for you." He hastened to take the cups of wine from her.

"Oh, he won't be back for two more days. He's gone off to visit with his fiancée's parents in Santa Maria del Cami. He hopes to get some kind of trading apprenticeship with her Father." She answered, unwittingly telling Leon exactly what he wanted to hear.

"That's a pity. But then again, I get you all to myself, don't I?" he replied with an innocent smile.

"Well, what brings you to visit our humble home, Leon? You haven't even contacted me since I left home. I mean it's great to see you, I do miss you and Mama but it just seems a bit strange. Where is Mama? I thought you both might have been trying to surprise me and catch me in my slovenly ways now I don't have Mama to keep me tidy!" She laughed with a lovely melodious chuckle and her smile reminded Leon of Sige. Her auburn hair and fresh clear skin spoke of her innocence. He had a momentary pang of reticence about his dark motives but shook it off and adjusted his expression to gain Anna's confidence.

"Well, actually, your Mama and I have had a falling out and that's why I came to see you. I thought you might be able to talk to her. Tell her I'm sorry, that I didn't mean to tell her a lie. But she won't listen to me, Anna." At this, his voice broke and affecting a near fall with his cup, just managed to put it on the table next to the couch he was sitting on.

"Oh, Leon, I didn't know! Are you all right?" Anna's innate empathy for others immediately surfaced and she quickly crossed to where Leon sat and put her arm around his shoulders. Leon had his hands covering his face by now, which luckily hid the grin that began to stretch across his face as he realised his plan was working easier than he thought possible.

195

"I'll speak to Mama for you, I'm sure she'll understand. She's probably just angry with you, she'll calm down soon." Anna comforted him.

"I don't think she will. She told me she didn't want to be with me anymore. What am I going to do Anna?" Leon cast a sideways glance towards Anna and noticed the tears forming in her eyes in sympathy for him, so he made his move.

"Can you just hold me Anna?"

"Don't you want me to write to Mama and talk to her for you, get this sorted out?" she asked, but actually was flattered that he had come to her to talk. He must really think her a woman now! As if having read her thoughts Leon said,

"You've grown into such a beautiful and caring young woman Anna. Aren't you courting a young man yet?"

"Oh, err no. I'm a little shy with the people here still. There are a few young men around but I don't know them very well yet. I don't get out that much unless with Xavier."

"I'm surprised. You're so lovely. Thank you for holding me. Won't you sit beside me on the couch?" he said as he gently pulled her from the arm of the couch down beside him. Anna was a little startled by the direction things seemed to be taking. She didn't want to give Leon the wrong impression but she could feel his nearness pressing against her thigh and a tremor of excitement rippled through her,

"Shouldn't we have some wine?" Anna voice trembled slightly.

"No, just hold me a while. It feels painful inside, just here. Put your hand on my heart, it will help soothe it." Hesitating, Anna acquiesced and almost jumped when she felt his heart racing under her hand.

"No need to be afraid, I think I'm being a bit affected by your loveliness. It's making my heart thump. Can I feel yours?" Without waiting for a reply, Leon rested his hot hand over Anna's breast and she let out a gasp of fear mixed with desire.

"I don't think we should be doing this Leon. I thought you wanted to sort things out with Mama?" Her voice was wavering as Leon ignored her and continued to stroke her breast gently, slipping his fingers under her waistcoat and over her quickly hardening nipple underneath the thin chemisette that she wore.

"It's O.K. little Anna, we can just comfort each other." His words sounding to her ears like liquid chocolate, melting her on the inside.

He slid his other hand round her back and pulled her close to his face and licked her ear. Anna had begun to groan with desire and she felt fire in her belly. She was a bit scared. These were new feelings for her and their intensity overpowered her immature resolve.

Leon continued to stroke and gently pinch her nipple while rubbing her back with his other hand. He swiftly moved to open her buttons as he felt her yielding to him. When he put his lips to her exposed breast and nipple, Anna completely gave in, gasping for him to touch her more. Then he used his mouth and tongue in quick little sucks and kisses all over her breasts and neck.

Leon took control completely and carried Anna from the couch, upstairs to her bedroom where after expertly removing her clothes, he ravished her gently at first. Still she urged him on; wanting more. She opened up so completely to his stroking that he thrust himself into her with a desire he surprised himself with. He wanted to pleasure her, wanted to make her remember having been made love to. For a while they were so engrossed in the surprisingly, to Leon, enjoyable lovemaking that he forgot his ulterior motive for initiating the situation. Not that it mattered. He had done what he'd set out to do.

The hardest part would be in the leaving. He was taken aback by Anna's earnestness and burning passion. She was a quick learner, by no half measure! They made love for several hours, Anna losing herself in such new and wonderful

197

sensations that she forgot completely about her mother or that she was with her mother's lover.

Only as it grew dark outside and they rested in sensual slumber did Anna begin to feel regret and guilt. She tried to rationalise her behaviour by telling herself that her Mama had said she didn't want to be with Leon, so why couldn't she? But was that true? How did she know how her Mama felt and how was she going to tell her? How could she explain to Sige that she had enjoyed it so much? Had she always wanted to do this with Leon? What if she didn't tell her? If Leon didn't, how would Sige know?

"Leon, what are we going to do? I feel awful about Mama. How am I going to tell her?" Leon kissed her into silence and there was no more said about how to tell Sige.

Over the next two days, Leon waylaid any talk of guilt or remorse by setting Anna's loins on fire with desire as he traversed her body up and down. He stopped short of the physical cruelty that he'd subjected Jade to, but took Anna in every other way possible. He thoroughly enjoyed quenching the light of Anna's innocence as the days and nights wore on and Anna became languid and dazed by the sheer satiety of sex at its most intense. He had her completely subservient to his will as he opened up the world of sensuality and snuffed out the desire for love for its own sake. He could do anything with her. Hadn't his spell as Marquis de Sade taught him that anyone could derive sexual pleasure from anything once they overcame their initial repulsion?

On the third day, Leon was up and getting dressed. He had to get this bit over with as soon as possible or he'd be right back into that little temptress' bed shortly.

"Are you sure you haven't had a boyfriend before, Anna? You seemed to have taken to sex like a fish to water. I don't think you should tell your Mama how you seduced me with all that pretend sympathy. I get the feeling you've wanted to do that for some time. The way you used to flirt and wiggle in front of me at your Mama's house, eh?" Anna's mouth had fallen wide open as she heard Leon say these words. Her eyes were ogling in disbelief.

"Me?! How dare you! You're the one who came looking for sympathy and wine. You're the one who started pawing at *me*!" Anna cried. Leon just laughed in her face.

"I didn't see you moving away. In fact, I seem to recall you asking for more the minute my mouth was on your tit!" He leered at her and licked his lips obscenely. Anna cried out and pulled the covers up to her chin.

"You bastard! You did that deliberately! You did it to get back at my mother, didn't you?" Leon's voice dropped to so low a pitch that Anna had to strain to hear him,

"*Si*, I did, little stepdaughter," he growled menacingly and grabbed her by the hair. He dragged Anna screaming from the bed and stood her naked in front of the mirror. He began to mumble some mad invocation, incanting and summoning someone called Sata to help him trace Sige. Anna was terrified. The mirror began to cloud over as if smoke swirled inside the glass. It was murky green and red streaked with black. Leon's voice became louder and more insistent as he repeated,

"Sata, let me see Sophia. Sata, open the realms and let me see Sophia. Become me. Now is your moment! Let her see me, let her see YOU!!" This last, he shouted in a terrifying voice, which was no longer recognisable as Leon but sounded more like a cavernous roar.

For a split second Anna saw a reflection of what was now grasping painfully onto her hair and she screamed in terror. In the looking glass bearing over her was a huge beast with the face of a lion, its fangs bared as it roared. She glimpsed an enormous tail thrashing about the room and heard things smashing behind her. The glass cleared again and she could see her Mama in the Hub with Rosita and Aluzzo. They were all looking up at the mirror as if way below. Her mother's face had gone deathly pale and Anna screamed to her,

"Mama, he..elp meee...!!" , not knowing if she would be heard. The beast that held her laughed with a sneer.

"Help you, she can't help you! She doesn't know how. She's too caught up in her own self-pity and hurt at what others have done to *her*. Hear the latest old Sige, dear Sophia, my adversary of times past, supposedly wise Sophia. How can your wisdom help you or your daughter now? I have had her, dear Sophia. I have taken her innocence as I took yours. I have raped, no I forget, she fell willingly, didn't you Anna. She loved it! But watch now Sophia, as I *do* rape her. As I destroy you both with my mighty sword, in one fell swoop." Sata laughed and laughed whilst Anna felt his sex grow alarmingly behind her.

Sige had been at the Hub for the final midday session of Momentary Silence with Aluzzo and Rosita when they heard the scream. They looked up to the rose window in the ceiling and saw there the reflection of Sata and Anna.

Sige's legs buckled underneath her and she almost collapsed on the spot. Aluzzo held her up as Sata spewed out his challenge. Rosita ran swiftly to the meeting area to reassemble the Matrons and Patrons, who quickly made their way back to their places in the Hub, gasping in horror at the image above them. Aluzzo urged Sige to the centre of the Hub and Rosita conducted the choir to the treble note A and bass note C that they had just been practising in preparation for this evening's full moon. Oils of Lavender and Geranium were still fragrant in the air, the burners not yet having been extinguished. The notes grew as Sata laughed maliciously, the scent floating upwards towards the window in the ceiling. The mother of oils, Lavender, will not tolerate bitterness, malice or jealousy and sought to infiltrate the image with compassion as the bass note climbed to a deep crescendo. The fragrance of geranium in its resonance with the archetypal energy of the Goddess and all feminine vibrations allowed the treble note of A to assume material form as arrows, letting them disperse through the energetic field to reach Sata and Anna. Anna visibly relaxed as an arrow pierced her side before disappearing. She felt cushioned and somehow shielded from the beast close to her. The Lavender began to affect Sata and Sige. He became angry at the softness taking hold of him and she began to feel her despair lift, the sadness falling away; helping to mobilise her energy. Sige began to intone and take full responsibility for her role:

"I am knowledge and ignorance. I am shame and boldness. I am shameless; I am ashamed. I am strength and I am fear. I am war and I am peace."

She raised her voice with great power above the pure tonal notes of the choir:

"Give heed to me. I am the one who is disgraced and the great one!"

Sata had been startled by her admissions and thought she was giving in until her voice was raised. It was enough time for the choir to raise the vibrations to produce a fountain of colours, cascading gold and silver, pinks and greenish blues. The gold and silver light shot up through the centre. The deeply gentle voice of Christos could be heard,

"Dearly Beloved! Let us go toward Union.
And if we find the road that leads to separation,
We will destroy separation.
Let us go hand in hand.
Let us enter the presence of Truth
Let it be our judge and imprint its seal on us
Forever..."

As the gold and silver light intermingled and shot through the window to the other side where Sata held Anna, it blinded the beast and he let his grip loosen and Anna was free. A transparent image of Christos materialised next to Sige as the notes became higher and their power shook the Hub, it moved towards and into her and she spoke again with twin voices, her own echoed by Christos,

"Abandon the ways of that Corruptor and approach me. And I will enter into you…And make you wise in the ways of Truth…Through me you will be saved and become blessed. I am Sophia, The Saviour Goddess of Light."

Sata gave a blood curdling scream and exploded into thick, black oily smoke. Leon's body was all that remained in the mirror, charred and frazzled without a breath of life.

Beautiful golden light shone around the hub and Anna walked out of the fountain of colour, a lilac dove cupped in her outstretched hand, to be wrapped in Aluzzo's cloak. Then the dove rose into the air and alighted on Sophia's shoulder. Just at that moment there was a commotion on the steps leading to the entrance of the Hub. Everyone turned to see what was going on. They could hear shouts and scuffling, then a darkly clothed figure stumbled into the Hub pushing past the two patrons at the doorway.

"So! What have we here? This looks very much like pagan devil worshipping going on. I heard your chanting and unholy prayers as I came up the stairs! Saviour Goddess of Light?! This is heresy!" Padre Josep was breathing hard and his usually pale face had reddened from anger and exertion as he stood quickly, recovered from his stumble, to his full skeletal height. The priest was glaring at Anna, who was still naked under the red cape and surrounded by Aluzzo, Rosita and Sige who were all dazed from the events moments before with, yes, there was no denying it, the Devil.

202

Black Magic & Bruises - <u>Glasgow -2000</u>

Not again!! I screamed inside as I started to recall images of the previous time I'd endured a confession of betrayal.

"I will not be the understanding, all forgiving woman. This is wrong!!" I said in a coldly controlled manner, fearful of my emotions overwhelming my sanity. That too would be a re-run. "But you will have to go. I will not fight to keep you with me because you made your choice when you got into that situation. So, I'll see you to the door. Goodbye Malcolm."

After Malcolm left, I slumped into a chair in shock. Memories flooded back to fifteen years ago before my first daughter was born. Gareth had taken to drinking regularly and since returning from our disastrous few days in France four years previously, his presence had become elusive and the relationship distant. I had decided to stop using the contraceptive pill because of its adverse effects on my health and had moved out of our shared flat to a friend's house taking my cat with me, but there were still occasional couplings for old times' sake. We seemed to be making half-hearted attempts at restoring something that was lost.

News of my pregnancy nevertheless filled me with joy and indescribable peace. Gareth only turned white with shock and remained speechless as he sat in the now dingy flat, with its dull mock wood wall casings and flowery wallpaper, an exact replica of the flat of the neighbour below.

"I don't care if you're not happy. I am." I said confidently while wondering why he was so shocked.

"Are you sure it's mine?" he slyly threw at me as I was making for the door.

"Unlike you, I've never slept with anyone else," I retorted, slamming the door as I left not yet realising the accuracy of my response. We struggled on through the ensuing months of the pregnancy but Gareth knew that I was resolved to having this baby whether he was around or not and didn't like it, becoming more aggressive as time went on. A shove here, a dunt there and more than usual attempts to undermine,

"Sleeping with you is like sleeping with a dead camel!" Was one of his more memorable slights at the time. Interesting, I remember thinking later, was he talking from experience?

We eventually managed to secure another flat to make ready for the arrival of the baby. Small but newly refurbished, the flat was clean and warm. Its one bedroom was given over to the new baby and me while the sitting room, with its well-designed kitchenette corner, was adequate. Gareth was not often there and when he was, his anger grew while my fear grew in proportion until I could no longer keep any food down. I had a regular visit to the doctor about six months into the pregnancy. The surgery was busy and the waiting room full and stuffy. People were coughing and spluttering around me. I felt weak and nervous. These days I was always feeling on edge and anxious, so jumped when the receptionist eventually called my name.

"How are you keeping, Morag?" the doctor asked when I sat down in his office.

"Tired doctor,' I replied, 'and not eating too much 'cause I just bring it back up." My gaunt pale face and dark-ringed eyes told their own story. He looked a little concerned and as I got up on the examining table with some effort. He pressed the cold stethoscope against my not very big belly.

"You haven't put on much weight, have you?" he commented disapprovingly.

"No, I'm still the same weight I was before being pregnant, so I think I've lost some?" The doctor's expression became more concerned as the session continued when he went on to take my blood pressure.

"OK Morag, the baby is becoming distressed and the heartbeat is faint so you need attention very soon. Go home and get some things then go straight to the hospital, please."

I was put in the Intensive Care ward on arriving at the hospital and wired to a drip. Only then did I realise the danger the baby was in. I'm not good away from home. I like my own creature comforts though was happier knowing the baby was being helped. I was kept in intensive care for two days and then moved to a less critical ward when the baby's heartbeat strengthened and it was out of danger.

While there I met a woman who had been spending time around Gareth's flat in the last year or so, a supposed friend of his sister. She had just given birth to a baby boy the day before I met her there and I held the child remarking on its shock of dark hair. The baby's mother smiled knowingly not meeting my eyes, immediately sparking suspicions I'd had over the last year since she'd been around, but which on voicing them at the time had had them dismissed by 'good' old Gareth. Nothing new there.

I felt better and bored after a few days and signed myself out of the hospital despite the disapproving looks and comments of the consultant and ward nurses. Gareth brought my clothes when he came to collect me. I carefully mentioned the coincidence while in the elevator as we were leaving,

"I saw Samantha yesterday. She's just had her baby. She'll probably be out soon. They're both fine. He's a lovely wee thing, amazing hair."

"D…did you?" he stuttered and fell very silent, his face visibly draining.

"Is something wrong, Gareth?" I innocently asked knowing my suspicions were now confirmed.

"No, no…Let's just get you home." His voice trailed off and there was no more mention of that new arrival for a while.

I tried to settle into nesting for the next few months until the arrival of my baby, but the constant tension and threat of violence from Gareth's binges kept me in a state of dread. Sure enough the threat became a reality soon after our daughter Jane was born and when she was just a week old, Gareth exploded one evening when I returned home from visiting friends. He had murderous rage in his eyes.

"Where have you been?" he demanded. "Why didn't you come back sooner?" He continued, barely waiting for an answer. I began to tremble and my heart was thumping in my chest for he wasn't being rational, it wasn't late!

"What are you doing out with my daughter this late? I've been waiting!" He roared into my face, his eyes gleaming as he grabbed my jacket and pulled me towards him and all I could see were the bloodshot eyes and his fist in my face, sporting a ring with an engraved red dragon, I didn't recognise. It's amazing the things you notice when in a state of terror. Then he pushed me away with a look of disgust.

"But Gareth…" I tried to explain but got no further as he lashed out with his fist again, punching me in the face and then head as he screamed at me to put down the child, whom I was clutching to my breast. But I couldn't. I was scared for the baby and for myself. Gareth kept punching anyway. Eventually I managed to get away from him and put the baby in the next room where she remained silent in frozen terror. Gareth grabbed me immediately from behind by the hair and threw me across the room. I landed sprawling in the baby's cot. It stopped only when the neighbours next door began banging loudly on the wall.

The next episode of violence was of a similar nature stopped only eventually by the presence of his sister. Gareth told me then, that the child I had held four months before in the hospital was his. He had been beating me up out of his own guilt. It stopped after that but for one more time.

The relationship was not redeemable and we decided to split finally at the end of the year. I had one more memorable event before that. With new beginnings always come endings and Christmas morning was to bring an unexpected visitor. It was one a.m. and the buzzer sounded. It was my brother and I let him in.

"Hi! Merry Christmas! What can I do for you at this time of the morning?"

"It's Dad, Morag. He's dead." His voice was husky with unspent emotion.

"You're joking?" I replied shocked, realising he wasn't joking at all.

"No, I'm not. He died this afternoon. Caroline found him." I immediately burst into tears and my brother left after a short time to go back to the family home since there was little to say in that dazed place of death. Neither of us had been up to any more attempts at Christmas cheer. Gareth was there and tried to comfort me but I needed no great comfort from him right now. But my marmalade cat was successful where Gareth hadn't been, meowing gently then nudging and pawing at my face whilst the tears flowed. Below the deep sadness there was both relief and a sense of joy that I would be alright. Our relationship, my father's and mine, had been difficult and violent in later years. The pattern was repeating itself again for me with Gareth and I knew my responsibility was, as with my father, not to accept the bullying, the violence or the pathetic apologies, but to be strong enough to walk away. Gareth saw my strength and resented it, so had one more go at me. The result being that I attended my father's funeral sporting a black eye disguised with heavy make-up.

207

And the day of the funeral had its own dark comedy. When we arrived at the cemetery after the service we were told that the wrong grave had been dug up.

"We're not really sure where the right one is, it may take a wee while tae find it", the priest mumbled apologetically to my mother, as I quickly clamped my hand over my mouth to stop myself exploding with hysterical laughter. So back into the cars and back to the house and the 'bun fight' with relatives and friends cracking jokes about what my father's response to this farce would have been, "Some bastard's stole ma grave, eh? Well! I better get it back quick or they'll get ma toe up their arse!" And there was Uncle Stewart, not letting us sit about looking sad, announcing:

"He'll be a long time dead!"

True... but it wasn't long, dead or not, before he repeatedly made his presence felt again in my own life.

I had moved on since Gareth, or so I thought, till now, when this man whom I'd been in a relationship with for the last year and just asked to leave, revealed his covert visits and assignations with some woman from work over the last few months. Now I understood why he'd stopped phoning so regularly. Had kept on not turning up when we made arrangements to get together, using pitiful excuses. Memories flashed through my body and mind, jolting me but not able to dispel my sense of disbelief.

The fall-out of this latest betrayal ensued for the next few weeks but I had friends like Maggie, who kept me from going quietly insane though not always so quietly.

"What's going on Maggs, I can't believe this. I must be jinxed or something?"

"Naw, I don't think ye're jinxed Morag. Maybe ye're jist no very good at choosin men, eh hen?" Maggie put her arm round my shoulders as she tried to console me.

"Thanks a lot Maggie. That makes me feel *a lot* better."

"Don't go in a huff Mo. Ye know, if he's gonnae sneak aroon wae other wummen, then ye're better aff wae oot him, d'ye no think so? Then ye widnae be sittin wonderin where he is or who he's wae. He's a sneaky wee shite!"

"You've got a way with words Maggs. I could think of some choice ones myself but I better not get started. Anyway, he's out the picture now. But I can't help thinking, ye know, what must I have done to deserve this happening again? I know what ye're saying about my choice of men though. There's definitely a pattern here, so I've got a lot of thinking to do." I was already holding my head in my hands trying to contain my racing thoughts.

"That's half your problem, hen. Ye think too much. Ye're gonnae go mental wae aw they thoughts rattlin roon yir brain. Gie it a rest Morag. Dae some o that meditation malarkey yir aeways on aboot. Maybe that'll help ye calm doon a wee bit, eh?"

"Aye, you're right Maggie. I'll give it a try but I'm not sure how long I can sit still just now. Thanks for coming over. I know I would go mental if I didn't have friends like you to call up and moan the face off."

"That's a back-handed compliment if ever a heard wan but nae worries hen. Jist gie us a shout if ye need some company. Don't shut yirsel away or ye *will* go radio rental, awright?"

That last remembrance of Spain was still powerfully engraved on my consciousness because I hadn't yet been able to recall past that moment when the Padre had discovered Sige and the others at the Hub. How had he known where to find them? Who had betrayed the *Alumbrados*? What had happened to them? I had been awakened in the early hours of the morning with Enrique shaking me.

"Mora, Mora! It's alright, it's just a dream!" I garbled what I'd just seen in a terror-stricken voice.

"Oh, Enrique, what's going to happen to them? The priest from the Inquisition…?"

"Slow down Mora. What is it? Tell me what you saw." He took me in his arms to stop me trembling with fear and I slowly told him everything that I could remember. I felt concerned that even though there had seemed to be some deep integration and I could still feel Sige's strength and wisdom, I didn't understand how they could have explained what they were doing in the Hub?

I phoned Mhairi later on that day to tell her of the latest visions and she tuned in quickly saying that she had a presence nearby that sounded a lot like Aluzzo.

"It's an old man. He's wearing a round black felt hat and red cloak. He has a white beard and twinkly blue eyes."

"That's Aluzzo! What's he saying, Mhairi?" I implored her.

"Just that although things were difficult, that they managed to escape with their lives. Speaking Woman is whispering that you will recall in the course of time, to be patient."

"What have I done to deserve this? What am I supposed to make of it all Mhairi?" I was close to tears wondering how I was supposed to be. What was I supposed to do with these dreams and visions?

"Just write them down and learn the lessons. Take the gifts that they offer and use them to improve your awareness and your way of being in the world." Mhairi encouraged me to be gentle on myself. We left it at that for now and I did eventually write down all that I could remember and as I had before, painted some of the most intense images, realising that although dreams and artworks are from the imagination and give form rather than invent, they can't easily be used to represent each other. Much was changed in the re-creation. And

I have still yet to recall what happened to them-to me. The pattern of betrayal had continued.

I also realised that I needed some objective input to the situation and sought the help of a woman recommended to me by a friend at the Buddhist Centre. Gayla called herself an 'Archetypal' healer and could, using intuition, read archetypal patterns in this and other lifetimes. This woman helped me put some of the raging emotions into perspective and clarified some of the things that had been happening which I had been sensing but had no clear evidence of.

"Just sit quietly. I need to check a few things," Gayla said. As I sat in front of her, she began to make many symbolic gestures with her hands. Some resembled turning over the pages of a book, in another part of the reading it looked as if she was reorganising files. Then in one instance she drew a labyrinth in the air and in others drew crosses and spirals. Then she asked me,

"Do you know anyone who practices 'Black Magic'?"

"Well, I've known people who dabbled and seen the effects. But no! Not directly."

"What about this friend or ex-friend?" She insisted.

"He does talk about it sometimes, why?" I wondered where this was coming from and where it was leading.

"From what I can see here someone has been trying to influence you with black magic but I'm just clearing the negativity now." What was going on? I'm a down to earth kind of person but life just keeps giving me strange gifts. Black Magic!? I could just hear Maggie if I told her that. "Tell them tae keep the coffee creams for me!"

Gayla did her thing with her hand gestures some more and when she stopped asked,

"How do you protect yourself, Morag?" Simple question you'd think.

"Emm...what do you mean? I don't do anything that I can think of, but I'd have a go if anybody tried anything on. A good swift kick if I got the chance."

"I mean, you've got strong clairvoyant abilities and are sensitive to these influences. So you need to do something to protect yourself from attacks, yes, but psychic attacks!" Weirder and weirder! But it did make a few things fall into place. "I suggest you use a visualisation surrounding yourself in radiant blue light. Like a ball all around you. Do it everyday. Prepare yourself before you go into company. OK?" Gayla then brought the session to an end declaring,

"You're a Volunteer. You chose to come back to help others improve their lives, to help alleviate their suffering. You must try to put this drama behind you as soon as possible and move on. You have a lot of work to do."

I felt much better after the session with her and quite calm, but regretted not asking the question that had been in my mind the whole time I was with her. Which past life is the one that was mainly affecting this one? Even so, of the remembrances I'd had, it still seemed that they contained more of the same events so that I was being betrayed again and again by friends and lovers.

"How dae ye know you've been reincarnated?" Maggie would ask looking highly sceptical.

"I don't *know*" I'd reply, "but don't you think that there must be some purpose to meeting people whom you've never seen before and being able to talk to them as if you've known them all your life? Or visiting a place for the first time and feeling like you've been there before, that it's very familiar? And I've told ye the ones I remember Maggs."

"But that's jist co-incidence and déjà vu, everybody gets that sometimes, it disnae mean anythin." Maggs insisted.

"How do *you* know? And just think for a minute what 'déjà vu' actually means, 'already seen.' If you've never been somewhere before and get that feeling the first time you're there, how else could you have 'already seen' it!? And what about having the same things happening in your life over and over again as if you just aren't moving on no matter what you do to change it or yourself?"

"So, whit? We've been over this already Mo. We're just creatures o' habit an you choosin bastards is jist a bad habit, that's all."

"Not according to some. Buddhists would say it's not co-incidence. I think it's important because after you've tried rationalising, tried the psychoanalytic perspective and still got nowhere; then all that's left is the spiritual, the unseen, the things in life that aren't logical. That can't be explained away! The only system which seems to offer a purposeful way of recognising the significance of these habits, as you call them, is in Eastern Philosophies. Haven't you heard of Karma?!"

"Mmm…is that that acrobatic sex you an Enrique used tae hiv?" was the reply I got to that.

Enrique was still around; in mind and heart, if not in person. I had eventually told him back then of my decision, but he had no interest in living in Scotland. When we left he was making plans to go back to Andalucía, though we still kept in contact now. We just got on with our separate lives. Doing what needed done. Though I'd obviously messed up again with Malcolm 'the Magician'! Would I never learn? No-one could ever replace what Enrique and I had, but I knew the risk I was taking when I decided to come back without him. I loved him still, with a burning ache that never left me.

Otherwise, life had been better in Scotland, since being back, than before I left over seven years before. I'd been able to restart my aromatherapy business here and had since completed further training in the more subtle stuff like the Usui System of Reiki, or healing with Universal Energy. I chose to study it because I couldn't deny the sensations passing through me when laying hands on people during massages, or the spirit guides that I seemed to have collected over the years, whispering in my ear trying to get in on the act.

Mikao Usui was a Buddhist monk from Japan and while on a retreat had an experience of a powerful energy descending through the crown of his head, clearing his doubts and learning how that energy could be used for healing. He went on to help many, many people during the Second World War and the system is now practised worldwide. My beautiful daughters were still not used to their weird mother.

"Mum, what are you doing now? Why can't you just be normal?"

"Sorry, don't know that word. It's not in my vocabulary, love." Paula flounced off infuriated.

She was twelve now and after taking her own time to settle back into a very different life in Glasgow, she eventually began to enjoy it. Some of that was down to starting the local High School within a few weeks after our return from Palma. Those cute boys! She had long blonde, but not so curly hair anymore, which glinted in the sunshine and with her sallow skin, made her look surprisingly Spanish. Her command of that language meant she could wing it with the boys. It was all about what to wear and how to wear it, and a modicum of disgust at how her mother dressed.

"You're not wearing that are you!" she said often about my proclivity for strangely shaped skirts and other odd items of clothing from the charity shops. She had taken her periods or 'Borne her Flower', as the Sarrapan women would say, about six months past and was suitably mortified, as young girls are, when I tried to congratulate her on the dawning of womanhood and give her a big bunch of flowers.

"Mu..um!. Stop embarrassing me. You better not talk about 'The Curse' in front of my friends. I'll hate you if you do, you know." No amount of ancient 'herstory' could convince her that it needn't be like that when she had menstrual cramps telling her otherwise. Her older sister, Jane who still had the shiniest brown hair, agreed with her little sister on this one having already had the experience herself. That and their opinion of my dress sense were some of the only things they did agree on. Daily fights over clothes and whose turn it was to do the dishes or "Could you tell HER to get out of the bathroom NOW!" were the everyday delights of mothering the girls, but I loved them fiercely. I was also happy that they shared a friendship with Maggie's daughter, Claire.

Maggie, of course, still thought I was off my rocker too and getting weirder by the day, but didn't complain when I practised my strange skills on her. Reiki and massages seemed to help alleviate or reduce some of the M.S. symptoms that she continued to experience.

"By the way, you *are* quite hairy, Maggs! Not quite Guinea pig proportions but still…"

"Listen, I'm doin ye a favour lying here getting slathered in cookin oil, enough o yir cheek!" Irrepressible woman! I did some effleurage strokes on her back using an essential oil blend of tea tree, geranium and lavender that I'd made up especially. "Mmm…That's excellent, hen." She mumbled drowsily.

"Have you been doing any research for that book we were going to write Maggs?" I asked as I worked on those legs of hers that sometimes just wouldn't hold her up any more. Kneading and stroking deeply to stimulate the damaged nerves.

"Well, I've been tryin oot some o they exercises wae Martin that ye told me about and they're no bad. At least Martin's no complainin! " I smiled, happy that some good was coming of my time with Enrique. Though, I still felt pretty much centred and continued my meditation practices, even the

Yab-Yum. I just never got to do it in the flesh these days; more's the pity. No, I wouldn't even have considered it with the recently departed 'Man with the Black Magic Box'. When I did mention what Gayla the Healer had said to me about that Maggie was off immediately.

"Ooooh..! Who knows the secret of the Black Magic Box?" she said in a mysterious voice, doing an impression of the old T.V. advert. "I dae an if he's at all like the hunk all dressed in black in the advert, tell him tae bring that box tae me an we can share the secret," she continued, cackling at her own joke.

"No mystery Maggs. It's only coffee creams left and you're welcome to him and them! I told you I was jinxed, didn't I?"

"They'll dae, they're ma favourites, jinxed or no." She always got the last word.

I got an answer to my unspoken question about *the* past life anyway. A few nights after the session with the healer I was having a bath. The water was hot and I was feeling drowsy. The room was bathed in candle-light and I could see the flame shining hazily. The plumes of smoke and steam were drifting up across the mirror on the opposite wall, in which I could see a blurred reflection of my body above the shoulders, lying in the bath. The mirror was steamed up and I inadvertently inhaled the acrid smoke from the candle to my right shoulder, on the shelf above me.

Suddenly I began to feel inexplicable fear, making me catch my breath. I could hear my racing heart echoing loudly in my ears, as my misted reflection in the mirror began to waver and undulate like the smoke. The candle sparked repeatedly as droplets of steam touched the flame and became as if echoes of gunfire, intensifying the terror that was passing through me. Then I thought I heard someone whispering close to my ear,

It's time to remember.

THIRD CHRONICLE

*"If only there were evil people somewhere insidiously committing evil deeds and it were necessary only to separate them from the rest of us and destroy them.
But, the line dividing good and evil cuts through the heart of every human being.
And who is willing to destroy a piece of their own heart."*

Alexander Solzhenitsyn-21st Century

The Steel Bullet – France 1944

Jacques Tralow was of average height with a slim physique and handsome boyish face, despite his thirty-two years. His dark brown hair used to reach shoulder length which he usually kept tied back, but now it was gone, shaved close with bloody scratches from the razor, emphasising his grey drawn face. His pale blue eyes were bloodshot and wide with fear. He lowered his head in shame, though he still felt a surge in his belly of that twisted power which had led him to this place. It was a small glimmer of the enjoyment he had felt at being in control of other people's lives. Or so he thought.

His former colleagues would never understand the ripples of power that surged when he thought he had everything organised. Jacques believed he had everyone suspecting everyone else, except himself. He had managed to control his 'gang' as the Germans called them, and sweeten the locals despite the dangers of them betraying him. He could come and go between his compatriots, though they would not call him so now, and the army Kommandantur of the recently arrived SS Das Reich Unit. Only the Vichy Milice gave him problems for a while, after sending out it's *traîtres* to locate and destroy his Resistance fighters.

Jacques had arrived back in France some eighteen months before. While in England, he had been trained how to operate a radio and underwent mock interrogations so that he could withstand procedures of a similar nature, should he be caught. Then there was some time spent on the bleak hills in the north of Scotland being stranded with few provisions in an area that the Special Operations Executive volunteers had no knowledge of, to test his abilities in escape and evasion using night and day orienteering. Training was carried out in Allied and German weapons, unarmed combat, demolitions and explosives. Additionally, communications and cryptography tutorials were also involved.

Jacques had proven he was able in directing and leading others with a strong capacity to organise resources. This ability to withstand the pseudo interrogators, his four years in the infantry before the war and time spent serving in the headquarters unit of the military school in Paris, led them to believe that he had what it took to organise and maintain a *réseau,* in one of the most strategic and dangerous areas of France.

As there were only six days each moon period when they could do the drops, weather permitting, Jacques was flown over the week after the full moon as was the usual practice,

"OK, are you ready Jacques?" the dispatcher shouted over the roar of the plane's engine. They were flying in a Hudson from the 'Moon Squadron', one of the RAF Special Duty squads based at Tempsford. From this two-engine low-wing monoplane, he would be dropped to meet the reception committee waiting on the ground.

"I can see the signal lights below. Your welcoming committee seem to have had a bit too much vino, old chap. Their inverted 'L' looks more like a 'V'!" the guffawing pilot joked. Hearing this only made Jacques more nervous.

"Do you think they've been caught? Could it be a trap, *non?"* Jacques was at this moment sitting with his legs dangling through the aperture in the floor of the plane fuselage, waiting for the red light to turn green, which it did just as he asked the question. He looked at Marie who was sitting calmly waiting her turn. She didn't appear scared at all. Then he remembered, this wasn't her first time being dropped, so of course she wouldn't be as nervous as he was. She smiled and nodded to encourage him knowing it was pointless to try speaking over the rattling fuselage and roaring engine. But she was mouthing what he thought looked like *"Bonne Chance!"* The dispatcher then shouted into his ear,

"You'll be fine. They've flashed the correct letter code in Morse. Good Luck!", then he slapped Jacques' shoulder letting him know it was too late now to change his mind. Jacques lifted himself up and pushed off down through the gap, falling fast into the near darkness.

"Sacre Cœur!" He muttered, feeling the icy chill of the wind as it knocked the breath from him. He could see bushes below and hills in the distance. His parachute began to open automatically, as his weight pulled the static line attached to the plane. As soon as he was clear of the slip stream, he began to plunge rapidly down 700 feet towards the flare path into the area surrounding Simoges. The landing came sooner than Jacques expected, hitting the grass with a thump, rolling twice. He sat there for a moment catching his breath and rubbing his bruised thigh at the place of impact. Then he stood and started to remove his equipment. There hadn't been much wind and the parachute had already collapsed. It took only a twist to release the harness before bundling it up for hiding.

He looked up to see Marie falling into the sky above him; a dark silhouette, for some reason, spiralling pretty fast. She was floating some distance to the right of where he was. He'd have to go look for her. By this time members of the reception committee were heading his way, at least he hoped that was who the figures in the distance coming towards him were, but got out his revolver as he'd been instructed, just in case it was Germans.

He left the parachute on the ground as he headed east in a crouch across the field, almost sliding along the grass in his haste towards where he could now see the dark figure of Maria hunkering down trying to grab her own gear. He hissed her name before he reached where she knelt and she turned towards him. Her eyes looked wide and glassy in the moonlight. They were both breathing heavily. He pointed to the approaching shapes that were shrouded in darkness, hoping to hear a familiar word of welcome though his gun was now cocked as were his ears. He heard then a deep voice whispering,

"Bienvenue." Then the code word followed and both Jacques and Marie let out long sighs of relief before responding to their welcoming committee then slowly moved towards them. Muffled slaps on the back and the glint of smiling teeth in the moonlight helped steady the tremble that had been making Jacques heart race. With caution, the two arrivals were quickly led to the waiting truck hidden in the nearby woods.

Being dropped near his home town itself was unusual, but it showed trust in Jacques' ability not to become overly attached to familial goings-on in the area and gave him a head start with contacts he'd made among acquaintances who were already involved in the Resistance movement.

Some had been trained previously like Jacques and had been flown in weeks prior to his arrival. Others here and across France, who were also involved, came from many diverse backgrounds and had been landed or dropped to serve as circuit or *réseaux* organisers like Jacques. Some were liaison officers, radio operators, arms and sabotage instructors and couriers. All these people had voiced support and a willingness to put their lives in danger to see the occupying German army undermined at least, but preferably defeated and forced out of France. They all shared a love of freedom and a desire to make their own contribution to France's liberation.

The night of the jump Jacques stomach alternated between feeling knots of dread and waves of trembling excitement. He veered from complaining of nausea to dizzy hysteria. He had no knowledge or inclination yet of the events that would eventually lead to his denunciation. He stood tall in company when he thought about what he was doing for the land and people to whom he was born.

Marie was a courier who would help Jacques both to establish stronger links with those in the area and help maintain their security measures. She was the other 'body' that was dropped with him. Marie, as he referred to her, though it wasn't her real name, hailed from Paris. He had not known her previously. She was ten years younger than he and they had come from different backgrounds. It was unlikely they would have met at all other than in circumstances such as these.

Marie was a strong-minded woman despite her youth. She was twenty-two, only just. She was tall for a woman by French standards, with short curly hair that outlined her rather square but well defined features. Jacques considered her work with him invaluable and he knew he could not have set up the *réseau* as securely or efficiently without her help. She had already put herself in danger many times carrying codes and messages back and forward across a large area, with Simoges being the base. Marie often had to travel on trains and move about in the streets alongside German Officers and soldiers. She had always handled being stopped at the increasing number of controls, exceptionally well.

Having been posted in the town since it was first occupied Marie's face was known to the security forces, and she had been called in by them on her return from Britain for questioning. She had resolutely stuck to her story about having had to go to visit a sick relative, returning because of the increasing restrictions on travel between the occupied and unoccupied areas of France. The British HQ had suggested on her last trip there that she should consider plastic surgery if called in for questioning again. This was usual practice for some agents in particularly front line positions amongst the Nazis, but Marie would have none of it. She would rather rely on her evasion skills than the surgeon's knife.

Jacques and Marie had hit it off well from the beginning since their characters complimented each other. Some would say they were opposites and it was not always pleasant when they clashed now and then; for Jacques explosive temper came up against Marie's stubbornness. The question of surgery was a case in point. Jacques tentatively broached the surgery issue when Marie was released from Simoges after the S.S. had recognised and stopped her at a control point on the way into the town, a few days after the drop back into France.

"Marie, isn't it something you should seriously consider?" he suggested.

"*Pourquoi?*" she came back with immediately, her tone defensive.

"You know why. They know your face too well. Do you want to be caught?"

"Of course not! But why should I take such drastic measures when the S.S. haven't been able to find proof that I'm doing anything wrong?"

"But that's just the point. They're looking for something. They do suspect you and it's only a matter of time before one of the townspeople may be looking for a favour from the Germans; like saving their own or a family member's skin or even just craving a taste of butter!" Jacques insisted, feeling annoyed now at her refusal to see the potential danger.

"They wouldn't do that!" she exclaimed.

"Yes, they would and you know they would. Don't play at being naïve Marie, because you're anything but." He thumped the table then, his temper beginning to get the better of him and turned to check if anyone had noticed.

226

"Losing your temper won't change my mind," Marie sniped at him while lifting her nose in the air and turning in her chair as if to distance herself from his criticism, which only enraged Jacques further. He abruptly pushed back his own chair almost toppling it as he quickly stood.

"Don't you see I care about what happens to you? *Sacre Cœur!* And you put others at risk, if you're with them. Why are you being so impossible Marie?" he hissed. Then he strode towards the door of the café, before he really lost his temper.

"But it wouldn't *be me* after I let them loose on my face with a scalpel, would it?" she growled under her breath. She'd got the last word and was satisfied at that. She watched the door rattle behind Jacques as he went off fuming at her stubbornness. She smiled a little to herself on realising how similar they seemed to be sometimes. In the last few months they had become as close as it was possible to be under the circumstances, without being able to share much of their past with each other. She liked Jacques but had to keep any further stirrings to herself. He was an attractive man even though ten years older and she never had been much taken by men her own age. They just didn't seem mature. Still like boys in fact. There was something about Jacques that intrigued her. He never seemed to notice women or more precisely, that she was a woman. He treated her at the best of times like a younger sister. He teased her playfully but never touching her even in affection. Sometimes she wished for more but knew in the work that they'd both chosen to do, anything more was not allowed, never mind wise. It was too risky a situation in case either of them ever got caught. But he must care, didn't he say so?

Marie remembered the only relationship of any duration she'd had from three years ago back in Paris. As a student at the Sorbonne she had met Phillipe who was only months older than she. He was a gentle soul who studied philosophy while she studied politics. They had had some fun and she had enjoyed Philipe's romantic attention. He was absent-mindedly

227

thoughtful, writing her poems on scraps of napkins and forgetting to give them to her until he changed clothes and emptied pockets on laundry day. He was taller than her but walked with a stoop as if something weighed heavily on him, pushing down from above. They had argued finally when she mentioned volunteering for the SOE. His beliefs did not run to participating in the war and she wondered how he had managed when the call-up had begun. He would not have been given a choice.

She was more of an action person, passionate about her country and her people. She couldn't just sit back and wait for it to be all over and do nothing while the Germans destroyed everything that was good about France. Her furious anger at the enemy, as she unequivocally considered them to be, had grown since her involvement in the Resistance. She had seen too much to ever feel neutral or submit to their domination like some had. These thoughts reminded her of her need to get going to finish organising what needed done for their latest planned attack. She sighed as she stood, putting out of her mind any fantasies about Jacques for now and left the café, checking that she'd left nothing behind and wasn't being followed.

Kommandantur Rudy Schnell had, as an officer of the *Shutz Staffel* or Protection Squad, taken his oath of allegiance not to the Party or the State but directly to Hitler. The S.S. had proved their loyalty almost a decade before, in Hitler's unleashing of the 'Night of the Long Knives' by purging the S.A., killing Rohm then arresting and killing other prominent leaders who had been their comrades.

Schnell had since risen through the ranks because of his no nonsense and unflinching attitude towards any of the duties that were assigned to him. He had also spent some time under Heinrich Himmler, before being posted for a spell with Karl Maria Wiligut, in the RuSHA department of the S.S. as

Lieutenant of the Pre and Early History in Resettlement Office. Many of the other members of the S.S. were wary of those associated with this office, for there had been stories about events surrounding the department's searches for occult objects to further their dabbling in Black Magic.

Schnell didn't mind that the junior officers and soldiers were in awe of him. The fear he sometimes glimpsed on their faces gratified him immensely.

The people of Simoges and all over France felt feelings of passionate hatred and deep terror for the S.S. who being renowned for their ruthlessness and were now stationed here. This was a result of Jacques' 'gang's' attempt to liberate the town of Tulle nearby from the garrison there where they had captured almost all the German troops and then killed them, for they could take no prisoners. But Schnell's unit had prevented them from finishing the job and after the Resistance fighters retreated the S.S. rounded up every man they could find, resistance fighters or not and hung 120 of those they questioned as a first reprisal. This had not stopped the *réseau* attempts and they were now trying to attack the garrison at Guéret.

Marie had been the first to notice Schnell's apparent interest in Jacques when they last had to take their documents to the town hall for checking. Jacques was slightly unnerved by this interest. There was at that time too much at stake with the organisation of the *réseau* beginning to come together into a coherent and efficient communications channel and also because of the recent attacks. They had managed to help trace the routes of several garrisons of German soldiers in the last few weeks and were ready to lay another explosives ambush that they hoped would slow down both movement of the ever-spreading German troops and destroy some of their ammunition into the bargain.

Damn these checks! Jacques thought. Nevertheless, turning out for them was the only way to alleviate any suspicions that may be surfacing. Both sides had their informers. It was a war like any other and everyone had their price. The 'black market' was as much about the buying and selling of people and forbidden words as it was about goods and foods.

"*Guten Tag*, Herr Tralow. Ees everything well with you and your *famille*? The Kommandantur commented as he passed by. He moved along in front of the nervous townspeople, who avoided his glance by keeping their eyes to the ground while they lined up in the town square, ever in anticipation of being questioned over something the occupying army had decided they were hiding. In light of the recent attacks in nearby towns everyone was more apprehensive than usual. There were extra soldiers on duty, appearing twitchy and bad-tempered, shoving some of those waiting roughly or hitting them with the butt of their rifles for no apparent reason. As if they needed one.

"*Oui, très bien,* Kommandantur." Jacques replied quickly with a nod of the head as he watched the German Officer move on. He was confused and made wary by this greeting for it could signify many unspoken things, some of which he saw in the eyes of his compatriots, passing as dark fear, mistrust and even envy in some. Marie whispered in his ear,

"Last week he was watching us more than usual. I've just now realised that it's you he's interested in."

"Why would he be interested in me? *Non, Ce n'est rien.* It's nothing." Jacques whispered back, trying to dismiss her observation for he couldn't think how Schnell would have any knowledge of their activities.

"Don't be so sure Jacques. Remember what you said to me about the townspeople needing favours? From the looks you're getting, they don't seem to like the idea of you being a favourite of the *Kommandantur*."

Strangely enough, Jacques did like the idea of being the Kommandantur's favourite and he couldn't help noticing how handsome and impressive he looked compared to the scruffy privates with their course battle dress. The officer was in his well-cut uniform, a silver dagger hanging from his belt and wearing a cap, high-peaked to the front. He covertly admired Schnell's aquiline nose and smooth skin surrounding piercing blue eyes and a full mouth that hinted at cruelty when he smiled.

All the same they were more alert from then on; it was no time to take chances. The Kommandantur never publicly acknowledged Jacques presence again for quite some time but soon enough did make his presence felt in a much more subtly powerful way. A way in which Jacques had never experienced before and consequently got him hooked into feeling the power that many of us end up abusing.

The day of the planned attack on the garrison's route towards Mirradoire, Jacques and his comrades were up and about early. The charges had been laid using well-hidden explosives in the bushes by the roadside. These timed bombs were wired to a main box, so that the explosions would synchronise with the passing of the trucks later in the day. Often they used 'Chianti' bombs but those were more useful for attacks against individuals or small groups of soldiers at times when they were milling about some roadside café.

The bottles were made of celluloid and split into two sections. Each was then filled with plastic explosives and topped up with wine, and the raffia cover completed the disguise. Now that the moon phasing was right they had to get their people into position to set off this planned attack and then get everyone clear to safe houses or be flown out this evening. It had been a week since the full moon and they hoped the weather would stay clear.

They were as prepared it was possible to be but they all knew that anything could happen to prevent or thwart their plans at any time. Jacques rode in the car with Jean Maurois, their explosives expert. Jacques turned to him,

"Are the explosives ready for detonation Jean?"

"*Oui, Jacques*. I've checked that everyone's in position and the wiring to the main box is set up to do what we want it to do. We are as ready as we'll ever be."

"Who will set the charges off?"

"*Moi*, I wouldn't risk letting anyone else do it. I need to be there in case anything goes wrong. Did you manage to find a safe house to get a 'sked' arranged? We need confirmation of the co-ordinates for the planes coming in to lift our people out."

"*Oui*, it's all in hand. Pierre managed to get through to HQ last night. He has the details."

It was risky, as were all their activities but they had to let the others know who was to fly out and it had to be this evening or not all, for their opportunities were few. The others were spread at intervals behind trees and in the fields along the route and they drove quickly tracing the route making only hand signals to acknowledge their presence and pass on the information regarding time of detonation. Jean would drop Jacques back at his cottage and return to check that the charges would go off.

On a road leading west outside Simoges, before coming into Mirradoire, there is a cottage surrounded by fields of golden wheat, bordering a wood of tall trees. It was a beautiful grey brick house. Jacques mother Anna Marie and father Vincent had inherited it on the death of his *grand mere*. It was a life of hard work for Jacques' parents with some lean times, as living in the *pays* could be, being so dependent on weather conditions. The cycle of seasons ruled their lives giving a natural rhythm.

Jacques favourite place was in the orchard at the back of the house where apple and pear trees grew. As a child, he often played hide and seek there with his older brother Michel. He had a special tree. It was the oldest tree in the garden and had a thick squat trunk with gnarled branches which in summer were heavily laden with fruit. From the age of five he learned to scramble up the trunk and swing from the branches or sit in the crook of a high branch to escape the daily chores. But his mother always knew where to find him even if he had run off among the fields. Jacques had been a little afraid of his mother when he was younger, for at times he would come upon her working in the kitchen or the orchard pacing around, seemingly agitated and muttering to invisible people. At times he heard snatches of one-sided conversations,

"I know he's being naughty again. He's trying to hide from me so that he doesn't have to help with the harvest. *Oui, Oui,* I'll call him in a moment."

"*Maman,* who are you talking to? I'm here, you don't have to call me."

"Ah, Jacques there you are. No-one *Mon chéri.* Sh...sh." She would say turning her head to the empty space beside her with some irritation at their seemingly insistent chatter. He got used to her ways but was always afraid it would happen when they were in town and others would see his crazy Maman.

Since his involvement with the Resistance Jacques had convinced his now elderly parents to allow the house to be used as a 'station', which meant that from here a school for training agents including wireless operators was run. They had reluctantly agreed and now had their living quarters on the top floor of the house, giving over the lower floor to Jacques and the Resistance. Their outhouse was sometimes used to make the 'Chianti' bombs, as well as exploding rats and coal bombs where the lumps of coal were hollowed out and packed with explosives. Likewise, with the rats. These devices were harder for the Germans to detect and helped in the campaign to keep them guessing where and how the Resistance would strike next.

That day, after Jean dropped him off, Jacques went to the orchard to sit in the warmth of the sun to await any news and make sure there was nothing and no-one around the farmhouse that would arouse the SS unit's suspicions. His parents spent most of their time inside now, taking little to do with his activities but every now and then his Mother would still become agitated. She would come down the stairs, wringing her hands, anxiously talking to the empty space. While she was sensitive and frail, his father was now very deaf and Jacques sometimes worried he had put them in too much danger. Still, he tried to be as careful as possible and now he was hoping that he would soon hear the explosives going off from the ambush in which they had planned to do as much damage as possible.

He sat on the bench he had put under the tree and his sooty black cat tried to get his attention by winding in and out of his legs. Jacques was no longer able to scale the trunk so easily to hide in its branches, but still always sought solace below them when he felt the need, whatever the reason. Jacques had barely sat down when he felt the weight of a hand laid firmly on his shoulder. The cat hissed loudly, it's back arching as Jacques cried out, swinging his head round, startled by this unexpected presence and the strange sensation of something passing through him like a mild electric current. He looked at the hand on his shoulder, noticing its owner wore a gold signet ring with an engraved red dragon. It jolted something in his memory. Where had he seen that ring before?

"My, we're very jumpy today, Herr Tralow? *Es tut mir leid,* I'm sorry for intruding on your reverie but I have been meaning to pay you a visit for some time." It was Schnell! What was he doing here? Today of all days! Did he know something; was there an informer in the réseau? Had he seen Jean drop him off outside? Jacques head was reeling and he felt heat and sweat rise on his face.

"Oh, Kommandantur Schnell, you startled me! I don't often have uninvited guests, especially not out here." Jacques stood, his words coming in a rush as he attempted to explain his startled response. "But, of course, for you I'm happy to make an exception. It's just a bit of a surprise. Can I get you something?" He started to move back towards the house where the cat had already gone, hoping for a chance to compose himself and to check that there was nothing incriminating happening in the house. But as he tried to pass, the Kommandantur caught his arm, preventing Jacques from going any further. Jacques felt his arm tingle and had to stifle the impulse to pull away while gulping down his fear.

"*Ja*, soon but there's no hurry, is there? *Darf ich...*May I..?" Schnell moved his hand to Jacques chin and lifted his face towards him. As he touched Jacques skin, the electrifying sensation he'd thought was simply fear coursed through him again, this time even stronger. Schnell smiled down at him with an expectant glint in his eye as he slowly removed his hand from Jacques face though trailing his fingers down his neck and bringing his arm round Jacques' shoulders.

"Let's just sit and talk for a while or do you have to go somewhere? Schnell raised innocent eyebrows.

"*Non, non*. It's just such a warm day I thought you might like a cool drink, *monsieur?*" Jacques was trembling all over and trying to hold it in check. Was it fear of the attack being uncovered and his part in it, or the strange effect when the Kommandantur touched him? He'd have to play along and try to turn the situation around. Schnell continued to watch Jacques, silently shaking his head and seeming to enjoy Jacques' discomfort as he bent to sit.

"*Non*, then join me here for a moment, Herr Kommandantur." Jacques hoped his trembling was not too obvious when he spoke and sat down again on the bench needlessly indicating the already taken space beside him, struggling to exercise some control over the situation, little of which he felt at the moment.

"Tell me about your unusual ring. I have noticed the other Officers wearing a ring, but yours is different *n'est pas?*" As the German officer sat, the expression on his face shifted with an alertness that gave Jacques the sensation as if Schnell could read his every thought.

"Yes, I can. Almost...Thanks to my ring." Schnell said into the silence. Jacques jerked again, feeling more frightened than ever. They didn't mention mind reading on the training course.

The Kommandantur continued, "*Ja, das ist wahr*-Yes, that's true. The other SS Officers wear the *Totenkopfring,* or Death's Head Ring given by the Fuhrer, but I received mine from my Grand Master, *Le Dragon Rouge* or Satan as he is usually known. The ring helps me track the energy of those I wish to know better and that enables me to pick up their thoughts. Your pattern is one I would recognise anywhere; we are old friends Jacques Tralow. While I amuse myself, this time round in the identity of the man you see before you, we could be of great help to each other, *Ja?* "

"Wh... Wh... What do you mean?" asked a white-faced Jacques.

Rudy Schnell outlined for Jacques that morning, the part he saw him playing in his plan. Did Jacques refuse? Yes, at first. Did Jacques feel outraged that Schnell thought this was the kind of person he was? Yes, for a while. But this was a man, if man he was, who seemed able to see into the darkest recesses of Jacques being and discern the pride and hunger for power that he had denied to himself. Jacques eventually came to relinquish all control, for the promise of greater gifts.

Schnell did seem able to read Jacques' thoughts and he could certainly read his face. In no time at all began to read Jacques body with hands that emanated such electrifying carnality that all Jacques' heroic self-righteousness was rubbed out with ease and left him feeling that he had been a fool to believe that helping; being in the Resistance movement was truly what was needed or what he even wanted to do. In short, Schnell exuded evil. So too, did Jacques become as he absorbed the carnal despicability of Schnell's manipulations.

236

They did hear explosives going off that afternoon, as expected. But by that time they were no longer in the orchard. Rudy had led Jacques inside under the premise of his thirst for that cool drink Jacques had previously offered. As if like a lamb to slaughter Jacques meekly followed, with the promise of satisfying a very different thirsty desire that had been mounting since Schnell touched him. His crotch was throbbing and growing each step farther into the house. He desperately hoped his parents hadn't noticed the arrival of the Kommandantur or heard the muted sounds of lust that they now made in Jacques bedroom. Sleeping with the enemy was to prove now and on future occasions, a world Jacques ran towards too easily. He was being dangerously sodomised by the Kommandantur when they heard the noise as if from a distance. Dangerous because what they did was illegal and punishable by death, and dangerous because Jacques now realised he knew this about the Kommandantur. Why was Schnell taking such a risk? But of course who could Jacques tell without incriminating himself?

The first explosions and gunfire mirrored their dual orgasmic disintegration and sealed Jacques fate. He now cared less about Liberation and Freedom and more about the heights and delights with a powerful lover he fantasised he had always wanted. Betrayal by the body was to be the least of his ensuing misdemeanours as he later, quickly made his way from the cottage through the fields behind the orchard, in the direction of Mirradoire.

Schnell had left from the cottage in his jeep after promising Jacques a share of the loot when the soldiers had finished rounding up the townspeople and emptying the houses of any valuables in Mirradoire. Jacques disguised himself using some old clothes belonging to his mother, but did not remove the uniform below that Schnell had made him dress up in to act out his fantasies. It would be a useful disguise and there was no time, for he had to move quickly.

Of course, Kommandantur Schnell knew about the planned ambush by the Simoges *réseau*. His link was none other than Jacques. Unbeknownst to Jacques before that morning, Schnell was able to pick up everything he planned. How did Schnell do it?

He explained to Jacques that they were joined through the ages and had many an association in times past. Schnell had only realised this after catching sight of Jacques when he had first been posted to Simoges. Rudy recognised his adversary with whom he hadn't had contact with for several lifetimes. The unusual birthmark shaped like a diamond on Jacques' neck had given him away that day at the town hall and was what had alerted Schnell, or rather, the German identity this man had assumed. He had developed his occult powers with the Thule Society amongst other adepts and over the aeons had had satanic links with his Grand Master whom he could call on using either his ring or if possible, covertly using the well in the town to scry for Jacques whereabouts and activities.

The dead and dying that afternoon included Jacques' former compatriots in the Resistance and the majority of inhabitants of the town of Mirradoire. As Marie later told him, the attack had been turned on the fighters as they waited for the trucks to pass. The trucks never came but a well-timed tank division did. The 2nd SS-Panzer Division Das Reich had been ordered to make their way to Mirradoire. The *Milice* had passed on information to the SS, that one of their officers had been captured and was being held in Mirradoire by the Resistance fighters and they had come to rescue him. The Der Fuhrer regiment rolled their tanks into and surrounded the town after taking care of the 'gang' waiting in ambush along the road. That had been only the beginning. Marie later told Jacques how an officer was heard to remark to the soldiers before they set off for the town itself, "Today, you will see blood flow!" Once in the town, they found no trace of the officer they were looking for and presumed him dead.

"We need to have an identity check. Get everyone to that open ground there!" Schnell growled menacingly at the Mayor.

"The *Kommandantur* has ordered everyone to take their papers with them and line up at the *Champ de Foire*. Hurry everyone, *s'il vous plait!*" the Mayor shouted nervously and instructed several men to go to each house, to let all the people of the village know. The SS had already begun battering on doors and barking threats at people young and old. The town's inhabitants, after fearfully gathering were then told that the Division would search their homes for arms and explosives.

"You women and children! Over here! Hurry children, line up together, like you do at school." This officer changed to a deceptively friendly voice to encourage the stunned and fearful-faced children to move. "Let's sing a song as we go." The children began a faltering tune interspersed with whimpers and sobs,

"*Frère Jacques, Frère Jacques, dormez-vous, dormez-vous…*"

Jacques arrived after crossing the bridge over the river, and moved up the road seeing the church on his left, notable at any time for its remarkable architecture with its superb ogival vaults, resting on four columns carved with numerous figures. But now, he saw the women and children being slowly marched towards him. He stood stock still in shock at the scene, every hair on his body standing frozen in terror on hearing his name, still being sung weakly by the children as they and the women were herded past him inside the church. His legs almost buckled and he broke out into a cold clammy sweat. The soldiers were attempting to blow the church up but the explosives wouldn't go off. Jacques heard some muffled bangs and the German soldiers cursing. Then silence before he heard gunfire, children's screams and smelt the smoke, hearing glass breaking as flames leapt from the now broken, stained glass windows. They had set the church on fire after shooting those inside, and were now roasting alive those women and children who had not

239

yet died from their bullet wounds. He hadn't moved an inch as he now listened to their screams from within, tears streaming down his face.

"All men over here, now!" an officer with his back to Jacques barked meantime and then proceeded to split the men into six groups as they hurried to where he stood. Several soldiers then took each group to one of the barns around the town. Jacques spotted someone who looked like the man he had promised to identify and this despite the horrors he had just witnessed, reminded him of why he was here. He followed this group across the *Champ de Foire,* dragging the weight of his feet but continuing to move closer to his own downfall. The nearest barn at the far-side of the fairground was Brie Barn. The doors stood wide open, a line of soldiers standing in front with a machine gun set up and levelled at the, almost sixty men that they had herded inside. Jacques forced himself to move cautiously, keeping his face covered with his mother's shawl, towards the barn seeing at once the man he had been hoping to find. All of the men inside looked very scared.

"Marcel, *ma chéri*! Why have they brought you here?" Jacques shouted in a falsetto voice, trying to sound like a concerned female relative, knowing it was a risk. Marcel turned to him with a look of incomprehension, not understanding who was calling to him or why, for he knew no-one in the village that was close enough to call him *chéri.*

Jacques then recognised the commanding Officer, who turned his gaze directly on him, a cruel smile playing at his lips. Schnell then immediately turned back to the appalling scene and to Marcel; abruptly giving the command, "Group, Fire!" The soldiers began shooting, aiming low to prevent the possibility of their captives escaping but Schnell made sure Marcel was their first target, having had him pointed out to them. Jacques panicked and ran, trying to avoid being mistakenly shot and to get to the place he had arranged to meet Schnell after identifying the fighter who had captured Schnell's fellow officer. Jacques had known Marcel would be hiding out in Mirradoire.

He was slowed by one of the village men falling into him after managing to escape from a barn and been quickly shot down in a hail of gunfire. Jacques was pinned under the weight of the body hardly able to breathe, having gone down under the full weight of the stocky man. His nostrils were filled with the stench of smoke, blood and the sharp smell of his own perspiring fear. Jacques could hear Schnell screaming at his men to finish the job.

"Did you get them all? *Achtung!* Now set those barns alight. Make sure no-one escapes!*"* The men in all the barns had been shot, preventing their escape if not dead already. Each barn was then set alight, one by one.

Jacques moved out from under the dead weight with difficulty only after the soldiers' boots passed his line of vision and didn't return. He motioned his head towards the dead man before leaving him, silently thanking him for saving his life. He could still hear screams and cries for help as he stumbled up to and over the fence and then into the woods, tears streaming down his face, keeping a look-out for Schnell's men. He had thought it was only Marcel and the loot that Schnell wanted. The massacre he had just been party to was incomprehensible but there was no turning back now, so he continued to make his way to the house in the forest to meet Schnell. He didn't know the woman who answered the door and led him inside, but somehow she looked familiar. Soon the Kommandantur arrived looking pleased with his afternoon's work.

"*Guten Tag, Fraulein. Danke schon* for your help today and of course for your hospitality these last few weeks," the Kommandantur said, putting his arm round her waist and pulling her to him. Jacques watched this with a look of bafflement on his face. What had made him think that he was special? He shook his head, lowering it in shame.

"And you, Herr Tralow. He did a good job, *Ja*? Or should I say 'she'?" he laughed, motioning his head in Jacques direction while looking at the woman, inviting her opinion. She nodded her head,

"*Ja, Herr Kommandantur, naturlich.*" She replied glancing with contempt at Jacques, while snuggling into Schnell's embrace.

Rudy instructed Jacques to carry-on as if he was still the *réseau* leader, before dropping him in the jeep, back at the cottage soon after. Jacques' role from that day on had been to sit tight, go about his usual business and wait for word of his share of the loot and he tried to carry it out to the letter. Marie arrived soon after to tell Jacques of the day's outcome. Though he knew the 'gang' hadn't succeeded in their efforts that day, his surprise and shock was well feigned when Marie arrived, tearful and ashen-faced, bearing news of the massacre. Jacques played along, as he knew he should, finding it easier than he thought it could be. Rudy seemingly had only uncovered in Jacques what was always there, an accomplished ability to lie and deceive even those closest to him.

"What do you mean? How could this have happened? We must have *un traitre* amongst us. How else would they have known? Who could it be?" Jacques exclaimed, his tone outraged and stricken. "It's my fault. I should have known someone was up to no good. What did I miss? Who do you think it could be Marie?" Jacques looked crestfallen and disconsolate at his seeming stupidity. Marie was quick to reassure him.

"I had no idea either. But we must find out as soon as possible. We can't attempt any more attacks until we both find out who the mole is, and till the town has grieved the loss of most of the people. We must contact Headquarters for replacement agents and get their help in tracing the informer."

"*Oui, bien sur*, we need to make radio contact with HQ, we can't run the 'station' here much longer. There's no way of knowing what the Germans will do next," Jacques added for effect.

They consoled each other and resolved to flush out the traitor but there was wariness between them, for they were two of the few remaining survivors of the Simoges *réseau*. They glanced at each other sideways when they thought the other didn't notice, Marie silently questioning Jacques luck and Jacques wondering if he had been convincing enough.

He later could not get images of how the village used to be out of his mind. It had been a peaceful town on the back of a hill grown from the riverside. People from Simoges, in happier times, would come to picnic or fish at the riverbank. Its variety of hotels and restaurants competed using either their renowned cuisine or the quality of hospitality to outdo each other. There had been three schools for the children of the village. One school at the tram terminus for the boys; whilst the two girls classes were held in the village centre. The infants' class was on the Nielly road. Among the many cafés, as in most of France, there were those bare of fancy fittings, having only a few chairs and a table. During his own visits to the village at weekends, Jacques had gathered with the men chatting and playing pontoon. Sundays were the liveliest since all the shops were open. The women hurried after mass to get their final items of shopping for dinner, while the men skipped mass and stayed on the café terrace enjoying the early sunshine. The villagers were not overly keen on the 'townies' who disembarked from the tram but Jacques was excepted because he lived halfway between both Simoges and Mirradoire. The highlight of the day was the dances at Andre's or Fredrique's or Saquouties. The young folk made the most of this opportunity to size each other up and many romances began with a dance at Saquouties.

Jacques remembered the last year that the Fair had been set up with gaily decorated roundabouts to celebrate the Feast.

People came from miles around and the village children watched wide-eyed and grinning with excitement at the stalls and bands; festooned with coloured flags, fluttering in a welcome light breeze in the heat of August, hoping their parents would give them a franc for a ride or two on the roundabouts. But it had been a while since that had happened. Life was duller, harder and devoid of joy during the war years with worries about the missing young men who were prisoners of war or conscripted for compulsory work in Germany.

Jacques thought numbly now, about the scenes at the Fairground he had witnessed and had been party to. The image and sound of the children singing as they did at break-time in school or in class, now engraved on his mind filing into the church, their voices thin and high with fear, singing his name over and over and he justifying, terrifyingly so; that it was not his fault, it was not his fault, it was not his fault.

Simoges city and the surrounding towns and villages were in shock and mourning for all who had lost their lives. The Germans crowed and strutted at their victory, giving the townspeople a harder time than usual after news began to trickle back about the massacre. Raids happened nightly in searches for receivers and radios.

Jacques half-heartedly carried on his pretence of commitment to the *réseau*. Doing only what was required to keep Rudy Schnell informed of the radio communications from HQ. He felt he had no choice, for his life depended on it but he could not prevent Schnell or Marie from picking up on his lack of activity. Jacques tried to stay at home. But within a short time the Kommandantur's car would drive by, not stopping except after dark but still making his presence felt. Jacques had nightmares at night, hearing the children of Mirradoire singing their song, his name on their lips before they were burned alive. He would see the eyes and face of Rudy Schnell hovering above the flames, his evil laughter echoing amidst the screams of the women. Schnell knew he had Jacques mind and body in his power and used him nightly. Jacques discovered the baseness of his lust for copulation and greed. He was caught between the two sides and his duplicity held him bound by fear of exposure; still cowardly hoping that no-one yet noticed the attention he was receiving. In this he was wrong. The one person in his life he could never hide from knew.

"Jacques, *qu'est que tu fais,* what are you doing? *Je ne comprends pas?* I don't understand. Speaking Woman whispers to me, she tells me you will not be allowed to forget what has happened this day. Even after your death which already shadows you now." Annemarie tearfully regarded him as she spoke in a defeated tone. "How could you do such a thing, *mon fils?*"

"You're crazy *Maman!* You've always been crazy. Muttering to your self and always spying on me. Imagining I'm up to no good. I only ever wanted to please you and Papa. Leave me alone and say nothing to anyone of your crazy ramblings, for you too will die if you bring suspicion on this house. You know what the Resistance has been doing here." Jacques had abruptly turned away from his mother that day, missing seeing Annemarie's head falling to her heaving breast, tears coursing down her face, already mourning her son's death.

Marie became evermore suspicious of him, when, after contact with H.Q. there was still no clue as to who the informer could be. Several times she tried to call at the house unannounced and uninvited, trying to find out what was happening with the activities of the 'station' but got no answer.

Jacques had wound things down there using the danger of the recent attacks as a reason to lie low. Marie seemed to be hoping to catch Jacques out in what, with whom? She wasn't sure. But the distance between them was greater now. Jacques increasingly supercilious manner only aggravated the situation. She felt he was assuming an authority he didn't have, in truth

245

had no right to, but was driven by a heart full of guilt and unbeknownst to Marie; his head was full of Rudy's promises of power, compounded by his constant desire.

Jacques was becoming unhinged, but to him it seemed he had it all. Schnell promised Jacques that he would be protected. Schnell promised to take care of him.

It was never to be. Jacques' so-called protector protected only himself. After the massacre was completed Schnell felt he had accomplished total corruption of Jacques and became bored with the sex; he'd had better. The Division under his command had orders to move on. Schnell meanwhile, ordered several soldiers to follow him to search the cottage under the guise of a usual visit to Jacques.

Marie realised, too late, about Jacques' involvement with Schnell after arriving at the house-this time on an evening.

"Marie, what are you doing here?" Jacques demanded after opening the door. She was the last person he wanted to see for he was expecting Rudy Schnell's arrival any moment.

"I haven't seen much of you these days Jacques. I thought you might want some company." She answered. "Can I come in?"

"No, you can't. You know how dangerous it is being out after curfew Marie! It's already past ten and you'll still have to get back to Simoges." He snapped.

"Jacques, I must make a report to HQ. I need to let them know when the 'station' can help restart the *réseau*. We can't give up now. Especially after what the S.S. did to all those people. The whole village! They were our friends Jacques!" Marie glared suspiciously at him with a look of contempt.

"Ah, *Bonsoir Mademoiselle...?*" Marie jumped having not heard Schnell approaching quietly from behind. "Did I just hear you planning something against the Fuhrer's Protection Squad?" Schnell looked pleased with himself, for he had been waiting for an opportunity to end this now pointless liaison with Jacques and stop the Simoges' 'gang' of resisters. This had worked out even better than he had hoped. Schnell pointed his gun at Marie's head and Jacques meantime said and did nothing to avert the situation.

"And you my *petit* Jacques, *merci* for your help in dealing with this and the rest of the traitors." Schnell lifted his other hand and stroked Jacques face. This time it was not desire but sheer malevolence Jacques felt in the touch, flinching as if burnt. Marie watched with horror and disgust,

"Jacques, *Sacre Cœur!* How could you…?" was all she managed to get out, almost choking on the words. Soon the truck arrived laden with soldiers who proceeded to take the cottage apart, finding the elderly couple waiting for them upstairs, giving no trouble as they were led away with Jacques and Marie to Simoges for questioning.

It seems Schnell and Jacques had other unfinished business. As he eloquently informed Jacques on his last evening; his aim from the start had been to bring him down.

"Too many times, you have usurped my power. In too many lives have I endured you're disdain. Remembrance of this life after it ends will be your reward. Our Fuhrer would be rid of all his enemies and I must honour his wishes. How would it look to leave a known traitor alive here in Simoges when all others are killed? *Das glaube ich nicht!* I don't think so! And their blood is on your hands. It will be with pleasure that I'll watch your pathetic life snuffed out, for you have snuffed out mine like a candle in other lives. We shall meet again but my power is on the increase whilst yours declines. I look forward to our next battle. *Auf Wiedersehen!*"

The click of his heels echoed interminably on the stone floor as he turned and strode away, malicious laughter thrown backwards in his wake. The cell door clanged shut and Jacques was left alone with his own twisted and destroyed mind. In the dank cold, sitting on filthy straw scattered around the stone

247

floor, he held his head but could not contain his conscience. No tricks would subdue its rising and the onslaught came. *'Frère Jacques, Frère Jacques, dormez-vous, dormez vous..?'* Over and over he heard the children's voices singing his name. He was so scared! He didn't know what to do, how did he end up in this situation?

All his life he had thought of himself as an upright person. How he had talked of injustice, raged and outraged about atrocities done to others, that how he and *son amies* were so lucky to have their freedom, their homes, indeed their lives! Yet, *it was him!* He gave them the information, the exact whereabouts, the names, locations. *Sacre Cœur!* Why didn't he give them shoe sizes too! He may as well have. He wondered what was to become of his parents and Marie. He had given the Germans everything and now awaited his own demise.

Ha! Truly that came when he began, not now, at the end. When he made the first step into the arms and pocket of the evil that was to become him. When he gave up the ghost, sold his soul and watched it disappear into the sea of malice that was to drown him. Now he coughed and spluttered his words of woe and self-pity, for what else can they be in the monologue of a hypocrite? Could he ask forgiveness? No, there was no forgiveness for acts such as he had perpetrated, though still he wished there was.

He wanted to get these memories out of his head but knew there was nowhere for them to go. There was nowhere to hide. Absolution would not come, execution would. By way of the steel bullet reserved for those judged guilty of aiding and abetting the Resistance. The way of madness would be a more just reward for those like he, Jacques thought. Death is too easy, too much like a release from the hell that life has become, though he knew he would pay again and again and again. Death is only a momentary release until the next time.

Night fell quickly and heavily as they came to deliver Jacques to his death and he followed with something like relief, for the children came with him, "*Frère Jacques, Frère Jacques...*" Darkness was all around as they took him out in front of the building. The soldiers wasted no time standing on ceremony. He was turned towards the wall and forced to his knees, then briefly heard gunfire, laughter and felt the impact at the back of his head. Confused, he lifted his hand to his head and it came away bloody. Jacques realised he'd been shot and collapsed face forward.

Blackness...then consciousness of a kind. Hovering above the killing fields at night. Down below, awareness of two soldiers lifting my body, each holding an arm and a leg. They half carry, half drag it into a shell torn building, where there are other dead bodies strewn around. They seem unsure what to do with it, and eventually dump it in a corner. Darkness again then many colours. Subtle pinks, blues, yellows and green floating around my consciousness. No body to speak of, but still a sense that I am. A disembodied mantra begins:

"Om Mani Padme Hum...Om Mani Padme Hum..." Over and over, as colours and consciousness fade.

Healing, Teaching & Losing a Friend – Glasgow 2002

I awoke sitting bolt upright in the bed. It was 2am. I had no
need to check the clock. In fact, it was 2am on the 2nd day of the
2nd month 2002. An auspicious day no doubt, and the dream I
had awakened from confirmed the sense of imminence that I'd
been feeling for sometime.

I was in a hall, its walls covered in brocade, with two
huge embroidered hangings depicting dragons at each side of an
arch. There was an old woman there, standing at a balcony
wearing a richly decorated kimono. She was holding in her
hands, two bamboo poles at least ten feet long. The poles were
bending with their own weight, leaning down over the ornate
rail that came up to her waist. I walked over curious and
concerned about what she was doing and how she was
managing to hold them up, for she looked frail and thin, her
silver hair piled atop her head, above a calmly smiling face.
"You need to learn to do this." she said, turning to look at me
with a smile of encouragement, but I felt puzzled. I couldn't see
the point. What was she doing?

I turned away and looked around. The walls were yellow
and the floor was of dark wood, as was a nearby closed chest.
Then suddenly, I caught sight of the dragons as they flew from
their hangings, became enormous above me, and began fighting

with one another. They were swooping down and around each other in arcs and spirals. It was more like a dance, but they were angry; roaring and attacking. I felt frightened when they came towards me. Their huge threatening, mouths agape before quickly disappearing on reaching me. Another woman came to stand beside me. She was taller and heavier with sallow skin and dark slanting eyes. Her hair was black and tied in a bun at the back of her head and she wore a plain kimono of midnight blue.

She put her hand on my shoulder and I felt an enormous surge of energy pass through my body. There was no pain, just raw power. She gestured with her hand towards the floor to indicate that I should lie down, giving me a green pillow for my head. I was wearing a cream silk kimono decorated with exotic flowers. I lay down. She continued to place her hands on different parts of my body and each time she did, I felt another surge of incredible energy move through me. It was neither pleasurable nor painful, just extraordinarily mind shatteringly gentle. She moved to lean over across my pelvis then put her hand between my legs and on up inside me. There was no pain, no sense of violation and again, I felt the gigantic surge of energy but not in any way sexual or intrusive. Just, though not merely, powerful beyond measure. One thought: I've just had a healing. I opened my eyes, the thought still present and there I was sitting bolt upright in bed, knowing that it was 2am on the 2nd day of the 2nd month of 2002.

"How dae I no get dreams like that? I get all the borin wans aboot money an worryin aboot the weans. Except, I did get wan a few weeks ago aboot flyin. That wis great!" Maggie was not too happy. She was by now confined to a wheelchair, her legs refused to support her at all. She was a veritable 'Bitch on Wheels,' and proud of it.

"What about the money one? Were ye dreaming about lottery numbers, by any chance?

251

"Aye, ye wish! I could be so lucky, lucky, lucky, lucky. I could be so lucky in wealth!"

"Very good! There's just no keeping ye down is there? You're an amazing woman Maggs, ye know that? I don't know how ye keep going." I was so in awe of the way she had handled her illness over the years, while bringing up her daughter Claire and still managing to keep her relationship with Martin strong. I remember when she described the day she went to the hospital for the results of all the tests they'd put her through five years ago, and was told what the diagnosis was. She told me she had bounced into the doctor's office feeling great, since physically it was a good day. Her symptoms seem to have receded and she was so grateful. But she visibly deflated on hearing the doctor's words as she sat opposite him, while he made his pronouncement. Her response?

"So, this is not just illness, this is M & S illness?" The doctor's face stayed straight and annoyingly sympathetic.

"Yes, Multiple Sclerosis. It is also known as M.S." He wasn't a fan of T.V. adverts or Marks and Spencer's then. Maggie sighed deeply as she told me this with a wry smile adding,

"Even ma jokes are not connecting anymore." I laughed but my heart was breaking for her.

"Oh, Maggs, Well I'm here now and we make a formidable team, don't we? I'll teach ye some relaxation techniques."

"Why, will that make ma jokes funnier?"

Later, I'd been looking out the folder I had with a whole Relaxation Course inside, going over some of the techniques I could help her with, when the phone rang.

"Hello, is that Morag MacAulay? This is Niall Walker. I run the Adult Learning Centre over at the Mount and I've just had your CV passed on to me. I wondered if you'd like to come and do a Relaxation class for our clients here?"

"Yes. I would." I had no hesitation whatsoever.

"Are you sure? I know it's not what you usually do but I just thought…" He said as if he was having second thoughts.

"Well as it happens I've just looked out my notes on relaxation so I think that's a good indication that you've called at the right time." I said to encourage him that he'd done the right thing.

"Really? That's a co-incidence isn't it?" He said, surprise in his voice.

"If you don't mind me asking, who passed my CV on to you?" I had no recollection of ever sending it to the Centre.

"Em…I'm not really sure. I just found it lying on my desk. But no matter, I've got it now and it would be good if you could come over and meet the client group, yes? How about Wednesday morning at eleven a.m?" He gave me the address before hanging up and it was all arranged.

I sat back a bit stunned. I never seemed to get used to the synchronicity in my life no matter how often it happened, but I had to acknowledge that I had had that strange sense of imminence and presence that I get every now and then. It usually means my Dad is hovering about minding my business. I'd reluctantly, got used to it over the years and didn't resist it as long as I didn't feel he was meddling too much. If I did, I would holler up in no uncertain terms where he should go and in the language he'd understand, "Dad, fuck off!" Like Father, like daughter.

So, when I woke up that auspicious morning on 02/02/2002, it was the day of the first relaxation class at the Centre. After the last remembrance I carried much guilt and I had many sleepless nights with a single mantra, *"mea culpa…mea culpa…mea culpa…"* although I did realise that all my life I'd been paying for that betrayal and still was. Now I knew where that strange feeling of déjà vu had come from all those years ago on that holiday in France, and more importantly, now I knew why I'd been plagued with one betrayal after another all my life.

I had since been given many gifts and opportunities unasked for and only the years of spiritual practice had helped me to recognise them for what they were. Even the painful experiences, had afforded me places to learn how to be a better human being. Even this most recent gift of helping many more by using the meditation experience and practice I had accumulated over the years, was initially painful.

I got to the Centre on time to meet Niall Walker and he took me to see a class that was in progress so that I could meet the clients. I had had contact with those with what is now known as 'Assisted Learning Needs' but not closely or for some years. For many of these individuals this label, politically correct as it is, tells only a fraction of their story and what people in these circumstances have to deal with.

Everyone sat around a large rectangular table that was covered with paints, brushes and pieces of material, wool etc. The tutor with them was getting the participants to decorate blown up balloons, making faces and hair for them. I was shocked at the appearance of some of the individuals, but was able to keep the expression from my face. One man, who looked fifty-ish had a huge head. Another, a very small head with no neck, his head appearing as if attached to his shoulders, while his eyes bulged from his face. I was introduced to each client and those who could speak said hello, those who couldn't, grunted. There was a bit of noise with the cacophony of limited expression that some of the adults had, including squeals, grunts, shouting, laughter and moaning.

I was shocked to the core on leaving the Centre. How they looked had stunned me. But what they were being asked to do had shocked me more. I thought it condescending and degrading. I cried for a few days for what I imagined those people's everyday situation to be like. It occurred to me that this, more than anything else, would be a class in compassion for me. It had immediately opened my heart and I recognised it as the place I needed to be to undo some of my own negative karma. It was the reason I had been learning the skills I had for the last, almost twenty years. This, more than the aromatherapy work that I did, was what I had come back home to do.

Niall Walker was a personable man in his forties and I developed a good working relationship with him. We were like-minded though being trained in different disciplines. His was more the conventional route of Social Care, whereas mine was the Spiritual route. The results were the same when the heart was engaged, in that, we both took a human perspective and had a desire to improve the quality of life for the clients that attended the centre.

I developed a format during the time I taught this group, where these individuals learned to be calm and tolerate others who couldn't relax or did in less obvious ways. I've come to realise that such adults were generally treated as if they were not as capable of learning and developing as other people, which of course wasn't true. But for this learning to be optimum it seemed that it had to start at the stage each individual was at. Not where others thought they should be or assumed they were. Even when the students experienced difficulties due to physical disability; and there were some individuals like Peter and James who were brought to the group in wheelchairs unable to move any part of their body unless it was moved for them, their carers were taught to help.

Peter though, loved his body to be tapped up and down his sides and his legs. This brought on a fit of the giggles from him, every time. There was in Peter, the essence of joy. He also responded well to Reiki or hands on. I would lay my hands on his head and neck and call on my spirit guides to help him with what he needed in terms of Universal Energy. Slowly his head fell closer and closer to his chest until he was asleep. Others, new to the group, looked at me a little frightened when they saw Peter's response. "Whit's she daen tae him?" they'd whisper to the other support workers. But the regular carers were used to how things were in the class.

On first meeting Peter I took his hand for he could not give it to me. It was warm, soft and limp and I stroked it,

"Who are you?" he said. I was stunned. I mean, from a Buddhist perspective this is the ultimate question. He said, could say, nothing, I mean *nothing* else except this phrase over and over again. I wanted to do prostrations at his feet.

James, well James was another Buddha and I considered him a soul-mate for he and I shared our birthdays. Like Peter, he could not move in any way or do anything for himself but when I played, as I always did, flute music in the background, he smiled and smiled and smiled, gently nodding his head to the music. James had no words and needed none for he had his smile and constantly exuded gentleness. I very soon realised I was in the presence of enlightened beings even though they could not talk, walk, feed, dress or in anyway do any of the things for themselves that most of us take for granted.

Like Maureen, a twenty-year-old young woman who looked like a skinny fourteen-year-old. She whizzed and spiralled round the room in amongst the other clients as we carried on with our warm-ups and Chi exercises. Sooner or later the deepening quiet had its effects and she would find a corner to curl up in, especially if I gave her essential oils on a handkerchief to inhale or if she allowed me to lay my hands on her, to try gathering some of that exuberant energy that flowed through and around her.

The general sense of those class participants was in their freedom of expression and for the most part this was seen in their innocent and spontaneous joy. I shared my joy in working with them with Enrique in regular cards, and calls which happened every month.

"Que tal cara? How is the work going?"

"Muy bien caro, I feel so blessed and full of gratitude most of the time. Living Buddhas, can you believe it!? If this is penance I'm all for it."

"You'll always be a Catholic at heart, won't you Mora? So, do you think that the times we spent together have helped you balance some of the events that you remembered?"

"I don't know Enrique. For all the experiences I've been through it doesn't feel like the end of it. How can it be if I'm to fully understand Karma and re-birth. I must have had countless lives though I'm sure not all were bad ones, but neither can there have been so few negative ones."

"Como! Are you feeling guilty for things you might have done but don't remember? Come on Mora, give yourself a break. You've helped many, many people in the last couple of years and you still are."

"Si, you're right of course caro, I'll just make the most of the gifts I've been given and not worry about what may or may not have happened, eh? I'm sure Mhairi or Speaking Woman will let me know if there's any more coming, anytime soon. So, can you come over for a visit? It's been such a long time since I've seen you."

"I'm not sure Mora, since I got back to Andalucía and into dance many things have changed for me too. I focus on my origins now. I teach African dance and it grounds my faith. I'm not sure how I'd take to Scotland, especially after the way you've described it!"

"Well, that was then. It's not like that now. I'm not like that now. I'm so busy feeling joy I've no time for self-pity. I miss you Enrique. You know I still love you. Why don't I meet you halfway? Maybe we could get together in Mallorca then. What do you say?"

"Bien! That's a better idea. I'll look at my work schedule and let you know when I've got a space and call you, vale? I still love you and miss you too Mora. Adios, Cara."

I continued to witness many small miracles in that Centre and others. When you regard people from the heart as full human beings no matter the outward appearance or the diagnosis, then you're rewarded with seeing them make great strides in awareness and therefore development, because they feel that they are valued. This is not something that needs to be verbalised. It's something that can be conveyed through the expression in the eyes, the touch of a hand reaching out to another or a smile.

I went from doing one class at the Adult Learning Centre and then over time, to several classes in Relaxation. Later, I added other courses in subjects and activities that I felt would be beneficial to these particular clients, like art and working with plants. My main objective was always what I could learn and for everyone to have fun.

My best teacher in the 'Art of Not Taking Myself Too Seriously' had always been Maggie. Even in the places I thought were the best, she could knock me out of my hoighty-toighty delusions.

"Whit're ye daein noo Mo? Ye think ye're a Buddha or somethin? Listen hen, there's people dae these jobs fir years an years. Dae ye hear them goin around talkin like they're miracle workers? Get a grip. So's that you found yir vocation, *again!?*"

"Okay, okay. I get the message. How are *you*, Maggs?"

"No great Mo. I'm gettin weaker by the day and the doctor was talkin aboot puttin me in the hospital. Now, that is a death sentence. I'll never get oot o there alive. They're dangerous places, them!" I could hear the weakness in her voice and started to feel frightened.

"Listen, do ye want me to come round and give ye a massage tomorrow, Maggs?

"Aye, that'd be great hen, but it's probably Martin needs it more'n me these days. I've no been near him for a while. I'm too sore an always tired. We cin jist aboot manage a hug noo an then." She sounded sad and there were fewer and fewer jokes as the months had gone on. Definitely a bad sign.

I was just putting my oils and stuff in my bag to head round when the phone rang. It was Claire and she was nearly hysterical.

"Morag, it's ma mum. She's collapsed! Ma da's wae her the noo, but the ambulance is on its way. Gonnae come roon quick, please? What am I gonnae do if anything happens tae her Morag. What am I gonnae dae!?" All I could hear were heart-wrenching sobs when she stopped speaking.

"Claire, I'm on my way. Tell your Dad I'll be round in ten minutes at the most. It'll be alright Love. I'm just coming." The girls had just finished their homework and where either just going out with friends or settling in to watch telly.

"Jane! Paula! I need to go right now! Maggie's collapsed. I don't know when I'll be back. I'll phone you in a while OK!" I shouted down the hall trying to keep the note of panic out of my voice. They both came into the hall at the same time looking a bit shocked.

"Will she be ok Mum?" from Jane quietly.

"She's not going to die, Mum, is she?" from Paula already becoming tearful and afraid. Paula was closer to Maggie but both girls loved her. She was a part of our family.

"I'm sure it's just a setback, girls but I'll let you know as soon as I can. I've got to go." I was halfway out of the door already.

"What about Claire?" I heard Paula ask her sister. She, ever thoughtful of others, would probably call Claire now. I got to the flats just as they were lifting Maggs into the ambulance and closing the doors.

"Maggs…" and the doors closed. "Martin I'll follow you to the hospital."

"Naw, it's awright Mo. I'll call you as soon as they let me know what's happenin'. Go back to your girls."

"Claire, can you go wae Mo, hen? The girls will keep you company till I get back, OK?" Martin was ashen-faced and Claire just stood looking at the ambulance doors unable to move or speak.

"Claire…Claire love?" I went to her and put my arm round her shoulders leading her away with me. Martin nodded to me and got into his car following the ambulance, siren blazing as it pulled away. It was a long night. Jane and Paula tried to keep Claire's mind off it by chatting about school gossip, but every now and then they would descend into silence. This was not the kind of silence that happened at my relaxation classes, the profound kind that comes out of deep relaxation. But was more like the calm before the storm. It was as if we were in suspended animation, frozen inside a moment of anticipation just waiting for the telephone to ring. When it did, we all jumped and ran at the same time. I got there first.

"Hi Morag, it's Martin. Maggie died ten minutes ago." His voice was flat and lifeless. He was relating only what was necessary and not yet connected to the meaning of the words he spoke.

"Oh Martin, no!" I gasped. Claire had been watching my face and now burst into tears again.

"Noooo……" My girls surrounded her from both sides in a hug and were soon to follow with more subdued sobs. I gave Claire the telephone and let her talk to her father. She wasn't able to speak, just sob. Presently I took the receiver and told Martin that we would be there in half an hour.

"Aye", was all he could manage. We got there in twenty minutes and Martin broke down on seeing Claire. We took turns going in to see Maggie. I said some prayers and sat and held her hand for awhile.

"Maggie, what am I going to do without ye? There's nobody tae keep me in check now. Who's going to tell me jokes and make me laugh at myself? Who will I have tae tell all ma weird adventures to? Maggs ye can't go, ye just can't." My heart was breaking and I sobbed and sobbed holding her cooling hand to my cheek. Soon I tried to pull myself together and let Martin spend some time before we all made our way home in a living nightmare. We all stayed at my house. Martin couldn't face their home just yet. I made up beds for him and Claire and we tried to get some sleep. Before I could sleep, I had to call Enrique, he would understand how I felt. He had met Maggie a few times on Mallorca when she came out to visit me. They had got on well and he knew how close a friend she was. Maggs had often felt like more of a sister than those I had by blood.

"Ah, Mora. I'm so sorry. Listen, I will to try to book a flight as soon as possible, *cara.* I'll call you when it's arranged and let you know when I'm arriving, *vale?*" If I had ever doubted his love before, I couldn't now.

Enrique arrived the night before the funeral just after midnight. He took me in his arms and I cried again as I had been doing, off and on for the last three days. I had gone round to the house with Martin and Claire the day after Maggie died and made some tea and something to eat for them while Martin made the necessary phone calls to the hospital, the undertaker and the church to arrange the service.

It seemed like Maggs would be home any minute from the Co-op where she had worked for ten years, until she couldn't any longer about two years before. Her characteristic bold coloured clothes were scattered around her bedroom, some already in black bags, for she had been doing a clear-out for the charity shop. Maggs had lost some interest in what she wore and how she looked since being confined to the wheelchair. Recently she had stuck to the easiest clothes because she needed help to bathe and dress. They hadn't the enthusiasm or Martin, the patience, for flimsy materials with lots of little buttons, no matter how colourful. The one item she had lots of, that kept that colourful spark, was her scarves. There were several dozen in every shade of pink, red, blue and green and combinations of them all.

I didn't try to clear her things, just tidied up a bit for now and sat on the bed and cried with an emerald green chiffon scarf close to the colour of Maggie's eyes, bundled against my cheek as I inhaled her favourite scent, 'Moonwind', between sobs. I began to feel an impression, subtle and soft, slide across my back and down my arms like a exquisitely gentle embrace and heard a soft but distinct chuckle that could only be Maggie. A breath and a whisper, *Ye cannae get rid o' me that easy hen!*

I swivelled my head around checking the room seeing only the curtains briefly move, except the window wasn't open.

"Is that you Maggie?" I gasped. "If that's you give me a sign." I waited patiently for a few minutes but there was nothing more. I needed no more signs to be convinced anyway, I just wanted to feel more of her presence. I didn't say anything to Martin for he had always been pretty sceptical about my activities and I had no wish to further upset him. I left the room smiling though and kept a sense of peace in between the bouts of grief that continued for the next while.

Martin had finished making the arrangements and after having a cup of tea with them both, I left giving hugs and invitations to come round anytime they needed to or just phone for a chat. Now they would have to start adjusting to life without Maggie and my heart went out to them, it was not going to be easy by any means. Maggie had had such a strong character that it would be hard for them to bear the loss of her humour-filled love of them and life.

Enrique stayed for a whole week after the funeral and we got to know each other all over again. The return of his smile and gentle ways helped soften the blow from the loss of Maggie and the girls too, were overjoyed that he had come, albeit under sad circumstances. They had missed him and needed the affection he gave freely, especially at times when I couldn't quite feel the enthusiasm they needed to help them move on with their lives, in what was a dark time for a while. But he had made a new life for himself again in Andalucía and would have to go back, leaving promises that he would return before long.

Mhairi came to the funeral and cried with us. It was a sunny spring day and the daffodils shone yellow against the fresh green grass in the cemetery. Even the sound of the birds' song helped us get through the day easier. There was joy that Maggs was at peace now and not in pain, or struggling to accept her dependence on others, in the way she had had to do in the last few years.

"She's dancing free now, Morag. Kicking up her heels and making the angels laugh. She's not far; just on the other side of the veil until it's time for her to begin a new life." Mhairi consoled me. Martin was ashen-faced and struggled to keep himself together. He clasped Claire to him as they stood to speak of her part in their lives. Maggs had chosen to be cremated and had asked Martin to scatter her ashes at the place they had honeymooned up North, and where Claire was conceived. Martin had planned to take Claire with him at their next anniversary.

"How's your work going Morag?" Mhairi enquired when we got to Martin's place after the service.

"Yes it's good. I've felt very blessed this last year working with these individuals. They inspire my practice and have made me look closely at how peoples' learning and development, physically and emotionally is intertwined. 'There, but for the Grace of the Goddess, go I', has been the feeling most of the time. I'm learning a lot."

"Yes, what's that expression? *'We are all learners, doers, teachers.'* From Richard Bach, I believe."

"Yes, I agree wholeheartedly. I'm just wondering what next. I have this sense that there's more to come. Enrique tells me not to feel so guilty for things I don't know I've done but I still feel that I still have more to bring to consciousness. Something that I must recognise, must remember; so that I can reach more people."

"Well, if it's there, it will come when you're ready. You can't hurry these things as you know. I can hear Speaking Woman whispering one word. Can you guess what it is?" She looked at me expectantly, sure I would know the answer and I heard a whisper in that moment.

"Patience?" I replied, just a little disappointed.

"Yes, of course Morag. The last thing you wanted to hear, but that makes it all the more authentic. You don't have an instant wish-fulfilling tree that can change your or others' life just because you don't like what's happening, you know!"

"If only! If that was the case I could have done something to help Maggs couldn't I?"

"Well, you've learned that you can't use these gifts at will to further your own wishes. That's not how it works", she insisted. "That's the difference between helpful and harmful practice. The 'good' works for the benefit of all and the dark side arises when there are selfish motives. What you told me of your last remembrance illustrated that clearly didn't it?"

"Yes, very clearly." I nodded emphatically in agreement. "So back to the biggest lesson, that I still haven't yet been able to accept...Patience." Mhairi smiled and hugged me, pulling me close to her.

"Yes. Especially now, Morag. It's essential under the circumstances. You have yourself and others to be mindful of here. They will need your support in the coming months and you have my support if you need it. I don't tell as good jokes as Maggie, but I can at least raise a smile from you now and then, can't I?" I smiled immediately with gratitude, for Mhairi had been a good friend and an important support through all the years of strange happenings. I was not sure how I would have managed to stay grounded without her matter of fact way of dealing with the Spirit world. It existed and needed to be listened to and respected, was Mhairi's take on it. Otherwise I could have felt ridiculed and afraid to acknowledge that other dimension that had so influenced my life.

Even Maggs had never quite believed much of what I related to her. That was more sceptical humour; that although it did keep me having to continually question my motives and not take myself too seriously, sometimes left me feeling that I was just being dramatic. I knew it was Maggie's way of protecting herself from the fear that what I told her might actually be true. Well, she had the opportunity now to see for herself. I wondered what she would make of the after-life. She had already made her presence felt in a small way since dying, so seemed to be taking advantage of that particular opportunity. I wished for her a good life in the next. One as free of suffering as possible, but that would be of her own making. She had led a life of helping others, at the very least by making them laugh when able and I was sure that would help.

The weeks went on with some difficulty without Maggs or Enrique and I turned my mind to researching my beginnings in this life. The question of past life influences was almost a fact that I had had to come to terms with, but there was also that lingering question about my present location in Scotland. I remembered how attracted I was to other cultures and how much I had come to learn about them, but what of my own ancestry. I loved Glasgow and appreciated it more since living abroad as I had on Mallorca. I quietly held a fierce attachment to my Scottishness, which showed in my culturallly soft-centred but gritty and sometimes sharp exterior. An important question for me was: where had the clairvoyant abilities come from?

Meantime the girls spent as much time as they could with Claire, keeping her from closing down into her own grief. She stayed with us most weekends and we had some good chats about her Mum, as Claire regaled us with hilarious stories of how daily life with Maggs had been. Martin had by now gone back to work and we eventually got around to clearing much of Maggie's belongings, except those that they both needed to keep her memory alive. I got the jade green chiffon scarf.

"She would have wanted ye tae have it Mo'. It's yir favourite colour isn't it?" Martin placed it in my hand, the white tissue paper it was wrapped in softly crushing as I accepted it, tears in my eyes.

"Thank-you, Martin. It's a beautiful gesture."

"Nae bother, hen." We hugged. Then he and Claire got into the car to go spread Maggs' ashes.

Epilogue

There are some…on whom divine favour has bestowed the gift of contemplating, clearly and very distinctly, with scope of mind miraculously enlarged, in one and the same moment, as though, under one ray of the sun; ever the whole circle of the whole earth, with the ocean and sky about it.

St. Abdomnan, *Vita Columbae*

Speaking Woman's Silent Thunder

Hear my whisper like silent thunder. Understand that to live in ignorance is to suffer. To survive is to find meaning in the suffering by relinquishing our ignorance. If there is purpose in life at all, then there must be a purpose in death and in dying. But you must find that purpose for yourself, for no-one can tell you what your purpose is. Be prepared to accept responsibility for what that purpose asks of you.

You have the chance to make use of, or let go the opportunities life provides to redeem your spirit. In this choice lies spiritual freedom. Fulfil your potential as a human being to be able to undo the conditioning of our current past so that you can transcend your circumstances and discover the guiding truth that will enable you when confronted with destiny, to meet it with equal spiritual courage.

What does Life expect of us? The answer consists not just in talk and meditation, but in right action and in right conduct. Your ability to respond, not react, is the essence of human existence. 'Life' is something very real and concrete just as life's trials are. They form human destiny, which is different and unique for each of you.

The redemption of humanity is through Love and is what brings us the greatest joy.

Morag is trying to fulfil her chosen destiny and by opening up to what is beyond only the rational, has been honoured with many gifts from other realms.

The Two Seeings or 'an da shealladh' in Scots Gaelic is that sense known as 'second sight' and is not always a welcome gift. It has the power of perceiving beyond the physical world to the subtle manifestations of Spirit. Some are born to see or sense this realm; some learn to develop the gift.

Morag wonders if it ever ends. Where or when does life end and the dream begin? Is there any moment when we are no longer responsible for our own thoughts and actions?

I may whisper in her ear at any time without warning. How will she respond? Will she be ready? Will you be ready?

Author's Note

The Chronicles in this book are fictional accounts loosely based on and entwined with some historical events with a fair amount of artistic licence.

The First Chronicle is set in an area that is now known as North Pakistan, but is considered to be the Indus Valley of prehistoric times. The people were of the Harrapan Civilisation, about which not a great deal is known. The culture went through several periods and is considered to have been advanced for its time. I have used creative licence in changing some details of course, also giving it a matriarchal base. The philosophy there-in is based on feminist readings of pre-Hindu culture.

The Second Chronicle relates events again which are akin to some that did occur in the 16th century on Mallorca regarding the Inquisition and the Alumbrados, but these particular events in the story are imagined and the characters purely fictional although some are based on the Gnostic Creation Myth.

The Third Chronicle is based on actual events that happened in the Second World War in France. The characters and their involvement are however, wholly fictionalised though some are based on historical figures. These events were shocking and tragic and I used them with the greatest of respect in honour and remembrance of the victims and their families.

More details can be found at:
http://bit.ly/wordsmith-jacqueline

Bibliography

Dakini   Teachings   by Padmasambhava , Yeshe
Tsogyal , Nyang-ral Nyima Ozer ; Shambala. 2004
Woman's Encyclopedia, Myths and Secrets, Barbara G.
Walker; Pandora. 1983
The Dreamer of Calle de San Salvador, Roger Osborne;
Jonathan Cape. 2001
In Search of the Christ-Sophia, Jann Aldredege-Clanton;
Twenty-Third Publications. 1995
The Essence of the Gnostics, Bernard Simon; Arcturus
Publishing Ltd. 2004
A Quiet Courage, Liane Jones; Corgi Books. 1991
Celtic Visions, Caitlin Matthews: Watkins Publishing. 2012

Jacqueline wrote *The Two Seeings* novel before '*The Scottish Witchfinder*', published by Fleming Publications (2018) the latter inspired by the case of 'The Bewitching of Sir George Maxwell' at Haggs castle in Glasgow, where she was born. Jacqueline formerly ran Poetry@The Ivory and is a former Chair of the Scottish Writers Centre. She had a Scots ballad published in the Long Poem Magazine (2012) entitled 'Dumbie & the Devil', chronicling the life of Janet Douglas, the protagonist in *The Scottish Witchfinder* novel. Jacqueline completed the MLitt. Creative Writing at Glasgow University in 2012. In 2013 Pothole Press published '*Inspiration from the Common Wealth of Writers to Boost Creativity*' as an e-book based on Ivory author interviews, and in 2015 it was published in print by Fleming Publications. She has before and since had several short stories, poems and articles published in various anthologies and health and well-being magazines and e-zines. The first of Jacqueline's YA Trilogy Obroni Tales, 'Slaves of Men and Gods–Book One' was published in April 2020 with the Independent Publishing Network.

www.flemingpublications.com

Print ISBN:978-1-83853-282-6

Credits
Two Seeings Front Cover Image: Gerry at Canva

Author Photo: Louise Ainsworth